S0-AVX-140

The Shadow of the Soulkind

Book 2

Steve Davala

Copyright © 2016 Steve Davala
All Rights Reserved
ISBN: 1522906894
ISBN-13: 978-1522906896

For Laurie
For her undying efforts in editing and being patient with me

And for the real Ash. Part of you still lives on in this story. I miss you buddy.

Acknowledgements

This book would not be here today if not for some special people.
Laurie, your constant editing, rewriting, and feedback were all invaluable,
even though I might not have been the greatest sport about it all the
time.

I never imagined my cover art could be as amazing as it is. Tanner
Thompson is to thank for this. He took an idea I had and, with his
incredible vision and talent, forged what you see. I am still amazed by
what he created.

Chapter 1: Lost

Magic coursed through Jace's body, intoxicating him with its power. The eye-shaped mark on his hand glowed brightly. Valor shifted in flight, spinning Jace's vision and leaving a momentary dizziness. He tried to shake off the lightheadedness and focus on the landscape so far below. Leaves on the sparse trees a hundred feet away and the small movements of tiny creatures between rocks and scrubby bushes became clear, even in the fading light of day.

Valor's eyes darted towards a slight movement of leaves. A strange sensation wound up Jace's spine. Was it instinct? Fear? A shrouded being scurried between boulders towards the camp.

"Something's coming," Jace called out. He severed his connection to Valor and drew his dagger from his belt.

Straeten doused their campfire with a handful of snow and stood up clutching the bladed staff he kept from Marlec's fortress. Stroud gripped their prisoner by the shoulder and held a sword at his side. If someone was coming to free Marlec's former puppet they'd have to fight for him. Karanne stood at the front and drew the string on her bow back quickly, aiming into the darkness. The creaking of other bows being drawn sounded behind Jace.

"Is it the Darrak?" Straeten asked.

Ash growled beside Jace and shook his snow-covered fur. Icy chunks flew everywhere uncovering his gray coat.

"Thanks, Ash." Jace rubbed his hands up and down the dog's back, scraping off the remaining ice bits. "What do you think, boy? Any Darrak?" Ash whined.

Jace readied his dagger to throw at anything that moved. His thoughts drifted to his Soulkind and the marks on his body. Could he use his magic to attack if it came down to fighting? He shook his head at the question. Of course not.

But I could use it to control minds.

A chill rode up his back. Where did *that* thought come from? He turned around, but everyone was staring into the distance. Even Dorne.

"Who?" Jace said aloud after hearing the name in his mind. He looked again at his companions, and more closely at the prisoner in black robes, the man who had once possessed Marlec's gloves.

"His name is Dorne," Jace whispered to everyone. He got several raised eyebrows and even a look from the prisoner in return. That was more than anything they'd gotten out of him in the past three days. Dorne returned his attention to the gloom and his eyes faded back to a blank stare.

"Hey, focus." Straeten waved at Jace to quiet down and pointed into the distance. Beneath a bundle of thick animal skins, a person raced from one slick rock to the next without slipping. Jace watched the newcomer then signaled to his friends. The party slowly lowered their weapons. Straeten relit the campfire with a quick burst of flame. The light shone onto the face of a dark-skinned girl.

She looked younger than Jace by about ten years, though the worried expression of her sharp features made it difficult to tell. She removed wrappings from her head revealing a thick, dark braid.

"My name is Nilen." She held her hand to her forehead in greeting. "A man took my mother." The girl batted away Cathlyn's offer of water and continued hastily. "There were monsters with him. They took others from the village, too."

"When did he take them?" Jace asked.

"This morning." Nilen paced, her hand never straying from the long knife at her waist. "But we don't know which way they went."

Stroud spoke quietly to Jace. "Our concern is the Soulkind. We must get these remaining artifacts and our prisoner to Myraton." When Jace didn't respond, he added, "She doesn't even know where her people went."

He was right. They couldn't do much good without knowing the direction, or anything about this area. He was lost. And this girl would do better with people who at least knew the land.

"I was sent to find you," Nilen said.

"You mean to find help?"

"No," she replied. "To find *you*."

"What do you mean?" Jace asked. "How could anyone know we're even out here?"

"You are Jace, aren't you?"

Everyone's eyes turned towards him. "Yeah," he said slowly.

"Then you must help us."

This day was getting stranger all the time. "But how did you know we were here?" Jace stammered.

Nilen grabbed Jace's arm and started pulling him. "Aren't you listening? We've got to hurry back to my village! That man took my *mother*!"

Turic stepped towards the child and put his hand on her shoulder. "We'll go with you. You can explain how and why you found us on the way." She calmed a bit and lessened her hold on Jace. "Who was this man that came to your village?" Turic continued. "Can you describe him?"

Jace, still baffled, listened for the response he dreaded.

"He was a foreigner. About his age." The girl gestured to Jace. "With red hair."

Jace jumped into Blue's saddle in one swift motion. Within seconds, the party was galloping after him towards the village.

Chapter 2: The Village

"Can't these horses go any faster?" Nilen asked over the sound of the horse's hooves.

Jace felt the creatures struggling both to bear their burdens and to keep their footing on the rocky hillsides. "Not likely."

"So how did you find us?" Straeten asked.

The girl cleared her throat. "The smoke from that fire you made. I could see it for miles, even in this wind. You don't make fires much, do you?"

"Not until recently, no." Straeten laughed. "So *why* did you find us? Is Jace that popular out here in the wasteland?"

Jace just shook his head.

"This wasteland is my home," she said defiantly. Karanne slapped Straeten silently on the back of his head.

"I've never seen Jace before," Nilen continued. "But our mystic saw him in a vision."

"A vision?" Jace asked. "What did he see?"

"He didn't explain it. He's our leader, he didn't need to. "

Well that wasn't much help.

"How did Jervis manage to take the people from your village?" Jace asked. He was foolish to think he'd seen the last of him.

The girl wiped her face with the back of her hand. "He and those creatures forced everyone to the middle of the village. He pulled some strange objects from his pack and showed them to each of us, then stopped when he came to my mother and Tanor. And after that, my mother... she..."

Jace waited for her to finish. She didn't.

Turic rode up beside them. "We already know Jervis had some of the Dark Soulkind. My guess is this abduction has something to do with them."

A man in red robes appeared on a horse behind Turic. Jace rubbed his eyes and the vision faded. He must've been getting tired.

Nilen continued. "This man, Jervis, took my mother and Tanor. And they just let him! My mother didn't say a word to me, or to anyone. I tried to stop her but she ignored me."

"I'm sorry," Jace said. "I don't know what happened to her. But we'll try to help. What about the other villagers who went with them?"

"They were different. They didn't go willingly."

"Which direction did they go?" Jace asked.

"No one knows," Nilen said. "Darkness fell on the town and we were all blind. By the time we could see again, they were gone."

Jace knew that magic all too well. Memories of the last fight with Jervis and Marlec in the tower came to mind. He had felt so helpless not being able to see.

Nilen scrambled off the horse and ran up ahead through the barren rocky slopes. "I know these hills. We are close now!"

"Hey, come back!" Jace shouted.

"Your horses are too slow," she yelled without turning around.

Jace thought about urging Blue and the other horses to move faster, but their heads hung low and their hooves dragged. Nilen would easily beat them on foot.

"You're okay, Blue. I don't think you're too slow."

She nickered in response.

A few lights shone from atop a low rolling hill several miles away. A welcome sight in the winds and deepening coldness. After a half hour, the group rode up the stony hillside where Nilen had sprinted and passed the tall gates. Charred blast marks scarred the stone wall at the entrance. Two men wrapped in furs stood up above watching Jace and the others.

Nilen yelled from just inside, "It's okay. They're here to help." Their bows remained drawn while the party passed through warily.

Nilen came to meet them. "Welcome to Varkran. Take your horses to the water in the middle of our village." She pointed to a pool past a few sturdy dwellings, low and rounded and made of stone. "Please, come talk to our leader. He has been waiting for you."

She tugged at Jace's sleeve after he jumped off Blue. He signaled at Stroud to follow. The people of the village watched from their windows, mere holes covered by animal skins. Their sad eyes followed Jace and Nilen up the dirt path.

Up ahead, Burgis and Tare passed a pen of unfamiliar animals stamping nervously. His brother kept walking, but Tare stopped by the stones lining the pen and waved Jace over. His hands twitched in excitement. A new kind of animal, something out of magic, right in front of him. The creatures stood taller than horses, with horns protruding from their shoulders and heads. Tare caught Jace's eyes with his own, a huge grin on his face.

"I think we've seen something similar to these," Jace said. "Back in the mountains hauling the Darrak's weapons, right? What are they?" he asked Nilen.

Nilen barely slowed her step to answer. "Many months ago they just appeared in the hills around us. Stronger than horses. Faster too."

Jace reached out to the creatures with his mind. Their random movements stopped. Each stared into Jace's eyes and came in unison to the edge of the railing holding them in. One puffed out a steaming breath. Jace approached, answering the call he somehow knew came from their leader.

Not somehow. The strange warmth that came from using his magic washed over him. The base of his neck tingled, no doubt from the mark that sat beneath his hair. He sensed the strength that emanated from the creature's body. He sensed the need to protect his herd.

"Come on!" Nilen called from up ahead, jarring Jace from the connection he held.

Before Jace turned away, the creature bobbed its head. Jace nodded back then caught up with Nilen.

"My grandfather, Kedan, can tell you what you need to know to help us." Nilen led Jace to a domed stone hut. Smoke filtered out of a hole in the roof.

"Your grandfather is the leader?"

Nilen nodded.

Jace silently walked through the doorway with Stroud, pushing his way past several thick animal skins. Many candles lit the small space, reflecting off a still pool of water set among smooth stones in the room's center. The light shone on the copper skin of an old man, wrinkled beyond years, sitting by the pool. Several layers of furs covered him. His cloudy eyes stared down upon a small metal rod in his hands.

Nilen bowed as she entered and kneeled off to the side. She motioned for Jace to approach. Stroud stayed at the doorway, watching with crossed arms.

"You heard our call for help," Kedan said quietly. "Thank you for coming, Jace."

"It was Nilen who found us, we didn't hear anything."

A slight smile appeared on Kedan's face. "As you say. But you are here nonetheless."

"Nilen said you *saw* me."

Kedan gestured to the pool in front of him. "The water shows me many things. It showed me that you would come to help us."

"We want to," Jace said from across the water. "But I'm not sure what we can do."

"Can you feel the magic?" The man stared at Jace. His milky eyes stood out against his dark skin. "In the stones around you?" He coughed violently. Nilen ran to his side. The old man stirred the shallow waters of the pool with the curved metal rod. "Use them," he uttered. "Use them."

"What do you mean?" Jace asked.

"Now you're just being stubborn." Kedan splashed some of the freezing water onto Jace.

Before Jace could decide whether to protest or laugh, something called to him. The water? He felt drawn to place his hand onto the stones at his feet. He concentrated on the ground beneath him, stretched out his mind.

Much like his own memories when he touched one of his stones, visions of Varkran filled his senses. Visions from the distant past when Kedan was much younger, visions from other mystics before him, right in this very hut.

Suddenly the skins lying across the door flapped open and there was Jervis, his red hair barely visible in the darkness. He stood with two others, a man and a woman. They approached Kedan. The mystic seemed to know the two... both townsfolk. Something about them confused him, though. The man placed his hand on the mystic's forehead and walked out.

Jace's vision shifted to the streets of the village, a scene of chaos filling his senses. Several Darrak ran through the streets herding people to the center. They lined them up, turning pockets inside out, removing cloaks and furs, and dumping out bags. The Darrak then forced about ten of them out through the gate. Villagers waved their arms about and cried out for those being taken away. Darkness settled over the town. The same darkness obscured Jace's vision.

They were leaving and he couldn't see them. He was going to lose them in this shadow. How had he seen through it before when Jervis attacked in Marlec's tower? An animal's cry cut through the screams of the villagers, a strange call he'd never heard before. One of those creatures in the pen. And then he remembered.

With a thought, he shifted towards those strange horned animals. Magic coursed through his body, pulling him into a whirling vortex until

7

he stopped abruptly behind one of the creature's eyes, Jervis' darkness gone like clouds blown away from the sun.

The villagers walked north past the borders of Varkran towards a range of mountains. A band of Darrak surrounded them.

As the images began to fade, he heard a voice calling from inside one of the huts beside him. His vision slipped out of the creature's and inside the dwelling where a pool of water shone with a bright light.

"Who are you?" Kedan called out.

"Jace."

"Why are you here?"

Didn't he already know? "To help you."

Jace stood, the vision fading instantly when he released his grip on the stones. He was back. He reeled momentarily before speaking. "What was that?"

Kedan smiled as he sat stirring the waters. "The vision I saw of you."

"So wait. You saw a vision of me, seeing this vision of myself?"

"Yes, but we have no time for that now." Kedan said. "Tell me what else you saw."

"I know which way they took your people," Jace said, still a bit confused. "North."

Kedan coughed again and fell on his side. Nilen reached over and helped him back to a sitting position.

"To the north through the peaks, there is a camp." Kedan struggled to speak with a catch in his throat. "A camp where many of these creatures you call the Darrak are kept and trained. You must save our people before they get there."

"We'll stop them if we can," Jace said. "Stroud, go get Cathlyn and Turic."

Stroud nodded and left. Jace turned back to Kedan. "But first, we've got to help you."

"There's nothing you can do for me," Kedan said weakly.

"We'll see. We have two healers with us."

Another spasm of coughing wracked Kedan's chest. "They…did this to me."

Jace remembered the villager touching Kedan's forehead in his vision. His head hung forward limply after the touch. Jace turned to Nilen. "How far to that camp he was talking about?"

Nilen shrugged. "A half day's journey, perhaps."

"Then they're already there," Jace said.

"No. They'll be taking the long way. For them, over a day, maybe two. But I know a short cut."

"Good." Jace fought to keep his eyes open. "I don't think we can go right now."

Nilen bit her lip and turned to the door.

Jace stifled a yawn right as Turic pushed into the room with Cathlyn. Turic rushed to Kedan's side and placed his hand on his forehead. Cathlyn, too knelt down beside him.

"When did he become ill?" Turic asked. "How quickly did this sickness progress?"

"It started right after my mother left. I gave him several medicines before following her. None of them worked."

Turic sat back, a deep frown on his face. "What do you make of it, Cathlyn?"

Cathlyn continued to examine him. "It's not a magic I recognize."

"It doesn't seem like Marlec's Soulkind caused this," Jace said. "At least we haven't seen it do magic like this before. Jervis brought other Soulkind with him. Maybe he found new Masters for them?"

Cathlyn pulled back her long brown hair into a ponytail. She closed her eyes and held her hands over Kedan.

"What is she doing?" Nilen asked Jace in a whisper.

"I don't know, I've never seen her do this."

Cathlyn breathed deeply, her brows furrowed. Was she trying to sense something? Jace felt the power of his Soulkind pulse at the corners of his mind, like ripples in a pool lapping at the edge of the shore. Maybe she could see the remnants of magic, too.

"There's something dark here," Cathlyn said with a shudder. "I can *see* the decay in him. Someone put it there." She closed her eyes and rubbed her temples. "Is only evil to come from magic re-entering the world?" She opened her eyes to see Mathes at the door listening. "Come in, Mathes. Maybe you can do something."

Mathes swept back his robes, and set down his bag. "I will try."

Kedan drew back when Mathes came towards him. "I don't need what you have."

Mathes smiled. "But I have some medicine that will help your mind gain clarity."

Kedan held up his hands. "I want my mind to be my own," he insisted. His clouded gaze shifted to Cathlyn. "Try again, please."

Cathlyn backed up. "I don't think I can help."

He held her with his gaze.

"Please, you must try," Nilen asked.

"I…" Cathlyn turned back to Jace, her eyes darting.

Jace placed his hand on her shoulder. "You can do it. Remember what you did for Turic back at the cave?"

"But that was before I could use magic."

"Was it?"

Cathlyn paused. She took a deep breath and reached out to Kedan. She looked back over her shoulder at Jace.

He read her unspoken request and beckoned to Nilen and the others to give her some room. "Come on. Let's figure out how to get your people back." Turic and Mathes walked off together, still discussing Kedan. Stroud stood waiting for Jace outside the door.

Jace knew what he was thinking. "These people need our help."

"My orders are to take our prisoner and the Soulkind back to Myraton," Stroud said. "We must warn Myraton about the Darrak heading east on Marlec's last command."

"But Jervis has Soulkind with him," Jace said but he already knew it was pointless. Stroud would follow his orders. Jace considered the cold presence of Marlec's gloves in his bag. Memories of Marlec's cage drew a cold shiver into his heart. "I guess it would be a good idea to keep Dorne and these gloves separated."

"So you will go after the villagers," Stroud said.

"Yes."

"And I will continue to make for Myraton and beat the Darrak there," Stroud said. "If I reach Jervis and the two with him, I will deal with them as I can." He clasped Jace on his shoulder. "I expect to see you in Myraton soon."

Jace nodded silently, an unsettling thought sneaking up on him. Was he going to be in charge now? With Stroud in his party, the burden never fully fell on his shoulders. He knew Stroud could keep everyone safe if he made mistakes. But who would protect them now if he failed?

They walked to the dwelling where the others waited. Jace swept aside the heavy animal skin holding back the bitter wind from his companions. His friends. Well, mostly friends. Brannon Co'lere, in his tattered purple robes, sat away from the others and edged even further away when Stroud entered. No one quite knew how to handle his betrayal. Turic insisted Marathas' lingering soul caused his behavior, but Jace suspected Stroud wasn't convinced. Maybe the burn marks across his arms had something to do with it.

10

Straeten offered Jace some of the food and drink Nilen left for them. Jace dropped quickly into a pile of furs and quietly ate. Turic entered with Mathes. "I think I may know what happened to him," he said. "The decay Cathlyn saw sounds familiar. One of the Dark Soulkind was altered from its original purpose of protection and fortification. Allar, you hold its twin."

Allar reached into his pack and removed the Soulkind he took from Marlec's tower, the shield he used to protect his sister from Jervis' blast. A Soulkind that had not claimed a Master.

"That shield is from a man named Newell," Turic continued. "One of the youngest of the great Soulkind Masters whose souls were trapped from Sarissa's locking. The twin Soulkind that was turned Dark was held by one called Guire. For years, Guire's Soulkind was slowly twisted, like many others. No noticeable changes at once, but soon the magic for which it was originally intended was perverted to cause sickness and decay."

"So you're saying someone is using *that* Soulkind?" Jace asked.

"From what happened to Kedan, it certainly seems possible. Old Masters returning from their rest is not uncommon lately." Turic continued. "I... have seen Marathas."

"What do you mean?" Jace asked.

"When Brannon gave me power over the Soulkind, Marathas tried to persuade me to do certain things." He and Brannon exchanged a look.

Allar gripped his shield tightly. "But I thought the souls were released from their Soulkind when Cathlyn awakened them all."

"It may be that some did not wish to depart," Turic said.

Jace felt ill. Marlec was bad enough. "In my vision, Jervis had two people with him," Jace said. "Do you have any ideas about who might control the other?"

Turic shrugged. "We have not seen the effects of the other's magic, so I cannot say. It will be revealed in time, I'm sure. But now, we must rest."

The small fire in the room crackled. One by one, they lay down and pulled up their thick blankets. When Jace heard Straeten snoring, he opened his eyes to see Turic watching the fire.

"Tell me what you know about Lu'Calen," he asked Turic quietly.

"Can't sleep either?" Turic let out a deep breath and turned towards Jace. "Stories of Lu'Calen's rule go back a thousand years. He was wise, ruling his land with respect and quiet power. If you want to know about his Soulkind, *your* Soulkind, that is a mystery. I still cannot believe you are actually a Master."

Jace smiled. Neither could he.

"I didn't learn anything from Lu'Calen before he left." Jace stared into the fire, remembering how the former master slipped away through the pool with Marlec. "Is it all lost?"

"He did not have powers over the elements like Marathas," Turic said. "Nor was he a healer. Whatever he used magic for remains hidden, but, no, I do not believe lost. Look at what you have learned. Your power to communicate with animals and your understanding of languages came from the Soulkind, perhaps magic he created."

"So he became king because he could talk to horses?"

Turic laughed. "Don't you see? You have made the Soulkind your own. You told me he *gave* it to you. There must have been a reason. May I see it?"

Jace reached into his pouch and felt around for the familiar smooth stone. Images of his past danced behind his eyes as his fingers brushed the other stones. He finally pulled out the Soulkind and handed it to Turic. The green stone appeared almost grey in the firelight, but the lines across its middle still glowed white.

Turic turned the stone over in his hands. "It has no other markings or extra 'baggage' if you will. A simple stone. So interesting." He held it out for Jace to take back.

"You!" a raspy voice shouted out. Dorne. Several people stirred. Stroud pulled his knife and Allar stumbled over to Dorne's side, his hand on the knife at his waist. Jace slowly put his stone back in his bag. The man's dull gaze returned.

Allar rolled up the sleeves of the man's black robes. The bindings on his wrists remained in place. Allar shifted his gaze from Jace to Stroud. "We should have killed him," he said. "He's still a Master. Even if Marlec is gone, he'll only bring us trouble."

"We do not know that," Turic said. "Perhaps he was only doing what he was forced to do. For all we know, he was just like us before Marlec possessed him."

Jace frowned. Could that actually be possible? His eyes settled on Brannon.

Cathlyn finally returned from treating Kedan, her shoulders slumped. "Kedan will make it. For now."

Jace motioned her to a makeshift cot on the floor and handed her a plate of food. Cathlyn lay down and yawned. She ate a few things but put the plate down before finishing. "Has anyone figured out our plan for tomorrow?"

Jace shrugged. "Not yet. I know I'm going after the villagers. Not sure what the others will do." He held his breath for her response.

"I'll go with you," she said. "I need to help the villagers fix this mess." Jace let out his breath as quietly as he could. Cathlyn's eyes drooped but they stayed on Jace.

"Are you all right?" he asked.

She opened her mouth to speak, but simply nodded. She smiled a goodnight and pulled up her blankets. Jace wondered what she left unsaid. The sound of the howling wind eventually drew him to an uneasy sleep.

Chapter 3: The Ride North

Before the gray of dawn arrived, Nilen swept back the thick furs on the doorway, waking them all. Jace sat up and stretched his neck after what only felt like a couple of hours of sleep and listened to the quiet outside. Last night, the wind was so constant he must have learned to ignore it. Now, without it, the village had an eerie stillness as if all life had just slipped away.

Even after they ate breakfast and walked outside, the feeling of emptiness persisted. A few small children peered around corners as the company prepared to leave but quickly scurried from their sight.

Straeten had already packed and came out to check the horses with Burgis and Tare. There was no doubt who those three would follow today. Jace waited quietly to see what everyone else would decide.

"I'll go with Jace," Allar said.

"You have a duty to the Guardians," Stroud said quietly.

"And to my sister."

Stroud nodded.

"I'm with Jace, too," Karanne said and glanced at Mathes. He said nothing.

"I am sorry I cannot go with you to free the captives," Turic said. "Since escaping from the Shadow Vale, I have been so weak. I will continue on the journey to bring the remaining Soulkind to safety."

Jace put his hand on Turic's shoulder. "You better hope Stroud there is a good cook."

"Indeed I do," Turic said. "And remember, you are a Master now, too, Jace. You will join us at the Hall when you can to help decide what must be done."

The remaining people, including Brannon, Kal, a Follower and a Guardian, would follow Stroud, taking Dorne with them. The Soulkind were shifted around to Stroud's party, all except for a couple.

"Turic, do you mind if I hold onto this one?" Allar held the shield up for Turic. "I know I am not the Master, but it may be useful."

14

"It is the twin of Guire which makes it quite important. It also expresses an affinity towards you even though you have not awoken it. It may be helpful in figuring out how to solve the present situation with Kedan."

"But how?" Allar asked.

"Perhaps what is done with one Soulkind can be undone with its twin. A balance, of sorts." Turic smoothed his beard.

A gust of wind blew through the doorway. Jace could have sworn he saw a shadow pass behind Allar.

"I will guard it with my life."

"Perhaps," Turic mused, "it may end up guarding you."

Cathlyn checked one last time on Kedan while Jace followed Turic to the horses. Mist surrounded his head from the horses' heavy breathing in the cold, still morning air. Along with the extra horses, the villagers supplied them with heavy blankets and food.

"Good luck to you, Turic." Jace clasped his old mentor's shoulder.

"And to you as well."

His good-bye stuck in his throat. Turic gave Jace's back a pat, and then led his horse to the east. Jace watched him go, then stroked Blue's sides and tightened her straps.

"Your horse doesn't look strong enough to make this journey quickly," Nilen said.

"You don't know Blue. She wouldn't let me go alone." Jace hesitated slightly before slipping the bridle over her head. She stamped on the rocky ground by his feet. "Okay, okay." He laughed while putting on her bridle.

Soon, they left the safety of the village and were on an icy path to the north. The wind picked up again, but not as badly as the night before. Still, Jace's head tilted toward the ground and shoulders hunched under its constant force. He waved to Stroud and his party. Turic raised his arm in one last farewell. The sun shone bright yet lifeless in the wasteland.

They rode on for about an hour through low rolling hills and a desolate landscape. How had the villagers survived out here? No trees or other greenery, and game seemed scarce. Nilen didn't seem in the mood for discussion, so Jace kept the question to himself.

"We've got to hurry now," Nilen shouted back from the lead.

"Where are we going?" Jace asked.

Nilen pointed her chin toward a narrow ridge of stone jutting down from the distant mountains. "To the shortcut I mentioned. It'll take hours off the way to the Darrak camp."

"That's almost straight up," Straeten said. "How do you expect us to climb it?"

Nilen smiled. "I can't believe you've made it this far in the wild on your own. Come on, I'll show you the way."

Straeten shook his head with a short laugh and followed.

When they arrived at the massive thrusting of stone several hours later, Jace dismounted. The house-sized rocks lay amongst much smaller boulders, apparently shorn off the mountain side.

Burgis glanced back and forth from one end of the massive cliff to the other, nearly a mile in width. He shouted over the howling wind, "You think the path will be safe with all this debris around? Even if we can find it?"

"No, but we have to take it anyway," Jace yelled.

Jace got off of Blue and stood beside Nilen. "You know where to go, right?" The wind nearly blew him into her and he stumbled to catch his footing. Up above, Valor fought to stay directly overhead and headed to the wall to rest. There was no way they could climb straight up here.

"I've never actually been here before," Nilen mumbled.

"You're kidding," Straeten said. "Well that's great."

"I trust her," Jace said. It was true. She might be small, but there was a savviness about her. She would find it.

A dust cloud was gathering beyond a few of the last rocky hills they just passed. "What is that?" Jace pointed.

"I don't know." Nilen scoped the area again and then rode west of the cliff, scanning the walls. The rest of the party shot nervous glances behind them as the dust cloud grew bigger. A low rumbling shook the earth. Ash's ears pricked up and he darted from side to side.

Jace caught up to Nilen on Blue. "So what are we even looking for?"

"Kedan told me there's a small stream somewhere on the cliff face, near the middle of it. We're close, I bet. We just have to hurry."

"I'll try to find that stream." Jace reached for a visual connection with Valor but dust clouds kicked up by the horses' nervous stomping distracted him.

Before the hawk left his sight, Jace stretched out again. He drew in a deep breath, trying not to focus on the urgency of finding the path but instead to slow down his mind. With a burst of energy, his vision spun as he was pulled quickly through a dark tunnel behind Valor's eyes. There it came to a jarring halt and what he saw was not his own sight. The vast wall of stone loomed before him, but also minute details, even individual stones down on the floor of the canyon.

"You see anything?" Straeten said.

Jace jerked his head towards Straeten while still holding onto Valor's sight. A sudden lurching in his stomach made him reel as the bird's vision spun with his own. With another deep breath he focused on the hills and rocks and the spinning settled. Between two dark boulders to the west, a slight trickle of water exited the steep hillside.

"We're almost there, just a couple of hundred—" Jace stopped short as Valor's sight shifted to the south along the rolling hillside. "Run!"

His friends mounted their horses and shot off to the west along the ridge line. Straeten dared to glance over his shoulder as the horses pounded ahead.

"What is it?" Straeten asked.

"I've never seen anything like them," Jace yelled into the wind. "And there's a lot."

"How many?"

"A lot." One of the giant dust clouds rippled and grew behind them, crowded with hundreds of indiscernible bobbing shapes. Jace jammed his boots into Blue's sides and she jolted forward. "Sorry, girl, but we're not alone out here." He yelled at his companions to do the same. The other horses followed Blue's lead.

Up ahead, the twin rocks he saw from above slowly came into view. Just a hundred feet further. Ash struggled to match their pace. Strands of saliva clung to the side of Blue's head. He slowed her down and fell behind his friends. Drawing to Cathlyn's side he yelled to get her attention.

"Are you keeping up all right?"

"What are they?" Cathlyn shouted as the horizon filled with their pursuers. Finally Jace saw the dark-skinned creatures through his own eyes—tall, four-legged beasts with scaled hides. Their muscles flexed with each stride.

"Whatever they are, they don't appear friendly." Jace finally reached the entry rocks. His heart pounded in his ears and his hands fumbled for a weapon. The creatures' sloped skulls seemed to cut easily through the wind, and their lips were pulled back to expose large teeth. He could almost feel those teeth clamping onto his legs.

17

Nilen scrambled off her horse, trying desperately to coax it into the narrow passage between the tall orange rocks. The beast was spooked by the entrance or the approaching creatures. Either way, it wasn't listening to Nilen and reared up.

"Can you do something?" Jace leapt off Blue.

"Me?" Cathlyn stammered, nearly tripping.

The pounding of the beasts was a thunderous roar now. It was clear they were coming straight at them. Their rage permeated the air. He and his friends were in their territory. Jace gulped. They were about to be trampled.

Jace grabbed onto Cathlyn's shoulder. "Yeah, you! You're a powerful sorceress now, right? Do something!" Jace's face burned. Cathlyn broke from his grasp and stared at her hands.

Jace turned to the approaching horde and reached into his pack to grab his Soulkind. He gave one more glance at Cathlyn behind her horse. Her eyes read nothing but fear. Panic emitted from his companions, and the horses, too.

"Get back! See if you can get them up that pathway!" Jace squeezed his Soulkind tightly and scanned the stampede. One of the creatures stood out from the others, taller and more solidly built. The leader.

Jace locked eyes with the beast and tried to force his way into the creature's mind. Power, like water building up behind a dam, welled up inside him. Coldness crept into his heart, and he hesitated. Straeten stood by his side and held up his hand. Flames danced around his outstretched arm then sputtered out. Straeten shook his hands.

"What are you doing?" Jace yelled at him.

"It's not my fault," Straeten shouted and tried again. Nothing.

"Jace!" someone screamed. "Do something!"

Jace would lose them all if he didn't think of something fast. He gripped the Soulkind tighter, cold in his grasp, and again reached for the leader. The power he sensed beyond his Soulkind slowly channeled into his chest. The chill in his heart crept deeper with the raging cries of the oncoming creatures. The leader reared and a shrill cry escaped its snout. The horde faltered. Jace's friends stood watching.

"Move! Get going through that passage!"

Nilen pulled at her horse. "He won't go anywhere!"

Jace shouted and pointed his hand at the horse. "Go!" he screamed. The horse jerked ahead suddenly and ran into the narrow opening, knocking Nilen forcefully into a boulder, and dashed up the path. Nilen lay dazed, blood dripping from the gash across her forehead.

Allar shouted and stepped forward with the Soulkind shield held up on his arm. "Leave us alone!"

The herd reached the group. The leader reared on its hind legs and smashed towards Allar, but his clawed hooves struck hard in mid air onto an invisible surface.

Allar turned to Jace. "I did it!"

More of the beasts reared up screaming. This time, their force crushed Allar down to the ground.

Jace held his hands up. "No!"

The next few minutes were a blur as the strange creatures fought with each other in throes of madness. Jace shouted at his friends to continue through the tiny passage. He saw flashes of Straeten and Cathlyn grabbing Nilen and Allar and shoving their horses up the path. Blue trudged behind the others, finally forcing herself through the stone entrance. They escaped with their lives, yet Jace's heart felt as cold as the Soulkind in his pack.

They followed the narrow path as it cut back and forth across the side of the cliff, inching ever upward. The screaming of the animals finally faded and soon Jace heard nothing but the howling of the wind. The line of people and horses in front of him shuffled their feet on the narrow pathway.

"Straeten, what happened with your magic?" Jace asked.

Straeten shrugged. "Something's felt different ever since we left that fortress. I haven't tried to use it since then, not to attack anything anyhow."

"The fire feels a little further out of reach," Karanne said. "Too bad Turic isn't here. Mathes, do you know what those things were?"

"No idea. But they appeared to be drawn to us in some way." Mathes glanced at Jace.

"You think they were looking for me?" Jace shifted his pack on his shoulder.

"Not you," Mathes said. "But maybe something you carry."

Jace felt the cold of Marlec's gloves creep into his back through his thick clothes. He quickened his pace.

Up ahead on the steep rocky trail, Cathlyn glanced back at Jace several times while she worked on Nilen's injuries. Those looks sent needles into his chest. Sure, they were in danger and could've used her magic, but he'd never spoken that way to her before. He couldn't let this sit much longer.

Burgis, pulling his horse and Nilen's at the lead, yelled back. "There's a clearing up here, we should give the horses a rest."

The party reached the top of the jutting rock. Dust still filled the entire valley from the creatures stampeding.

"I'm going to check out ahead," Straeten called. "Tare, you coming?"

The tall silent boy stood up, giving Ash one last scratch behind his ears, and nodded. The dog scrambled to his feet and glanced at Jace as Straeten and Tare made for the ridgeline. His tail perked up and one ear flopped over. He didn't want to miss out on this.

"Go ahead, boy!" Jace said. Ash tore off towards the top of the mountain pass to the north.

Jace approached Cathlyn and put his hand on her shoulder.

"Cathlyn, I'm…I'm sorry."

Cathlyn didn't respond.

"I didn't mean to yell, I only—"

"Wanted me to do *something*. I know."

"Why didn't you?"

"You don't understand. I feel like something awful might happen when I use the magic."

"But you awakened the Soulkind. That was a pretty good thing. How did you do that, anyway?"

Cathlyn rubbed her arm and again didn't answer.

"You know, you've been pretty quiet about everything since you left Beldan."

"Everything is fine. Really." She turned to him. "What about you?"

"Me? What do you mean?"

"That was intense in the valley. I've never seen you get that upset about anything before."

"I'm sorry," Jace said. He walked several paces away from her and kicked at some rocks.

"You seemed like a different person."

"I don't know what happened. I just snapped. I'm sorry I yelled at you."

Cathlyn knelt to fill her water skin from the cold stream heading down the path they just climbed. "I wanted to use my magic. I just don't think I can control it. I feel like I could really hurt someone accidentally."

Jace took a deep breath. "Have you tried anything else with it, after the tower? Something small, like lifting that rock, or something?" He motioned to the ground.

"I suppose I could try." Cathlyn pointed her hand at the fist-sized stone and furrowed her brow in concentration. Seconds passed. Her hand shook. The stone started to quiver.

"There. See, you can do it."

The rock exploded into thousands of shards. Jace turned and covered his face but not before getting pelted.

He laughed as the pieces rained to the ground. "I see what you mean. Remind me never to ask you to pick me up."

"It's not funny." Cathlyn punched him in the arm. "I could really hurt somebody."

Jace frowned at Nilen. "I know how you feel."

"Something else happened down there," Cathlyn said. "After the yelling." Jace started to walk away but Cathlyn grabbed his arm. "I mean it, I saw something."

Jace stopped. "What do you mean, you *saw* something?"

Cathlyn paused. "No one else could, I think, but I saw the magic when you pointed at those creatures. What did you do with it?"

She saw something? He didn't really want to talk about it, but this was Cathlyn. "I...I made a creature do what I wanted it to. I felt its fear, anger, and I just...twisted it to do what I wanted." He felt Cathlyn take a step back behind him and he turned around.

The expression on her face made his guts wrench. The look softened and she placed her hand on his arm. "You saved my brother. Thank you."

"But you think I did something wrong," Jace said.

Cathlyn sighed. "It's not that simple. I can see your magic all around you. I can see how it flows into you through your Soulkind. What you did down there, it didn't feel right. It didn't look right."

He waited for her to continue. Instead, she kicked a rock on the ground, frowning, and then looked off to the side.

"What? What else do you want to say?"

"Would you ever use it on a friend?" She lifted her eyes to his. "Would you ever use it on me?"

His heart started to pound. He stared back at her and swallowed hard, trying to rid his mouth of the sick taste. What was she asking him? Would he control her mind? No. He wouldn't. Not ever. The pounding in his chest grew louder.

But he could.

His face heated up. He clenched his fists. "Look, I didn't want to do it, okay? I've never done it before, I'll never do it again. It's not like I had a choice. It's not like you were doing anything." As soon as he said it, he wished he could take it back. "I'm sorry, Cath."

Cathlyn took a breath and brushed past Jace towards the others. "I'm going to check on Nilen." She walked quickly away.

Great. He'd done it again. It was bad enough the first time. What was wrong with him?

Cathlyn knelt down next to Nilen and placed her hand on her forehead.

Nilen's injury was his fault too. The horse. Did he have a choice then? No, he'd needed to get his friends to safety. He scanned his arms for any sign that the new magic had left its mark on him. He didn't want any reminder. A few small symbols were next to the eye on his hand. Were they new? He concentrated and sensed their connection to the eye, his sight magic. He sighed in relief.

Allar approached but didn't say anything.

"You all right?" Jace asked.

"I wanted to apologize."

Well, that was different. "For what?"

Allar sighed. "I couldn't stop them all."

"Yeah, but what you did slowed them down. There were too many, and they would have crushed us before we got up that hillside. I didn't know you could use that thing."

"I'm not really sure I can."

"What do you mean?" Jace asked.

"I don't know," Allar said. "Like back in the tower. Something took over and it all sort of happened on its own."

Something moving on the path caught Jace's eye. "Well that's strange."

"What is it?" Allar turned around.

"I thought I saw someone up ahead, but I guess it was nothing."

"Well, get a little rest. We're almost there, according to Nilen. And next time I'll stop the stampede. Don't worry." Allar smiled and gave Jace the salute he had taught them what felt like months ago. First two fingers up and the others down.

He waited to see if Allar would send a barbed threat about his sister, but it never came. They hadn't come for a long time now.

Jace returned the salute and waited for Straeten to come back. He didn't have to wait long.

"Right over the crest of this hill you can see everything," Straeten huffed. "We looked right into another valley. This was a short cut, for sure."

"Did you see anything else?" Karanne asked. "Signs of the Darrak camp?" She shoved her water skin into her pack and hoisted it over her shoulders.

"Nothing yet, but if we're lucky we'll cut them off."

The two mountains stood ominously to either side of a line of cliffs and hills that went on for miles to the east. Jace felt Valor soaring above and Ash walking underfoot as they readied their horses for the push ahead. He led the party up the path quickly, wondering what they would see in the next valley. They still had a ways to go.

Burgis and Tare walked alongside each other having a conversation without words. Spoken words, anyway. Simple gestures led their interaction. They laughed between themselves about something or other.

"How long have you talked like this?" Jace asked.

Tare glanced at Burgis but Jace sensed Tare knew the question was meant for him. Burgis motioned for him to continue. A series of hand gestures flashed past Jace's eyes. He smiled to himself. He could tell what some of the motions meant. From what he gathered, this was something they came up with together a long time ago while hunting in the woods.

Jace said, "That's pretty amazing." It must have been some relief that Burgis could at least understand him. A pity though that no one else could.

A strange energy awoke inside him, warming him from his chest out towards his arms and legs. The power continued coursing through his arm and hand to his marks. Tare would in all likelihood never talk again, but maybe he could have something even better.

"I haven't taught anyone my magic yet," Jace began awkwardly.

Tare shrugged.

"I guess I never thought about it until now." Jace snapped and hit his fist. "So, what do you think?"

Tare stopped walking and looked at the ground. He gave a small nod. Jace nodded in return and took a deep breath. Now what? He thought back to Brannon holding onto his hands so long ago in Beldan.

It hadn't worked with him, but that was only because he was already a Master.

Jace reached out and grabbed Tare's hand. He tried to focus his mind on his magic, on moving it to Tare. Nothing.

"You two look cute up there," Allar called out from behind. Straeten laughed.

"Don't worry, you're next." Maybe it needed to be more specific. Jace focused this time on the black eye on his hand and reached to that spell. The pool of energy he sensed before pushed itself against his thoughts again. He welcomed it and suddenly his hand warmed and the symbol started to glow. The markings blurred a moment. Was it his mind playing tricks or had they actually shifted?

Tare's eyes widened at the symbols. In a moment, the back of Tare's hand began to glow too. He held it out in front of him, staring at it with a broad smile on his face. The small patch continued to glow briefly, then formed into a black mark in the shape of an eye, not as big or elaborate as Jace's, but clearly a smaller copy of it.

Straeten slapped Jace on the shoulder. "Looks like you have a Follower!"

Jace examined the symbols on his own hand. Something had definitely changed. The line right below the main eye on his hand was new. And something else was different. A presence in his mind. Tare's.

Tare still stared at his hand. He held it up to Burgis who'd been watching the whole time, wearing a grin as big as his brother's.

Jace patted Tare several times on his back. A Follower.

His Follower.

Tare ran back and forth to the others on the desolate trail showing off his new mark. That grin never left his face. Many times he turned to Jace and raised his fist in triumph.

"That must feel pretty good." Straeten placed his arm around Jace's shoulder.

Indeed it did. He had given someone else this magic, something he created. And it fit Tare so well. But how would he know who to pass it on to next? Or was that even up to him?

Up ahead, Mathes waved his arm to get their attention. Jace jogged to catch up. Past the craggy hill to their left lay the next valley. On another ridgeline of crests going to the north, a series of rocks jutted up creating a natural fortress. The tan spur that they had just climbed pitched down quickly into the valley and disappeared as it met the gray hills on the other side.

24

"That has to be it," Jace said. A sharp gust of colder wind blew up the hill into their faces.

"But did we get here before the Darrak?" Mathes asked.

The Darrak would be coming from the east. They had to go clear around the mountains, many miles further than this shortcut. Jace took a deep breath and sent Valor to scout out the approaching enemies. The bird circled twice above their heads and then slowly flew higher and off to the right.

They'd need a place to prepare an ambush. There was little chance they could defeat them head on. Especially if they had Jervis to face along with the Darrak. The valley floor was wide with few places to hide. Finding the villagers' exact path without being spotted would be difficult.

Nilen walked over to Jace, cradling her arm. Several cuts ran across her face. He wanted to apologize, but what could he say without giving himself away?

"The path is not as steep on this side as it was back where we came up," Nilen said.

"That'll make at least part of this easier then," he said. Only barely. Could they really pull this off? Some powerful magic would definitely be helpful. Of course, he could make the Darrak do what he wanted. Just one more time. It would be quick and easy.

He glanced back at Nilen's hurt arm and his heart went cold.

No. He had promised Cathlyn and himself he wouldn't. And he'd made another promise long ago. Never would he harm another Darrak unless necessary. But did he really have a choice? He would think of something. If they could just find a good enough point to get the jump on them.

"How many did you say took your townsfolk?" Jace asked Nilen.

"Four or five, I'm not sure."

Allar pointed to the bottom of the ridge they were on. "There. That looks like a place they'd have to go through. The path and stream cut through that rock. Good enough for an ambush. I'll go check it out."

As Jace led Blue down the slope into the valley, he thought about what Mathes said. Had the creatures really been drawn to them? He shivered. If something called those things, could it also call the Darrak?

The rock structure they walked on dropped at a steady but shallow slope. By the time they hit the bottom, the sun had already reached the gloomy mountain to the west, casting long shadows from the jagged top onto their resting place on a huge archway. They sat quietly glancing both ways along the quickly flowing stream below. Valor hadn't spotted anything yet. Hopefully the Darrak hadn't already passed this way.

"What are we going to do when we encounter them?" Straeten asked. "How are we going to free the villagers from the Darrak? And Jervis? They're not going to let us just take them."

Jace stared at the knife a Darrak had once taken from him. The etchings seemed so precise, almost artistic. How could such a creature make something so beautiful? He would stick to his promise not to harm them. Now Jervis was another thing. Jace's temperature rose. On top of everything else, Jervis was a kidnapper. Well, he'd pay for it.

"Allar," Jace called out. "What does it look like?"

Allar stared at the arch and the stream about twenty feet below them. "We set two bows on either side of the archway down behind those rocks. You stay up here to keep an eye on things and let us know the Darrak's formation. Now, we need to move the horses off this bridge so the Darrak don't smell them."

Tare stared at the mark on his hand as he walked along. Jace could sense him trying to connect with his horse. It was as if a light glowed inside the tall quiet boy, but kept faltering. Jace sheathed his knife and joined him.

"It just takes a little while to get it," Jace offered.

Tare's face shone bright red. He must have thought no one could see him trying.

Jace put his hand on the horse's chin and it stopped. "Like this. Now see yourself through his eyes."

Holding the horse's chin with one hand like Jace, Tare focused on its eyes. The mark on Tare's hand glowed briefly and Jace sensed a flow of magic stream from his Soulkind into it. Tare flinched and let go of the horse. A smile spread on Tare's face.

"See?" Jace said. "You can do it. The more you practice, the easier the connection will become."

Tare beamed.

"Pretty good teaching, Master," Allar said.

"Thanks," Jace responded. "Seems like you have a good plan, yourself. Did Stroud teach you this?"

Allar shrugged and glanced into the valley again. He saluted Jace before turning to go.

26

Jace watched him lead another horse up the hill. Strange that he wore the shield Soulkind on his arm outside of battle. Perhaps it was just wishful thinking. At least it functioned as a shield if nothing else. Jace squinted. Was Allar limping? Maybe he'd been injured from the stampede. He'd ask Cathlyn to take a look.

Cathlyn. They hadn't talked since he snapped at her. For the second time. Suffering, she'd barely even looked at him since then.

Something called to him and he glanced up. The news he'd been waiting for. Valor wheeled into view as a tiny speck and circled high above the valley. He was probably too far away to make a connection. Still, it wouldn't hurt to try. The sooner they knew about the Darrak, the better.

The familiar warmth began to grow within as he reached out for the magic, reached out for the hawk flying so far away. This time, he didn't see Valor with his own eyes, but somehow sensed where he was flying. The magic continued to envelope him in warmth while he reached for the point in his mind that he knew to be Valor's place. With a jarring movement, his sight shifted through the air and into the hawk's.

Not too far away after all.

"All right, Valor," he spoke in his mind. "What can we see from up here?"

The hawk peered hundreds of feet down onto the valley floor to the bridge where Jace was standing. So strange. Even from this distance, he could see the details of the wind blowing through his hair.

His sight shifted around the valley floor in swift motions, taking in all the gray stones and mountain peaks. Valor swung to the east and followed the stream, both steep and rocky. It would take the Darrak a while to walk anybody along it.

And there they were. The party from Nilen's village. Even with Valor's exceptional vision they appeared little more than insects stumbling along.

"I see them!" Jace shouted out to the others, still attached to Valor. Nilen quickly ran to his side.

"Where?"

"They are a few miles away, maybe five. At this rate, they could be here in an hour or two."

"Can you see how many Darrak there are?" Allar asked.

In the deepening shadows, he couldn't be sure. "Four? Five?" He pulled his sight back to his own eyes.

"Is my mother there?"

He didn't know what she looked like but was pretty sure he'd know her if he saw her. She'd probably be with Jervis. No luck with that yet, either. "I can't tell from here, but Valor is going to stay up there for a bit, following them. I'll keep watch."

Nilen sat silently. Karanne put an arm around her shoulder.

"We'll get ready, then." Allar started telling people where to go.

"And get that leg checked out," Jace added.

Allar shot him a questioning look. Cathlyn went to his side without a glance at Jace.

Chapter 4: The Rescue

Every fifteen minutes or so, Jace reconnected with Valor to check on the Darrak. The more they connected, the less Jace worried about Valor's endurance. The bird could clearly soar for hours on the updrafts.

It was getting harder and harder to see as the sun sank further behind the mountain and he still sensed no sign of Jervis. Jace's mind began to drift as he sat on the stone bridge, absently stroking Ash's gray fur. His Soulkind found its way into his hand. He rubbed its smooth surface, receiving flashes of different memories. First he plunged off the roof, next he saw Lu'Calen as the former Master and King of the land, then Marlec.

Before he knew what he was doing, he had his pack off and was taking out Marlec's black gloves. They were thick and heavy, but lighter than they appeared. Jace placed them on the ground then turned them over, wondering at the construction of metal scales, clasps, and layers of material. Where was the stone all Soulkind possessed from the start?

. He grasped two scales and tried to pry them apart. Its master's soul was gone now, but something remained, something that existed long before Marlec even touched the gloves. Darkness. He held one up.

The next thing he knew, his hand was inside.

A low growl emanated from Ash's chest. Jace glanced up to see Ash backing away, his hackles rising behind his neck. With a start, Jace wrapped the gloves in a thick cloth and shoved them back into his pack.

"It's okay, boy," Jace whispered. "Come here."

Ash stepped towards the edge of the bridge.

"Ash, come here!" Jace said in a firmer voice, but Ash kept his distance. Jace caught Cathlyn staring at him, but she turned away when he met her gaze. Nice. Two of his friends wanted nothing to do with him. With a grumble, he walked over to where Karanne and Straeten talked on the south side of the bridge.

"The Darrak don't like bright lights," she was saying. "Back in the fortress, I used Fireflash to blind them for a bit and then we did the rest with swords." A small ball of light spun around her hand. "Who first?"

She held her hand towards Mathes. He turned away without a word. Big surprise there. It didn't take with Burgis, and she didn't even try it on Tare. He was Jace's Follower now. She reached for Straeten's hand, though it seemed a long shot. They both followed Turic, but only a Master can teach new magic.

Straeten's eyes widened at a glowing circular pattern forming on his palm. With a big grin, he made the Fireflash appear and disappear in and out of his hand.

How about that? Maybe Turic misunderstood how magic passed on. Didn't seem likely, but then again, magic had been dormant for so long, who knew what else they'd discover?

Nilen gazed at the spell with wonder in her eyes. Jace knew magic was new to her, as it was to him just a short while ago. She reached her hands out tentatively when Karanne came to her. It might have been relief in Nilen's eyes when no lines formed on her palm.

No one else could learn the spell. "Isn't there any other way to rescue them?" Jace asked. "Without killing the Darrak?"

His question was met with confused stares.

"But, they took my mother," Nilen said.

"Something is *making* them do it."

Nilen grabbed a bow off the ground angrily. "They're evil, that's what's making them do it. And we've got to stop them any way we can."

Jace shrugged and stood beside Karanne. She was scratching her palm fiercely. "Something wrong with your hand?"

"I don't know. Maybe using the Fireflash is making this-" In the distance, a great booming reverberated in the canyon walls. A few drops from the looming gray clouds turned into a cold steady rain. Jace felt Valor calling. He gazed up into the darkening afternoon sky where Valor swooped low over rocks about a half mile to the east.

"They're here!" Jace shouted, and ran to the middle of the bridge. Everyone else hurried to their positions under it, keeping their eyes on Jace giving signals from the top. Straeten stood on one side and Karanne on the other. Burgis and Tare held their hunting bows at the ready with extra arrows stashed at their feet.

A bolt of lightning flashed just to the north, followed by ground-shaking thunder. The rain slammed into Jace's face with a gust of wind.

30

Along the stream to the east he finally spotted the group approaching. The wicked shapes of four Darrak herded their prisoners. The people stumbled beside the torrent of water, their arms tied behind their backs. The rain poured off their hunched shoulders and they didn't even try to ward it off.

Jace turned to the southern mountain and saw Blue trotting down the path towards him. He flailed his arms, motioning for her to hide. If the Darrak saw her, it would all be over. "Go back, Blue!" he yelled. She continued forward.

Under the cold of the pouring rain, he tried again with his mind, "Go back!"

She reared up suddenly, kicking loose several rocks beneath her hooves, then headed back up the hill. Jace breathed a sigh of relief.

Another blast of thunder sounded through the air. Downstream, the waters churned against the rocks from the storm emptying into it.

Jace signaled to the others that the Darrak were almost upon them and how many there were. Valor swooped over the bridge, calling out a sharp cry. The wind blew him off course but Jace got his message. He ducked down low to avoid being seen.

The Darrak's dark scales shone black. Two led at the front, and two prodded the prisoners with their spears from behind. Their black eyes glinted in the dying light as they trudged along.

One hundred feet.

Fifty feet.

And suddenly they stopped.

Jace sensed his friends' confusion.

The rain increased its pounding. The rivulets coming down from the mountain feeding the stream grew alarmingly in size and speed. Within moments, the small waterway through the valley began to fill up to its banks and then overflow with grinding froth.

His friends started to back away from the stream as it overtook the rocky path. With a brilliant flash, another bolt of lightning struck the mountain to the south, shaking the air with a resounding blast of thunder. Jace heard another sound. A sharp neigh. Not Blue again.

About fifty feet away, Blue moved haltingly towards Jace, fighting against his command to stay away. "Blue, I said go back!"

Jace stopped shouting. She wasn't alone. Behind her, two Darrak were sneaking down to flank Jace and his friends. Blue stood her ground and tried to stop them with her flailing hooves.

She had been trying to warn him.

"No!" Jace screamed as Blue twisted awkwardly under the Darrak's thrusting spears. He ran to the end of the bridge towards them. Time slowed. Blue fell sideways into the rocks. A searing hot rage and hate welled inside him, clouding everything else. Everything but his regret for forcing Blue to stay behind against her will. Her will to warn him. Suffering! Her message was so clear now, but only when it was too late.

The Darrak moved down the slope toward him with an almost liquid speed. Jace stood shaking, his hand outstretched toward the leader, his burning anger drawing his will. He bore all his rage onto that single Darrak. With a sharp clench of his fist, he twisted and gained control over the energy.

And he had it. With a flick of his finger, the Darrak impaled the one beside him in the chest with his spear. With another thought, he sent the Darrak to finish the others running upstream.

"Jace, no!" Cathlyn yelled at him. She reached both her arms to the sky.

Before the Darrak could finish the job, a blinding flash of lightning arced through the sky and exploded into him. The shattering rock threw him down and sent Jace skidding several feet.

The archers fired arrows at the Darrak surrounding the villagers but they charged harder after the attack, thoughtlessly yanking arrows from their bodies. Another wave of arrows slammed into them but they kept on running towards the overhang. There was nothing they could do. His friends would all die.

Cathlyn stood beside him with her arms outstretched again. Another bolt, even fiercer and brighter than her last, smashed into the bridge near the rest of the party. The molten bits of stone shattered violently before the terrified and now blinded Darrak.

He caught glimpses of the others fighting but could only think of one thing. He turned to where he last saw Blue.

She lay motionless on the ground, spears like twigs jutting from her side.

Chapter 5: The Decision

Jace pushed past Cathlyn up the hill amidst the sound of falling rocks. He barely noticed her collapse from using magic. A bolt of lightning flashed across the skies, this time from the storm, illuminating the still smoldering crater up ahead.

Jace rushed over to his old friend, his faithful steed from so long ago. He knelt down and placed his hands on her now still flanks. Why had he forced her to stay? Somewhere, deep in his consciousness, a warmth slipped away, leaving a hole filled with cold nothingness.

Gone.

Cathlyn walked up behind him quietly. "Jace," she started with a shaky voice.

"It's all my fault," he uttered. "I brought Marlec's Soulkind, that's why they came this way. I forced Blue to stay behind when she tried to warn me."

"You don't know that," she said. But she didn't believe her words. And he *did* know that. If he hadn't forced Blue behind she would still be here.

Straeten ran up the hill, stumbling to a halt when he saw Blue's broken body. "What happened?" He knelt beside his old horse and pet her. Cathlyn stepped back and covered her face with trembling hands.

Jace stared at Blue's still body. The emptiness she left behind consumed him. That and the burning taste of guilt. Sharp rocks bit into his hands as he clenched the ground to steady himself.

"Jace, let's go!" Burgis shouted up the hill as he ran. "Several of the Darrak ran to the ridge up there. We couldn't get them all after that lightning blast chased them off. We've got to get out of here." He paused when he saw what had happened. "For the suffering, Jace. I'm sorry." He pointed up at the mountains. "But we have to go. Now."

Jace followed his gesture towards the stony ridge now appearing as the storm receded. Great fires lit the tops of the crags. He took in the chaos left from Cathlyn's wrath. Giant cloven rocks with shear fractures lay strewn about at unnatural angles. If the Darrak upon the ridge hadn't seen this, the escaping ones would soon alert them.

Down by the swollen stream and across the broken bridge, Nilen was freeing her friends and giving them water. She skittered from one person to the next until at last she came to a stop and sat with her head down.

She now knew what Jace suspected all along. Her mother wasn't with them. Where was she? And where was Jervis? Jace let the downpour drown away the questions and caressed Blue's mane.

The freshly shattered rocks began to dam up the stream, threatening to flood the freed prisoners. Mathes led them to where Jace now rested by Blue. Jace stared at Cathlyn, still voiceless.

"I wasn't fast enough to save Blue from the Darrak," she said slowly.

From *him*, isn't that what she meant? As Jace patted his old horse's side one last time, he noticed a twisted dark mark on his forearm. He rubbed at it but it didn't come off. This one was different from the others. Sharper corners, thicker strokes. Almost like fangs. He quickly pulled down his sleeve over the mark. Cathlyn seemed to be taking stock of the damage she caused and Straeten was still looking at Blue. *No one noticed.*

He took a single stone from the ground beside Blue. A jagged gray shard. He squeezed it before placing it gently into the pouch of stones at his side.

"We can't leave her like this."

Karanne stood by his side and whispered to him. "I have a way." She showed him the marks on her hand and he understood what she meant to do for Blue. He nodded once and turned away.

Ash quickly clambered up the slope. He whimpered when he caught sight of Blue then quietly licked her face. Something else broke inside of Jace when he saw this. He reached out to pet Ash and the soaked dog leaned on his leg, as defeated as Jace felt. Ash lay beside his fallen friend's body and rested his head on hers.

Jace stood up, tightened his pack, and hoisted it over his shoulders. Everyone seemed to be staring at him. He felt sick. "Let's just go."

From the corner of his eye, he tried not to notice Karanne's brilliant flash of light pierce the dark. Afterwards, Karanne walked to his side and showed him her hand. A fresh mark appeared by the already numerous ones circling the central pattern. She reached out for his hand. "I've taken the memory of her spirit, Jace. Let me give it to you."

Jace backed away.

Karanne raised her hand again. "Jace, you *need* to take it."

"I don't want it."

He backed further away from her. The memory of Blue dying before his eyes sank into his chest. His mind crumpled again and unwanted tears stained his cheeks.

"I don't ever want it."

The climb back up the ridgeline wasn't easy. The slick path flowed with water from the rain. The remaining horses had an even harder time at it. Jace lagged behind. He walked in a daze, turning the jagged gray shard over in his palm until he found himself beside Nilen and the freed prisoners. He didn't really hear much but got a sense of how they were feeling from their sharp words and darting glances. They were scared.

Nilen asked, "What happened to my mother? Why isn't she with you?"

An elder woman of the tribe spoke up. "Your mother and Tanor separated from us soon after we departed from Varkran. But the creatures didn't say anything to us, and struck us if we spoke." Bruises and cuts covered her dark-skinned face. She must be someone who liked to speak her mind.

She had another mark on her, this one on her hand. Jagged and brutal looking, like shards of glass. Some shared the symbol on their own hands, and others had similar symbols on their necks.

"You know how to use magic?" Jace asked.

The villagers all glanced furtively at each other, almost guiltily.

"I believe so," the woman said, her head hung low. "We are cursed. They called us their 'Followers,' when they took us from Varkran."

"Who did?" Cathlyn asked.

"Lunara, Nilen's mother. But she is not her mother anymore."

Nilen's shoulders sagged. "How do you know?"

"Right when we left our village, she made us call her *Fay*. And Tanor is now called *Guire*. They left to the east, but not before they touched us and put that evil inside of us."

So Turic's guesses were right. One of them was Guire and they were embodied souls who decided to stay after being released from their

Soulkind. But who was this Fay? Jace glanced at Cathlyn, but she turned the other way. Even after everything.

"And they were going to force you to teach the Darrak up here, at this training ground?" Mathes came closer to stare intently at their marks. The old woman nodded.

"What magic did they teach you?"

"They didn't *teach* us anything." The lady motioned to the people behind her. "They forced their magic onto us. They left some with the power to cause great sickness. Whatever they touch soon dies." Most of them wore thick furs around their hands. Jace took an involuntary step backwards. Was this the magic that made Kedan so ill?

"What about you?" Nilen asked quietly, toying with the chain around her neck. "Do you have that type of magic?"

The woman frowned and scooped up some water from the rushing stream and let it drip from her fingers. The liquid turned abruptly to shards of ice.

"I have cold magic now." She placed her hand on her chest. "It chills my heart. They *know* where we are. They will send the Darrak to claim us."

"We won't let that happen." Cathlyn gave Mathes a look.

He responded with a slow nod.

The climb down the other side of the mountain proved to be even trickier now that the night had completely taken over. The rain had stopped, but was replaced by more gusting wind. Torches weren't working, so Karanne and Straeten cast the Fireflash magic to light their way. The two flames spun around them, showing the jagged rocks at their feet. At least that magic still worked.

"Why would anyone choose to live out here?" Straeten asked between gusts. "You know there are warmer places in this world, right?"

Nilen smiled. Jace thought he heard the word "baby" escape her lips.

Even though the villagers stumbled from their excursion, none slipped or injured themselves upon the sharp rocks. They were tired though, and it seemed only a matter of time before their surefootedness failed.

At the bottom of the hill they discovered a few broken bodies of the creatures littering the ground, remnants from the bloody stampede several hours back. Jace stepped carefully around them. He had never seen anything like these strange, three-toed beasts before, and yet he knew them somehow. They were not evil things with the intent to kill him and his friends like he'd assumed. Like Mathes said, they'd been drawn. Could the gloves really have been the cause? Without anyone commanding them? The whole thing was starting to give him an uneasy feeling. Well, even more uneasy.

He took a deep breath. "Maybe you should go on without me."

They all turned to him, several with incredulous expressions. "For the suffering, Jace," Cathlyn started. "We're not going without you."

"I think I can lead anything else off your trail if I go."

Straeten walked over and cuffed Jace hard against his shoulder. "You heard the lady."

Jace tried to laugh, but only let out a strange cough. He didn't feel like laughing. Not yet.

If they wouldn't let him leave, he could at least try to find out if there were more of those creatures about. Their fault or not, they were dangerous. It was too dark to use Valor to see anything out there, but perhaps he could sense the creatures like he did with his own animals. The magic flowed through him as he reached out. There were the familiar presences of Ash and Valor. A vast emptiness opened up inside as he thought of Blue but he quickly backed away from it.

Nothing. No raging anger like he sensed from those creatures before, nor anything else. He was probably just being paranoid about the gloves anyway. Still, it was time to get moving. The villagers were placed on the horses, some of them doubled up.

The storm faded and the waxing moon rose over the mountains to their left, showing through a break in the clouds. The pale light lit up the way enough for Straeten and Karanne to douse their magic. No point shining like a beacon to anything out there.

After a couple of hours, Jace came up to Cathlyn. How should he talk to her? Seemed like they hadn't spoken in forever. She gave him a small smile. At least that was something.

He couldn't put it off any longer. She had to have seen something wrong about Marlec's gloves and his own magic. "Back when I first controlled those creatures and Nilen got hurt, you said something about how my magic didn't look right. Did you see anything like that this time on the bridge?"

Cathlyn kept her eyes locked on the ground. "It was strange. I saw darkness pour out of you into that Darrak, saw you twist its mind."

Jace rubbed the mark on his arm. Could she sense it even now as it lay dormant inside of him? "Don't tell the others, all right?" Cathlyn nodded. "Did you see anything else I did?"

"What do you mean?" she asked.

Jace paused. "Before the attack, I was looking at Marlec's Soulkind and… something called the Darrak. I'm sure of it."

Cathlyn glanced back at his pack. "I didn't see anything."

Jace shifted uncomfortably. "Nothing from Marlec's Soulkind?"

"Nothing. But that doesn't mean nothing happened. I heard that the magic he used could never be seen, until it was too late."

"You mean by Sarissa?"

Cathlyn nodded. She was talking more, and that was good. But that rift was still there between them.

"Speaking of Sarissa, I can't believe what you did back at the bridge. That was amazing. You—"

"Stop," she said, still not even glancing at him. "I nearly killed everyone. It was too powerful. It was lucky that no one got hurt."

Jace rubbed the bruise on the back of his head from when he had fallen from the blast she summoned. "Well, not *no one*." Her expression hardened. "I'm sorry, I was just joking."

Cathlyn nodded, a sad smile on her face. "I know. And I've missed that. Just being with you and Straeten, you know?"

Jace nodded. It had been a while. So much had happened since they'd left Beldan.

"I need to tell you something," she started. "It's been killing me for such a long time now."

"Okay. Let's have it."

She closed her eyes and took a deep breath, then blew it out. When she opened her eyes again she looked directly into Jace's. "Do you remember back in Beldan when you found out you couldn't learn from Brannon?"

"Yeah," he said slowly.

"Well, I lied, Jace. I didn't pass that test. But I told you and Straet that I did."

Jace's mind spun for a second. He didn't know what he was expecting, but it wasn't this.

"You were so happy for me, despite your pain. And I let you experience that pain alone. Not a day goes by that I don't feel so guilty about it. Especially after what you said about friends not lying to each other."

38

"What are you talking about, you knew how to use magic without a Soulkind."

"But I didn't know that then."

So she wasn't perfect either. He should've been mad that she'd lied, or at least hurt. And yet, the slight dent her lie put in his guilt was worth it all.

"Don't worry about that, Cath. Straet did the same thing, sort of. We're friends. And friends forgive each other."

"I promise not to lie to you again. Deal?"

He smiled and squeezed her hand. The new mark on his arm burned in his mind. Could he make the same promise?

"What is it?" she asked.

"Nothing." He kicked a big rock off the path. Pain shot up through his leg. "Um, I'm just worried about Nilen's village. Do you think they'll be all right?"

"Those two, Fay and Guire, they'll be able to tell the Followers were freed, won't they?" Cathlyn asked.

It made sense. Even Jace could tell Tare was marching behind him right now. "Yeah and I don't know what we can do about it. If the magic ties the Masters to their Followers, they'll be able to find them no matter how far they go."

"I've been thinking about that," Cathlyn whispered. "There might be a way to free the Followers, but it could be dangerous."

"Free them?" Jace asked.

She looked up ahead at the others walking beside Karanne and Mathes. "I can sense the dark marks on them, feel the magic waiting inside like a sickness."

Jace instinctively covered his arm with his hand.

"And I feel like I could just…pluck it out of them."

"Like you *plucked* that stone from the ground?"

"Funny. I guess I asked for it. But this is serious," she said. "That's exactly what I'm scared of. If I'm going to try anything, I need your support."

Allar caught up to them quickly from behind. "We're almost back now." He pointed up ahead at a group of rounded hills in the distance. A glow from the village welcomed them. He placed a hand on his sister's shoulder. "Thanks for what you did back there."

"Well, I'm glad you were able to draw the Darrak under the bridge. That was a good plan."

Cathlyn fell behind to talk to Allar, but first sent Jace a parting smile. He returned it, but was glad she'd left. She could sense the darkness inside him, whatever she said.

They continued their ride under the rising of the moon. As soon as they crossed the gates into Varkran, the people erupted in shouts and cheers. Children began to run towards their parents, arms outstretched and tears running down their cheeks.

"Stop!" Nilen yelled from in front of the returning villagers. The children slowed down hesitantly. Nilen held up her hands and stared with regret into their young faces.

"They are sick."

"What?" the villagers shouted out. Some of the infected reached past her for their children but her look stopped them. It felt as if a dam were about to burst and Nilen was the only thing holding it all back.

Jace took a step towards her to help, but she gave him a small, almost imperceptible, shake of her head. He halted immediately. These were her people.

"They will be in the main hall," Nilen called out. "Go back to your homes until we have found a way to help them."

Slowly, the crowds obeyed and dispersed. When there was enough room to move through the streets, Nilen led the affected villagers towards a large structure in the center of town.

"Should we help her out?" Straeten leaned over and whispered to Jace.

Nilen knelt beside a small crying child watching his mother pass by. She laid her hand on the child's back and spoke softly.

"She's almost their leader," Jace said. "Let's give her a chance to prove herself."

After the group reached the hall, Jace and Cathlyn headed to Kedan's hut. Cathlyn pulled back the flaps at the doorway and hurried inside. A pale light flickered out into the street, casting eerie shadows onto Jace's legs. He took a deep breath before entering.

Candles lit the room, but most were close to burning out. The pool in the center lay perfectly still, as did Kedan. Jace exchanged a worried glance with Cathlyn and knelt beside her.

Thick sores marked Kedan's face. He breathed fitfully in his sleep, the thick blanket beneath him offering little comfort. An old woman by his side rocked back and forth, repeatedly chanting in a low voice as if Jace and Cathlyn weren't there.

40

Jace's foot accidentally knocked against the metal rod Kedan had used to stir the waters in his pool. He picked it up, its smooth metal cold and heavy in his grip. The designs carved into it seemed familiar, not unlike the style on his dagger. Could it have also been made by the Darrak?

A sparkle at the shallow bottom near the stones caught his eye. His hand with the rod moved almost on its own toward the water. The surface made no sound as the rod broke through it and began to swirl. The sparkle became a glow.

A gust of wind blew the skins on the door open. Jace quickly put the rod back on the floor just as Nilen scrambled to Kedan's side. All the poise she'd held in front of the village crumbled, replaced with the worry that had been etched on every other child's face.

Cathlyn shook her head when she finished examining the old man and rested her hand on Nilen's shoulder.

"Thank you for your help," Nilen said quietly. "Both with the villagers, and my grandfather."

Cathlyn whispered to Jace, "I'll stay and watch over both of them." Jace nodded and left to give Nilen some privacy. He heard her quiet sobs from outside the hut.

Jace walked into the nearly empty streets. He tucked his hood closer to his face to avoid the howling wind and the stares of the villagers watching him from their windows. Their faces, too, showed fear, fear for the friends and family that returned but were not the same.

He headed for the warm hut he camped in the night before and found Valor perched on the rooftop. He saluted him, but Valor kept glancing back and forth. "You see anything up there?" Jace felt too exhausted to look through his eyes. The sounds and the warmth coming from the hut called to him.

"I've got to get inside, I'm about to fall over. You going to be okay?" He glanced up again but Valor had already flown off. It wouldn't be the first time Valor left during the night, but with the temperature dropping and the wind gusting, it would've been nice to have him close.

Jace stood in the doorway for a moment. Villagers had brought plates of hot food, clothes, and buckets of hot water. His friends were already inside, resting on makeshift beds. He couldn't take another step and tumbled onto a pile of furs. Straeten, already cleaned and apparently well fed, sat next to him and held out a plate full of steaming meats and a metal cup.

"Eat up. We're probably not going to get a meal like this in a long time."

Jace grabbed the plate and the cup of clear liquid. The heat of the drink burned his chest and made him cough. Straeten and Burgis laughed and raised their cups to each other as if sharing a joke. The warmth of the strange drink swept through him, making the emptiness in his stomach clearer. He shoveled the sliced meat into his mouth.

"Anyone seen Ash?" Normally, the dog would've been glued to his side during a meal like this.

Jace's eyes were drawn to the back of the round hut where Tare sat. Tare waved to him and pointed to the ground where Ash lay quietly. Jace sat by the dog's side. Ash didn't even budge.

"You miss her too," Jace said scratching the silent dog. "If I could go back, I'd stop it all from happening." Still nothing. Well, what did he expect? That Ash would jump around like nothing had happened?

"Come on, buddy, you've got to eat something." He held a scrap right in front of the dog's nose. Ash's bushy gray tail thumped a few times on the floor. He lifted his head to help Jace eat the rest of the food. Jace smiled and scratched his ears. "Good boy."

"What's the plan for tomorrow?" Karanne asked.

Everyone turned to Jace. "What are you looking at me for? Can't I rest for a minute?" He shoved his empty tray onto the rough stone floor. The others fell into awkward silence and picked at their food. The night grew even darker outside.

Allar finally spoke up. "We're going to need more horses. Only a few are ours. Chase, Rhila—"

"I'll take Chase," Jace said firmly.

"I always ride Chase," Allar said. "What's wrong with Rhila?"

Straeten threw a chunk of flat bread at Allar. "Come on. She's Blue's daughter."

"Sorry, Jace." Allar said, brushing crumbs off himself. "I'll ask someone about getting more." He avoided Jace's eyes.

Straeten gestured to a pile on the floor by the doorway. "They've given us food and furs, that'll last us for a bit. I figure we get ready first thing when the sun is up to go after Turic and the others."

Jace picked up a pack of the supplies and nodded in approval before continuing. "Cathlyn wants to help the people who got infected by that spell to prevent the Darrak from coming back here after them. And them from causing more damage to others."

"Then we wait for her," Allar said.

42

Jace downed the rest of the strong drink and motioned for Straeten to give him a refill. Straeten slowly reached for the enormous leather skin resting on a hook on the wall. "You sure?"

Jace's mind swirled but he gestured again with his empty cup. Straeten poured, but his eyes fell on the gray stone Jace fiddled with in his left hand. "It wasn't your fault about Blue," Straeten started.

Jace scoffed. "You didn't see everything. I sent her to die."

"I'm sorry." Straeten sighed. "But you didn't mean to do it."

"I see what Cathlyn was saying about magic now. It only ends up hurting things."

"Not all magic," Straeten said. "Hey, I know. Why don't you try to teach me something now?"

"You don't give up, do you?"

Straeten laughed and shoveled more food into his mouth. "When it comes to food and bugging you, nope."

Jace laughed but then stared at his arm, at the dark mark. His smile faded. What if he accidentally taught Straeten that new spell? How long before Straet would use it on people? Sure he could do his best to control it, but for how long? Jace was barely controlling it himself. Could he trust others to hold back?

Come to think of it, why was he even worried? Straet already followed another Master. He nodded to Straeten, returned the gray stone to his pouch, and gripped Straeten's hand. He concentrated on the eye and on not letting his mind drift to any other spell.

"Now, this probably won't work since you've already got fire." It didn't take long before Jace felt the magic course through his body and into his friend's. His eyes widened at the tiny mark glowing brightly on Straeten's hand.

Jace laughed. "I think it worked."

"What is it? What did you give me?"

"Same one I gave Tare. It lets you see through an animal's eyes."

"No way."

In the back of the room, Tare sat next to Ash, staring into his eyes. "Tare's back there, why don't you give it a go with Ash, too? Just concentrate on—" Before he could finish, Straeten was already up and in the back of the room joining Tare in apparently confusing the dog.

Another Follower. It seemed Turic really had misunderstood learning new magic. Well, at least something was turning out good from this trip. Jace downed the rest of his drink and promptly fell asleep.

That night he dreamed.

On his arm, the mark from the dark spell began to grow. Like a snake, it crept around his hand, his arm, and soon covered his entire body. He couldn't breathe. His vision clouded over.

Through the haze, he caught glimpses of people fighting. His friends. Straeten, the same dark mark on his arm, yelled at and hurtled fire at the others. Karanne fought back against him with her own fire. With a flick of Cathlyn's wrist, trenches slashed open upon the earth and boulders tumbled around them.

The gloves on Jace's hands dragged him down, pulling him into the mud swirling at his feet. His friends reached for him, but they weren't trying to save him, only grasping at his gloves. The earth began to swallow him.

With a furious yell, Straeten yanked the gloves off his hands and danced around with them, letting Jace fall into the earth. Mud filled his mouth. Darkness fell over him.

With a start he found himself outside the cabin wandering the stony streets of Nilen's silent village. The gusting wind finally stopped and the bitter, still night air chilled him to his core. A thin blue light shone from behind the skins on Kedan's doorway, beckoning him towards it. He pulled them aside and walked into the peaceful hut. A strong glow surrounded him.

The radiance emanated from the pool in the center of the room. Kedan sat up in front of the waters, stirring them gently with the metal rod. Jace sat down across from him.

"You're better," Jace said with a sigh, happy to see the sores gone from his skin. "Cathlyn helped you."

Kedan smiled, but only briefly, and kept stirring.

"You will bring evil to your friends if you continue this way," Kedan said in a deep voice, not quite his own.

"I know. I am already drawing it to this village. I'm afraid I'll bring more Darrak here, or those beasts we saw on the way to the north."

Kedan nodded.

Jace rubbed his forearm where the twisted mark began. "So, what do I do?"

"You could stay with your friends, knowing what might happen to them," Kedan started.

"I can't do that to them."

"Or you could seek me out for help."

Jace tilted his head. "What? What do you mean?"

That voice. It wasn't coming from Kedan, it came from the water. Kedan stopped stirring to hand Jace the metal rod and in his own voice said, "The waters will show you the way."

With another jolt, Jace woke up from inside the hut, his friends safely sleeping. Ash's head shot up from beside Tare and Straeten. Jace hushed him down with a wave of his hand. Quickly and silently he walked to Kedan's.

There was no blue light glowing from the door this time. As he swept the furs aside, he heard only soft weeping. It came from Nilen, who sat next to her grandfather. He laid perfectly still, sores still spotting his face and arms. Cathlyn knelt beside him, her eyes on the stones in front of her. Jace entered and joined them on the floor. He put his hand on Cathlyn's back. She flinched at first, and then she, too, started to cry silently.

"You must sleep," Nilen whispered to Cathlyn. "The night is late."

"Nilen, I'm sorry," Cathlyn started.

"There was nothing you could do." Nilen took a twisted silver talisman from around his neck. With more tears, she placed it around her own.

Cathlyn stood up and walked to the door with Jace. She clenched her hands tightly.

"I'm sorry, Cath."

"All this power," she said, shrugging. "And I couldn't help a sick old man." Jace put his arm around her shoulder and helped her back to the hut. "I can't even walk, much less rip magic out of people. What do we do now?"

"I don't know." He felt something in a side pocket of his leggings, a cold metal. The metal rod Kedan used in the water. How did he end up with it? However he got it, it was his now. Given by Kedan. He now recognized the voice in the water. And despite what he'd said, he knew exactly what to do.

Chapter 6: Alone

Jace quietly gathered his things from the hut and slipped out, just like a thief in the night. He laughed at that. The still night with its chilling air surrounded him on his way to the center of the village. The cold actually felt comforting. Invigorating. He didn't know what was going to happen but at least his friends would be safe.

He stopped. Someone was watching him.

Ash.

He turned around. The mangy gray-haired dog peeked out at him through the animal skins on the hut. Jace knelt down, his hand outstretched, and held his breath. Ash, slowly at first, then at a trot, made his way over. Jace wrapped his arms around his friend and took the deep breath he couldn't quite do before now. Ash didn't blame him for Blue's death. He was just mourning in his own way.

Ash hooked his paw over Jace's forearm. He whined softly, the moon reflected in his dark eyes.

"No, you can't come with me." Jace stood up and the dog's paw slipped off his arm. "Sorry, buddy. It's too dangerous. I've got to run fast and far and I don't even know which way I'm going." He didn't want to admit the greatest dangers. Jace scratched him once more behind his ears. How strange that he once felt foolish trying to speak with a dog. Ash cocked his head to the side and sat quietly.

"And you've got to watch over Straet and the others while I'm gone. Think you can do that?"

Ash tilted his head and wagged his tail briefly. Jace patted Ash's head one last time. "So long, friend."

He hastily scribbled a good-bye note on a scrap of parchment and left it at the doorway under a small rock. He nodded and headed through the town into the west. He felt Ash's eyes on him the whole way. He'd come bounding toward him if he asked, his body seemed almost aquiver waiting for that call. And he almost gave it.

Better to say goodbye now than to lose another best friend.

Like a fresh wound reopened, his heart ached for Blue. His old companion was gone. Gone not only from the world, but from some place inside him. He'd always felt a connection to Blue, but only now with her gone did he realize just how much a part of him she'd been. Could he handle this much pain?

Karanne could give him a memory of her spirit. To help him.

No.

He couldn't take any more guilt from the attack, and if Blue blamed him during her last moments...

Maybe it was a coincidence, but ever since Blue's loss he felt something...*wrong*... inside of him. Some sickness. Only one dark mark on his arm for now, but how long before another appeared? And if the coldness that burned into his back from Marlec's gloves kept calling, he'd made the right choice in leaving his friends.

His friends.

Cathlyn wouldn't agree with his reason for leaving. She wouldn't understand that his presence endangered them all. She'd just say they all needed to stay together. Maybe she'd even try something with her magic to make him stay. And what about Straeten? He'd want to be with Jace no matter what. A not so small part of him felt like just waking him up right then and leaving together.

Best to get going soon before he thought more on that. But which way to begin? The voice in the vision told him the waters would show him the way. What waters? There was nothing around here but snow and ice. He'd have to figure that out later, at least for now he would start heading back west towards the mountain cave where they last found the dragon. Would he still be there?

The ancient beast had to have survived the Darrak. How else could he have seen the vision? Not only would Graebyrn be alive, but he would remove the mark and the darkness growing in Jace's Soulkind. And end Marlec's magic as well.

A creature calling drew his attention to the pen near the village entrance. Those horse-like creatures they passed on their way in. How long ago it seemed now. He walked warily toward them, extending with his mind that he meant no harm. The leader of the burras snorted and craned his head over the others to see Jace.

Jace raised his eyebrows. Burra? The word just popped in there, like it did so many other times.

Jace stared at the gray haired leader. Horns pointed down from the side of its head and from the bony plates on his shoulders. Nilen said they were fast.

Jace hesitated. This thing looked dangerous. He could use the magic to... To what? Force this creature to do something against its will? Jace's shoulders sank and he turned away to the west, adjusting his pack for the long journey ahead.

A whooshing sound came from behind. Jace turned to see one of the burras leaping effortlessly out of its pen and then walked right up to him. He smiled and reached up to its massive shoulder. The burra lowered it slightly. An invitation to climb up? The leader still stared at him from the pen, never once looking away. Jace raised his hand in thanks and thought he received a nearly imperceptible nod in return.

He grasped onto a curved bone and yanked himself onto the creature. It had short but coarse fur over its muscular shoulders. Jace could sense its power, like it was ready to explode at any moment. Its shoulders were broad and Jace found he could straddle its back with room to strap his gear around the horns. The creature bucked at its new rider. His first time. This wasn't going to be easy for either of them.

Before leaving the town, Jace turned back to Valor sitting atop a hut in the moonlight. "Well?" The hawk twisted his gaze to the hut then back at Jace.

"No, Val. He has to stay here. And so do you."

He raised his hand in the salute for a last farewell. A sudden rush of feathers sounded in the air followed by the clamping down of sharp talons onto his shoulder. "For the suffering, Valor!" Valor's grip remained tight. "You're not going to let go, are you?"

Valor stood tall, his eyes on the path ahead. Was there any point in trying? Valor respected Jace, but had a mind of his own. "Promise you'll fly away if I tell you to, all right?"

Despite the pain in his shoulder, Jace smiled. It all felt different with a good friend at his side. Luckily, Valor could take care of himself out there.

With Valor pulling at his curly hair with his beak, Jace nudged the sides of the burra. It leapt fiercely towards the edge of town and in a few seconds he was climbing the hills. He glanced back as he departed. Through thick snowflakes that just started to fall, the faint glow of Varkran slowly disappeared behind a hill. He shivered in the chill night air.

After a while, the rhythmic pounding of the burra's hooves almost lulled Jace to sleep. Everything blurred past with exhilarating speed, and Jace hardly felt the rough ground at all under the heavy but smooth footfalls. Had he been riding for an hour? Two? He sensed that the creature could last much longer, but he didn't want to risk it.

It was a "him," he could tell.

After all this running he felt even more confident about leaving Ash behind, although the part of his mind where the dog's spirit lay ached a bit. Ash wouldn't have been able to keep up with the burra. But for the suffering he would have tried.

"So, what do I call you?" Jace reached around and touched the side of the burra's head. The creature responded with a quick turn of his neck and a low growl. Jace quickly pulled his hand back. "I'll ask later then," he mumbled.

The moon sank ahead of him into the mountains. The beast finally came to a stop in a clearing at the bottom of a rocky crag. The wind was already starting to blow stronger and colder making him glad he had brought some clothes and other gear from Varkran. He pulled off a fur-lined blanket from the burra's back and threw it onto the snow-covered ground. He fell upon it and sleep quickly took him.

He woke to the sounds of the wind, the dripping of water, and the shallow but loud breathing of the burra. He splashed his face with icy water from a small pool beside his camp. The morning sun crept over the hill in the east. His friends back in Varkran were waking to the same sun and would soon find him gone and the letter he left.

Yawning, he pulled out some of the food that Nilen had packed, mostly dried meats and some hard bread. Valor happily tore apart a small rodent for breakfast. "So, what do you eat?" he said softly to the burra.

The beast turned his large head around to stare at Jace then away to face out onto the rocky plains behind.

Looming to the south, Jace saw the giant mountains, Retzlaff and Rabiroff, where he had left Graebyrn. How far could he have traveled after that attack? He could barely move then, much less flap his wings to fly.

Drops of water fell into the pool at his feet. He reached for the metal rod he was given at the village, and also for his Soulkind. When he took his stone out, he realized he had not looked at it for a long time now, not since the incident on the stone bridge. His heart started to pound. It had changed. Dark metal covered the back of it and three smooth sharp claws crept over the front.

What had he done? He tried to pry the metal from it. He pulled out his knife and tried to scrape them off.

Nothing.

The metal wouldn't even bend. Frantically, desperately, he put it into the water. Maybe he could scrub it off. His hand started to ache. First a dull pain, then more intense when he tried the knife again. The pain emanated from the mark.

"I'm afraid it won't come off that way," a deep voice called from a distance.

Jace dropped his stone in the shallow water and glanced around the campsite. He saw no trace of the dragon. Instead an image appeared in the ripples of the small pool. His Soulkind, distorted by the water, grew more twisted as the dark metal crept across its surface.

"What have I done to it?"

"You know what you've done."

Jace felt the voice wavering, weakening. "How can I fix it?" He closed his eyes and reached out to the dragon. But he was gone.

Jace retrieved the Soulkind. Icy cold drops fell off its metal claws into the water. As he watched, the illusion faded. The twisted metal subsided, but not entirely. There was enough to remind him. Rubbing the smooth green stone with his thumb, trying to avoid the remaining metal claws, he tried once more to call the dragon.

This time he felt a distant pulse away towards his left. Finishing his meager breakfast, he grabbed his blanket and approached the burra, careful not to spook him. The beast let out a loud huff when Jace climbed onto his back.

The burra rose to his feet. Jace held on tightly to the curved bones around its neck, guided the creature to face the direction he had sensed the pulse, and gently nudged him to go. With a sudden jolt, the burra leapt off the rocks with more power and confidence than any horse Jace had ever seen. And he'd thought he was fast last night. Tears streamed from Jace's eyes from the wind. Now he knew for sure Ash would not have been able to keep up. Valor, however, dove and soared upon the gusting winds right behind.

Jace thought about the friends he left behind, and those heading to Beldan already in search of Jervis. Like the rocky countryside blurring past, he left them in his wake as he sped past.

His companions were out of his hands.

Chapter 7: Gone

Cathlyn awoke the next morning. Something was wrong. The pale light of the day filtered in through the door as it flapped gently in the breeze. She turned to her companions. Everyone but Jace was still in the hut.

The others slowly woke around her. Karanne arose and ran her fingers through her red hair. "Wake up," she said to a groggy Straeten and stripped off his blanket. Straeten groaned.

Cathlyn walked through the doorway, allowing the full sunlight inside. The covering of freshly fallen snow made the early morning silence more profound. No Jace. "Have you seen Jace around?" she called back to Straeten.

Straeten stumbled outside. "In case you didn't notice, I just got up." He grabbed a piece of flat, hard bread and a strip of meat from the basket by the door. Then he just grabbed the whole basket. "Don't worry. I'll bring it in for everyone. Eventually."

Cathlyn noticed a note stuck to the outer wall. She reached for it, but Karanne got to it first and read it aloud.

"'I had to leave. It's not safe for you to have me around. Ask Cathlyn. She knows. I will meet you back in Beldan when I figure something out. Please take good care of Ash.

Jace.

P.S. Karanne, don't come after me. I'm calling in One of Four. I think I'm down to two now, right?'"

Karanne read it again silently then handed the letter to Straeten, grimacing. Cathlyn stood beside Straeten and read it over his shoulder.

"What does he mean?" Straeten said. "How could he do this?" He ran off towards the horses.

Cathlyn put her hand on Karanne's arm and led her inside. Soon, Burgis, Tare, Allar, and Mathes were up and watching Cathlyn intently.

"He…he did something with his Soulkind. He thinks it was caused by Marlec's gloves. Some sort of spell, I'm not really sure. He never let me have a close look."

"He told you this?" Mathes asked.

"In not so many words."

"I've said it before, magic will only bring darkness." Mathes stared at her hard. "We need to get to Beldan." He stood and walked out of the hut.

The others continued questioning her. "I think he was afraid the gloves would make us do things we didn't want to do, as well," Cathlyn said.

Karanne sat with her back against the wall and her head drooping. "You knew he felt like this?" she asked. "And you just let him go?"

"You think I'd abandon him if I suspected he would leave?" Cathlyn asked. "You know I'd never do that." Karanne nodded in agreement.

Minutes later Straeten returned. "I didn't see any of our horses missing. He can't have gotten far. We've got to go after him."

"Slow down," Cathlyn said. "We need to figure it out together. Burgis, Tare, go see if he left any trails."

"Got it." Burgis slapped his brother on the back on their way out of the hut. Tare gave a sharp whistle. Ash bounded up from the back of the room and followed them outside.

"What about the rest of us?" Straeten said.

"We wait for them to come back. I've seen them track food in the middle of nothing, if there's any trace they'll find it. While we wait, we have a village of infected Followers to deal with," Cathlyn said. "Also, Kedan is dead."

The others murmured. "This day just keeps getting better every minute," Straeten said while stuffing a shirt into his bag.

"What did Jace mean by *One of Four*?" Allar asked.

Karanne gave a humorless laugh. "It means I can't go after him."

Allar glanced at her sideways but she offered no explanation.

Straeten said under his breath, "It's something that happened in the Guild a while back. He saved her or something. He never talked about it really. Some big favors she owes him now. I remember the first time he called in on the Four. It was big, but not this big."

Karanne walked out of the hut just as Nilen walked in. The girl seemed to stand taller than before. Kedan's talisman dangled around her neck. "Is it true that the Darrak will come back for the Followers?" She sat down beside them.

Cathlyn said, "One of the Followers said that the Darrak would track them here."

"But if the only Darrak who knew of them are now dead, how could the others know?" Straeten asked.

Cathlyn shrugged. "Fay could sense them and send more Darrak."

"Great. Any other good news?" Straeten jammed more clothes into his pack.

"I'm afraid we don't know much about this magic," Cathlyn said. "I only feel that we are being watched."

"If you could heal our villagers, then Fay couldn't see them, right?" Nilen asked.

Cathlyn's eyes widened at the request. "But, I couldn't help Kedan."

"In a dream last night Kedan told me you would help. He told me to trust you."

Cathlyn stared at the walls.

"And Jace is gone, too, I see. Kedan spoke of that, as well."

"Did he happen tell you where he went?" Straeten asked and tightened the straps on his bag. "He kind of just took off. I just need a direction, that's all."

"I don't know," Nilen said. "He did say that he didn't want to be followed, though."

Straeten laughed softly. "We'll see how that works out for him."

Nilen stood in the doorway. "*One must honor the wishes of his friends,* Kedan always said."

"Even if he makes stupid wishes?"

"If you truly call him your friend, you will know what to do."

Straeten threw his pack over his shoulder.

Cathlyn sized up the young girl. The world out here was harsher than she'd ever experienced. Nilen was strong, though. Making all sorts of decisions for her people. And now Cathlyn had to make one, too. Whether to use her magic. What if she couldn't help the villagers? What if she only ended up hurting people?

She sighed. But then who else had any chance of helping them? And who was responsible for waking up that magic in the first place? The wind blew some of the powdery snow into the room. She stood up.

"Where are you going?" Allar sat up from the furs.

"I'm going to check on the affected villagers. See if I can…help them." She paused and then added in a whisper, "Just make sure Straet doesn't do anything *too* foolish, okay?"

"Not much chance in that," Allar said.

She pushed her way out the door and into Mathes.

"This could be an important test." Mathes followed her while she walked to the hall where the villagers were being kept.

"You think I should stay and help?" Cathlyn slowed her step. "I thought you were eager to get back home."

"If you could learn how to remove magic from them," Mathes said, "maybe you could remove it from the Darrak. Or even from Guire and Fay. You could stop them all at once."

"Sarissa tried that, and failed."

"Did she? She managed to stop the evil that was caused by the Soulkind."

"But she used the Lock to do that. I can't hope to do what you're saying without it. And Jervis and his new friends are heading towards Myraton with it."

Mathes nodded. "Well for now, at least you can try to help the people here."

"I don't know." Cathlyn rubbed her arm. "What if I do something wrong, only make things worse?"

"What if you save them?" Mathes led her to where the villagers were being held. A group of children clustered outside the main hall. Many were talking through small windows to their parents inside. Some tried to reach their hands in, but older villagers gently pulled them back. Children too young to understand wailed in the streets.

Cathlyn hesitantly walked to the front door. The temperature dropped. Blotches of ice covered the walls and the long stone table in the center of the hall. Nine villagers sat there, about half shivering deeply beneath thick blankets, and the rest wearing merely robes and seemingly unaffected by the cold. A few stood weeping beside the wall. Seeing the children's hands in the window from this side made Cathlyn's heart ache even more.

The old woman Cathlyn talked to on the way back from the Darrak camp called to her and Mathes. "What are you doing in here? You know we are cursed, yet you still come." Like the others in robes, she showed no signs of shivering.

"Nilen sent me here. She thought maybe I could help." Cathlyn twisted her hands together. "I don't think I told you my name earlier. I'm Cathlyn, and this is Mathes. He can maybe see things I can't."

The old woman touched her forehead in greeting. "My name is Lanor."

Cathlyn listened as the others told their names. There were old and young, men and women. Most wore confused expressions, others stared blankly at the tables. Lanor pulled back her sleeve to reveal the black mark on her forearm. Cathlyn took a closer look at the sharp lines of the woman's symbol. A young man pulled back a thick fur blanket to reveal the symbol on his neck. Cathlyn took a step closer but the man backed up so quickly he tripped over a stone bench. She held up her hands and apologized. The man sat down further away.

Mathes whispered to her, "I think I recognize those symbols now. They are of an ancient text."

"What do they mean?"

"I'm afraid I don't remember much."

"At least try to remember where they come from." Cathlyn focused on Lanor's symbol. As the old woman put her hand down on the stone table, intricate frost patterns spread across its surface.

"This happens to all we touch," Lanor said.

Cathlyn shivered. Mathes wrote busily in a journal. "It is as if those two... *Masters*... wanted them to infect the land. And, if they were being sent to that camp, to train the Darrak in their magic as well." Mathes kept scrawling on the parchment.

This was the beginning of a dark magic plague. One that would affect everyone. The cries of the children cut into her thoughts. She had no choice.

"I will help you get rid of this curse."

Chapter 8: Torn

Straeten kicked at the snow on the ground and stubbed his toe on a rock.

"I'm sorry," Burgis said. "But we couldn't find anything. It's like he just flew out of the village."

"Suffering!"

Ash shrunk back from Straeten's yell.

"Sorry, boy," Straeten said softly and scratched Ash on the top of his head. "I just can't believe he left without us. How come you didn't follow him?"

Ash cocked his gray head sideways. "Just asking." Straeten sighed. Too bad he couldn't get an answer back like Jace could. Allar walked up beside Straeten and gazed out over the small village nestled on the hill.

"If those Darrak are coming here to get the villagers back, we've got to do something. We can't just sit here." Allar scanned the surrounding hills and rocks. "This town was well built, and there are only a few entrances. See the stone walls surrounding it? We could funnel… Why are you looking at me like that?"

Straeten laughed. "Did they teach you all that in Guardian school?"

Allar shrugged and began walking as he scoped the village. "It just…makes sense. Anyway, I was saying we'd need to funnel them into the town over here and—"

"And what's wrong with your leg? Did you hurt it somewhere?"

Allar stopped and gave Straeten a sharp stare. "It's fine. Now, stop interrupting. We're going to need to retaliate somehow. The villagers can fight, you think, right?"

Straeten walked alongside Allar. "If they're anything like Nilen they'll be fine."

Allar pointed. "We need to fortify those walls, get archers up there. We have to move quickly. I'm going to find Nilen."

"All right, boss." Straeten said. "But I'm going after Jace."

Allar didn't stop walking. "We could use your help around here. Who knows what's going to happen with those Followers?" Allar absently pointed behind himself directly at the hall the villagers were in. "And Cathlyn told me to make sure you didn't do anything stupid."

Straeten laughed. "Slim chance, there."

"That's what I said."

"Nice," Straeten said. "Don't you think he needs our help too?"

Allar shrugged. "He's always been fine on his own."

"You don't know him like I do, then."

Allar turned around and squinted at the building the Followers were in. "What do you think is going on in there?"

"I don't know. Cathlyn went in earlier to see if she could help. Maybe she knows."

Allar headed straight to the doorway, limping even more heavily than before. Straeten hustled to catch up and overheard Allar telling the guards to let him in. They hesitated, but a shout sounded from inside and he pushed his way past them anyway. Straeten followed behind him, shrugging to the guards.

Inside, Allar stood in front of a long table with about half of the Followers moving away from Cathlyn and Mathes. One group of villagers scrambled past the table and knocked over a few chairs in the process.

"What's going on?" Straeten rushed to Cathlyn's side, the Fireflash pulsing in his palm.

Allar limped toward the Followers. "They have the taint of Guire in them. It's slowly eating at their minds."

One of the men shouted at Allar, "Get *him* away from us!" He rubbed at his red, watery eyes. A line of white spittle lined the side of his face. He shoved aside a chair and ran at Allar.

Allar pulled back his cloak from his right forearm, exposing the shield-like Soulkind. As the crazed Follower jumped, Allar swung his arm into the man, crashing him soundly back into the pile of others. Cathlyn winced as if struck.

The five huddling Followers shot glances around the room like cornered animals seeking an escape. Any escape. Allar held them back with his Soulkind in front of him.

"I can see the sickness in them," Allar said. "The corruption. I know what it is that they suffer from. And I can end it." He raised the Soulkind up above their cowering bodies.

"Allar, no!" Cathlyn said.

A soft glow emanated from the smooth metal surface of the shield on Allar's arm. It grew brighter until it covered the five villagers in the corner of the room. The light seemed to wrestle with the darkness above the Followers until grabbing hold of it all. Allar pulled back with his shield arm, making a fist. The light began to follow his movement away from them, but also pulled the darkness into it like a rag soaking up water.

Anguished screams sounded from the Followers. A thin strand of the darkness stayed tied to them, and seemed to be pulling their very life out.

"Let them go, Guire!" Allar called out in a strong voice. He pulled harder, but the screams intensified as he did so. Nilen ran into the room but stopped when she saw what was happening.

The floor began to creak and groan between the Followers. A crack opened abruptly and a large hand pushed its way through it. Boils and sores covered its diseased skin. It opened and closed its grip, pulsing. Pus oozed onto the floor as it reached out towards the mass of darkness above the Followers. It latched onto it and slowly pulled it back to the Followers along the thin dark tether that connected them.

Allar fought to hold on, to pull the curse from them. "Sarissa?" he shouted. "Help!"

Cathlyn hesitated but then pointed her hands towards the dark tether. A beam of pure white burst from her palms and pierced the evil hand, severing the connection in a flash of energy. The beam continued through the thick wall, disintegrating rock and mortar into a pile of dust. A scorched area spread out on the ground nearly twenty feet from the hole.

"I will come and take them!" a dark voice echoed throughout the hall. Cathlyn cringed and held her head from the pain shooting through it. The massive hand grabbed one of the Followers around his puny body and thrashed him side to side like a dog mangling a knotted rag.

"Enough!" Allar called out with a clear voice and pounded his fist into the ground. A crack in the floor raced from his fist to the hand and then widened, unearthing a bright light. The hand dropped the motionless body and then crumpled and twisted like a writhing spider in its death throes. Finally it sunk into the crack and disappeared with the fading light.

The darkness now hanging over the Followers spun within the glow from Allar's shield. As it revolved, it shrunk and grew brighter. Allar held his hand over the pulsating sphere until it disappeared in a tiny flash.

A cold breeze blew in from the gaping hole in the wall along with the daylight. The villagers in the corner stood up and stared at their hands. The red had gone from their eyes and they looked up at Allar with smiles. Allar stood silently, scrutinizing them.

"Allar!" Straeten called out. "What in the suffering just happened? Allar?"

Allar stood motionless, staring out among the freed Followers.

"Newell," Mathes called out from behind.

At this, Allar looked over his shoulder briefly and then limped out of the building through the new exit Cathlyn had carved. Mathes wrote quickly in his journal. Nilen tentatively walked towards the villagers and Cathlyn followed.

Nilen knelt down next to one of the smiling people. The young woman was searching her body for the mark that Guire had put on her, but it was gone. The others also had no marks, except the one who had been slammed around the room. Bruises and lines of blood crept down his cheeks, but somehow he still lived. For now. Cathlyn frowned and gestured at Straeten with her head to the door.

"What?" Straeten asked, still dumbfounded. "Oh, go check on him? Got it." Straeten quickly ran out of the building after Allar with Ash trotting along.

"You've really helped us," Nilen said. "I don't know how to thank you."

Cathlyn rubbed the pain in her temples. "This is not over yet. He'll be back, and not just to take what he thinks is his."

"Then we'll run," Nilen said.

"But I couldn't release Fay's Followers. She'll sense them."

"We can still fight," Nilen said loudly and stood up. She rubbed Kedan's talisman absently with one hand. "But first, we'll send my grandfather up to the spirits."

"You don't have much time," Cathlyn said.

Nilen nodded and walked away towards a group of villagers gathering in the streets.

Cathlyn turned to Mathes. "Why did you call Allar *Newell?*"

Mathes stopped his frantic scribbling. "Many reasons. The last person to use that Soulkind before Sarissa locked the magic away was named Newell. And since Allar was clearly using its magic…"

"Are you saying Allar is a Master, too?"

"Not exactly."

"What does that mean?"

"Your brother wasn't responding to his name for one. And for another, he has that limp. Did you notice?"

Cathlyn frowned. "I still don't understand."

"Legends tell that Newell and Guire were opposites. Each Soulkind has a balancing magic. Newell's Soulkind is used for protection and building. Guire was, or is, the Master of disease and suffering. Before Sarissa locked them into their Soulkind, they were bitter enemies. Guire, it is said, caused a disease that Newell could only stop by taking it into himself. Before the end of it, the disease affected his leg so badly he could barely walk."

"So, are you saying Newell's soul is still around? And attached to his Soulkind?"

"Despite you freeing the souls from the artifacts with the Lock, some decided to remain behind. To gain power, like Guire and Fay."

"And what about Newell?"

"To protect against Guire, most likely."

"So why doesn't Allar just become the Master of that Soulkind? Why doesn't Newell just give him the power?"

"*That* is a very good question."

Straeten rushed over to Allar with Ash leading the way. He grabbed Allar's arm. "What was that all about?"

"I don't know what just happened. I mean, I saw it, but…"

"But you did some serious magic there." Straeten laughed and slapped him on the back.

"It wasn't me." Allar glanced at the Soulkind strapped to his arm.

"Huh?"

Allar picked up his pace.

Straeten asked, "What do you mean *it wasn't you?*"

"It was like I was trying to remember a dream. I could see what was happening, but I didn't have control over anything. I felt the magic go through me when the curse was ripped from those people, but it didn't come from me." He took the Soulkind off and placed it into his pack.

60

"Why did Mathes call you *Newell?*"

"I… I don't know."

"Well whatever happened, you saved those people. It's too bad it didn't help Fay's Followers, though."

Allar frowned back at the building.

A strong gust of cold wind blew in from the west followed by a clear, low bell. Straeten silently scanned the town. People headed out into the stony streets to the town's center. Straeten and Allar followed to find hundreds already gathered, staring at Nilen upon a large stone.

"She looks so little there," Straeten whispered.

"Don't let her hear you say that," Allar said.

Burgis and Tare patted Straeten's shoulder in greeting. A group of villagers, hunched over in the biting wind, jostled one another and pointed at Allar. Young children clung to some of them with a death grip.

In a clear voice, Nilen spoke. "The Darrak will return for our cursed villagers." The crowd murmured loudly until she raised her hands. "We must leave our homes, for now. Our new friends have offered to help us. They will remain behind in Varkran to give us a head start."

Straeten cocked an eyebrow at Allar.

"That would be my sister," Allar said with a wry smile.

"But are we even sure they're coming here?" Straeten said to Allar quietly. "What about Jace? He's all alone out there." Ash's ears perked up.

Allar said nothing.

The crowd murmured and pointed but Straeten couldn't hear what they were saying. Allar looked like he did, though. His face turned a shade of crimson.

"Take as much food and water as you can carry," Nilen called out. "We leave within the hour."

Straeten was amazed at how the villagers accepted these directions with so few words. An hour? How could anyone be ready to abandon their home in an hour?

Cathlyn caught his attention and pulled him aside. Burgis, Tare, Mathes, and Karanne joined them as well.

"I know it sounds dangerous," Cathlyn said. "I just think we should give these people as much time as we can. And with the magic we have, we might actually stand a good chance. You don't have to stay if you don't want to."

"I think it's pretty clear what we're going to do," Allar said. His eyes ended on Straeten who stared at the ground, his hand resting on Ash's head.

"We'll need to move as quickly as we can back to Beldan after this is over," Mathes added. "Our town needs help as well."

"I agree," Cathlyn said. "But this is happening now and we can do something about it."

"And perhaps die trying," Mathes said.

"I'm not giving up here." Cathlyn folded her arms tightly across her chest. "Now, one important thing. Nilen said they don't want us watching which way they go."

"So we can't talk," Karanne said. "Makes sense. What about the cursed Followers? Are they going to be all right?"

"Nilen knows that they might draw the Darrak to them. She's willing to take that risk, and some of the villagers are as well. A few are going to stay behind and fight."

"We certainly could use some help with the plan here," Allar said.

"We have a plan?" Straeten asked.

"It better be a good one," Mathes said.

Chapter 9: The Path Back Home

Five days and nothing but snow and wind. Turic hunched forward on his horse, avoiding the harsh weather as best he could. He rubbed his saddle-sore back with numbed fingers.

Stroud, always the steadfast Guardian leader, sat tall upon his horse next to Dorne and shot watchful glances occasionally at the quiet man. It was as if Dorne was in some kind of trance. Able to move and eat, but never interact.

Brannon Co'lere also spoke very little since the Shadow Vale. Turic kept a close watch on the former master of his Soulkind. He remembered what had happened to Stroud, who still bore the scars from Brannon's attack. Turic often wondered if the anger festering from that betrayal would ever go away.

Another wailing blast of wind bent everyone's heads down in its path. "It's almost as if she is trying to slow us down," Brannon uttered between wind gusts.

"Fay? But she must be far away by now." Turic held the red gemstone in his hand. Daylight glinted off its multifaceted surface, no longer covered by the gold wings from when Brannon was its Master. "It is possible, I suppose."

"Can you use it somehow, against this cold?" Brannon pulled his robes and furs tighter around himself.

Turic pushed up his spectacles. With a short laugh, he said, "All those times I asked you to try something new with the Soulkind, and here I am not trying anything myself."

He hadn't created anything new since his bright beam of fire had vanquished the Darrak in the fortress. The marking on his forefinger forever reminded him of that destructive spell. Yes, he had needed that magic, but as Cathlyn said, there was much danger in magic.

Now that he had time to think, perhaps he could try again. He held the fiery Soulkind tightly and let his mind sink into the gemstone. He tried to feel its warmth, to surround himself with it all.

A warm, pulsating sensation started in the center of his chest. Startled, he lost control and it ceased. He reached for it again, this time imagining himself stoking the flames by adding kindling. *Now to form a barrier against the cold.* The feeling spread to his arms, to his legs, and then to the tips of his extremities.

He gently pushed the warmth right outside his body like a bubble. The ring of magic left him yet he felt its glow next to his skin. His horse nudged upward into Turic's hands as if in thanks. And that was it. The air was warm. The wind ceased.

He searched himself for a mark but found none. He let the magic go, to try it again. His horse shook his head in protest. The fierce wind immediately tore the furred hood from Turic's head.

Again he focused on the magic, starting in his chest and moving outwards. The magic moved quicker than before. He repeated the process a couple of times to practice summoning it at will, each time a little faster.

A circular mark suddenly glowed brightly across Turic's wrist, and then dimmed leaving behind dark lines. "Interesting," Turic mumbled, staring at the mark.

"What is?" Brannon asked.

"Well, the mark didn't appear until I tried the spell several times. I never heard exactly how it all worked." He smiled as he turned his wrist over to see the whole pattern on it. "I just created a new spell."

Barsal pulled his horse alongside Turic. Several strands of his long hair escaped his hood and blew out in the wind.

"What is it, Master?"

"I told you to call me Turic. I just created something to help with the cold. I think you might appreciate it if this works."

Turic closed his eyes and called upon the magic again, this time mentally expanding the barrier around the entire party. Did it work? He opened his eyes to see that his companions weren't huddled over anymore. Barsal and Kal removed their heavy furs and cheered. Stroud even relaxed his shoulders ever so slightly.

"Would you like to learn?" Turic asked Barsal who watched him in awe. He nodded. Turic reached out for his hand.

Though he had passed fire magic to the Darrak back in the fortress many times, he had yet to teach it to another human since Beldan. How long ago that seemed. So few of those Followers still lived.

Barsal's hand was cold. Turic focused on the new magic and closed his eyes.

Nothing.

He peeked out of one eye and glanced at the newly formed mark on his hand. He half expected it to glow when he taught someone but it did nothing. Barsal turned his hand over and furrowed his eyebrows. The mark the Fireflash formed on his palm dominated the surface as a large circle containing several strange markings.

"Come here," Turic said to Brannon. "I would like to try teaching this to you."

The look of relief on Brannon's face made Turic smile.

Stroud rode over between the two. "That's not a good idea."

Brannon shrunk away from Turic and Stroud, letting his horse fall several steps behind.

"It is only a simple spell, Stroud. And he is over the madness that consumed him. Marathas is gone."

Stroud scoffed and rode his horse back to Dorne and Gerant, the only other Guardian in their party. "I hope you know what you're doing."

Turic motioned for Brannon to come closer again. Brannon hesitated to move, his head still low. "Was it true what you said about Marathas?" Brannon whispered, looking nervously from side to side.

"I have not seen him for a long time, not since you gave me the Soulkind. Now let me see your hand."

Brannon offered it to him hesitantly, but shook with excitement nonetheless. Turic closed his eyes and focused on the spell. This time, the moment their skin touched, he sensed the mark on his hand warm and the magic move from within him towards Brannon. A pulse of warmth left him. Brannon jerked abruptly.

He opened his eyes to see Brannon smiling down at his own smaller mark. He started to smile, too, but then remembered Barsal. Why had the magic not gone to him? Turic pondered this for a moment while the horses made their way along the snowy path. "Now, what is the difference between you and Barsal?" The marks on his own hand from the Fireflash spell were lighter than those on Barsal's, nearly faded.

Could he still use it? He focused on the circle on his palm to call upon the spell but nothing happened.

"Well, that is strange."

65

Chapter 10: The Defense

Karanne walked with Nilen towards Kedan's silent body. Nilen stood tall for a few steps then her strong demeanor crumbled as she stooped beside her grandfather. She appeared like the child she was, the weight of loss heavy on her back. The quiet of the hut enveloped them.

"My father died a long time ago," Nilen said. "I don't even remember him."

Karanne reached for the white stone necklace she kept hidden beneath her shirt. "You lost so much, and then became the leader of your village. These are no small things."

Karanne knelt beside Nilen and placed her hand on Kedan's cold forehead. Sudden warmth emanated from her palm and it glowed faintly. A new mark formed next to the symbols in the center of her hand, much like the ones from Blue and Mitaya and the others she had collected.

From that mark, images and feelings flooded into her, almost too many to process. Within moments, Kedan's life became fully known to her. His fears, his passions. His love for his granddaughter.

Karanne peered into Nilen's eyes. "Your grandfather was proud of you."

Nilen gave Karanne a questioning glance. Karanne gently tucked the loose hair from Nilen's braid behind her ear, and then offered her hand. Nilen reached for it tentatively. Karanne had already tried and failed to teach her the Fireflash, but then, maybe she could give her something else.

Instinctively, Karanne raised her hand and placed it upon Nilen's forehead. The warmth erupted from her palm. Suddenly Nilen's eyes widened and filled with tears. A strong sense of relief flooded Karanne. Kedan's memory had needed to be shared.

"I don't know how you just did that, but I can… *see*… my grandfather. He is… Thank you."

Karanne smiled.

"I want you to take this, to give to my mother, when you see her." Nilen pulled a golden necklace out from under her cloak and placed it safely into Karanne's outstretched hand. "Please."

Karanne glanced at the golden chain in her grasp as Nilen headed back to her people waiting for her outside. Memories of her past life as a thief glinted around her head like the necklace shining in the fading sun. This would have fetched a fair price back in the guild. With a sad smile she wrapped the necklace up and stowed it in a safe pouch on her belt.

A pang of remorse ripped into her then. She closed her eyes and clasped her own necklace tightly. Why couldn't Jace have said goodbye? She stepped outside of the hut just as some of the villagers came in to prepare Kedan's body for burial. In only a short time, the village was alive with preparation to leave.

"Seems like they've done this sort of thing before," Mathes called to her.

"Nice that you're talking to me again." Karanne harshly pulled her red hair back into a ponytail. She couldn't even remember the last time they spoke.

"They're a nomadic people in their hearts, I believe. They will find a new home. They don't really need our help."

So that was his reason for breaking the silence. Karanne slowed her quick walk past the robed scholar. A thick layer of stubble covered his usually clean shaven cheeks.

"We should hurry and catch up to Turic and the others," he said. "They are only a few days ahead."

"We told these people we would help them." As she walked past the hut, she noticed a clearing with several burial mounds. Not many, but enough to show this was home. If it were hers, she'd want to hold onto it. All this fighting couldn't be in vain. "They won't be able to protect themselves from the Darrak without us."

Karanne joined Allar, busy ordering some of the villagers on a defensive fortifying task. Burgis, Tare and Straeten set to work adding stones and sharpened bones to the tops of the wall surrounding the village.

Mathes shouted above the din of the workers, "Even magic used with good intent will eventually fall."

"You doubt us?" Karanne shouted back.

Mathes stepped closer and lowered his voice. "I doubt you will ever back down from a challenge. But just because you learned a few new tricks, you think you will never do wrong things? Magic *will* twist your actions. As it did with Jace."

"You don't know him," Karanne said. "And I'm starting to think you don't know me."

Straeten stopped hammering and walked slowly towards them with Ash at his side.

Cathlyn took a step backwards. "She's right. Jace is fine." Cathlyn mumbled something unintelligible and tried to turn away but not before Karanne planted a solid grip on her shoulder.

There was more.

Things didn't often frighten Karanne. She *always* found a way out. And Jace was the same way. Okay, he was in the middle of nowhere right now and she felt concern for that, but there was something in Cathlyn's voice and eyes that chilled her heart and made her fear for him.

"What *is* it?"

Cathlyn exhaled slowly. "Marlec's Soulkind wasn't always evil. It started out simple, just like Jace's."

"What does that have to do with Jace?" Karanne asked.

"One small change here, another there, and finally Marlec was able to use his gloves to manipulate those around him." Cathlyn paused for a moment. "Jace thinks he may have started down a similar path."

"Why didn't you tell me this before? How can he be out there by himself with this in his head?" She turned and stared into the surrounding hills.

Curse the One of Four.

Chapter 11: The Attack

Karanne was up before dawn checking the perimeter of the town with Allar to ensure the structural reinforcements were in place. The sun broke over the mountain tops to the east, making Karanne's hair shine like fire, yet a chill settled over those awaiting the Darrak's return. No wind touched the skins hanging from the doorways of the huts, no birds called out. Even the strange creatures in their pens were silent.

Allar examined some of the traps he'd created with sharpened animal bones and piles of heavy rocks. "I barely remember doing any of this." He took a few steps back.

Karanne shrugged. "Mathes might know more about what's going on with you, but I don't think he's ready to talk about it."

"Could you talk to him for me?"

"I think he's even less ready to talk to me." She kicked absently at a stone in the path.

"Well, he hasn't looked at me since I started carrying this shield. Am I becoming like those Followers? Just someone else's tool? I wish I'd asked Turic when I had a chance."

They made their way back to the front of the village. A fortified pile of stones blocked the entrance, appearing almost melted into place. Straeten sat there stroking Ash behind his ears. Karanne eyed him carefully, noticing his packed bag. It was never far from him.

"The last of the villagers left late last night," Straeten said. "No one saw which way they went, just like they wanted."

"I guess we wait then?" Burgis yelled out from atop an abandoned hut. Seems he always had a bow strung and an arrow close at hand these days.

"Keep an eye on those northern hills," Allar shouted. "We all remember what's up there."

A couple of the ice magic Followers had remained behind to help out. Two men and a woman. Unlike the day before, they kept to themselves, sitting outside a hut in their animal skins and staring at the ground.

"Sad about leaving their friends and family, I suppose." Straeten looked at them and squinted. "They're acting kind of cold, though."

"Not funny, Straet," Cathlyn said as she and Mathes approached the gates. Karanne tried to avoid making eye contact with Mathes but couldn't quite help herself. Mathes didn't seem to have the same problem.

Cathlyn gestured with her hands as she conversed with her old teacher. She had been Mathes' top student, just as she'd been Turic's before he left the Hall. Maybe she would know what was going on with Allar. Karanne approached Cathlyn to ask, but stopped to watch the Followers heading towards the break in the village wall.

The woman in the group raised her hands above a pile of boulders in front of the openings and closed her eyes. The two men behind her did the same and started a low chant. At first nothing happened, but then the air around Karanne chilled suddenly. A trail of ice crept along from their feet across the stony ground. When it reached the pile the frost grew from the ground. Like vines, it stretched up through the cracks between the stones, sealing and strengthening them until a solid wall of ice remained, cutting the village off from the Darrak outside.

Allar walked over and gave the ice a couple of hits with the back of his arm. "That's solid," he said to the woman.

She started when he spoke to her. "Thanks," she managed to say after a moment. She furrowed her brows and rubbed her temples.

"You should do this mending around the sides of the town as well," Allar said. "Now, if we take position up there, and…"

He continued out of Karanne's earshot as he walked along the border of the village pointing up to various points to strengthen. The three Followers walked behind him adding the ice to the walls when needed.

Karanne's eyes fell on Tare standing next to the strange beasts Nilen left behind in the pen. She and her people had taken most of them, but thought Karanne and the others might need them as well. How, she hadn't a clue. They didn't exactly seem like the trainable type. Tare locked eyes with one of them much as Jace often did with Ash and Valor. Several of the beasts raised their hooves towards him, perhaps in resistance? He waved them down then attempted the connection again.

70

She approached Straeten and Ash quietly. "Come on," Straeten muttered. "Just a direction, anything." Ash twisted towards Karanne for a moment and then resumed staring out into the distance. Straeten straightened up.

"You doing all right?" Karanne asked.

He nodded. "Burgis will let us know if anyone is coming." He shifted uncomfortably and readjusted the furs around his shoulders. He pulled his pack closer to himself.

"Afraid that thing is going to leave without you?" Karanne asked.

"What do you mean?"

"Never mind," she said with a half-smile.

"I can't believe you're letting the One of Four stop you from going after him," Straeten said. "He's pretty much your son, don't you worry about him?"

She turned away. Jace could definitely take care of himself, he always had. Still, she did worry. All the time.

"He's safer than we are right now," Karanne answered. "If he'd stayed here, those Darrak might get those gloves he's been carrying since we left that valley."

Straeten slowly nodded. "I guess you're right."

Karanne's eyes widened. "I mean, he's still in danger though."

Straeten shrugged and went to go stand in front of Burgis and Tare. He took his bag with him.

Karanne let out her breath. That was close.

"This wait is killing me," Straeten said. "Allar told us he'd be back about an hour ago. Anyone see him?"

Burgis pointed to the other side of the village. "Didn't he go that way with those villagers, icing up the walls a bit?"

Minutes passed. Straeten tightened his grip on his staff.

"What are you all waiting for?" Allar said from behind.

Even Karanne jumped a bit at his return. "For you. Where did you go?"

"We were just checking the outer defense." He pointed over his shoulder at the three Followers walking closely behind him. They stared in silence and continued to the center of the village.

Straeten forced a laugh as they left. "They're a lively bunch."

"They were a bit quiet, I suppose."

"Quiet?" Straeten said. "I've seen corpses that looked like parties compared to them."

Karanne rubbed her arms and watched them sit down on top of a long stone wall out of earshot. "Did it just get colder around here?"

"Yeah," Straeten said. "Are they ok?" He gestured to the Followers.

"They were a big help," Allar said. "Nothing is getting through now that they sealed the walls around us. We'll be able to trap the Darrak in a bottleneck they made around the south wall. Once we force them through, we'll have them."

"You make it sound so easy," Straeten said. "You've seen those things fight, right?"

"I've seen you fight. We'll be fine," Allar replied. "Now, stay alert and keep your eyes open."

The wind, though not gusting as heavily as it had through the day, sent an icy chill over Karanne's skin. She paced back and forth in front of their hut while Tare and Burgis kept watch above them on the roof with Straeten. Mathes sat next to the smoldering fire in the center of town, throwing on the villager's logs crafted from animal dung. At first she had cringed at the idea of that, but the fire didn't smell at all, and its short flames put out fairly intense heat.

The villagers also left them some food, mostly dried animal meat. Allar passed some to the group. He offered some to the Followers who stood apart from them, but they ignored it, talking quietly among themselves.

"More for him," he said, eating a piece of the meat and throwing some up to Straeten.

Karanne climbed to the top of the hut to spy out across the hillside. Even with her height she had to stretch her neck at some points to see above the ice walls. The bottleneck area to the south seemed a good enough plan to contain the Darrak. But would they be able to fend them off? The recent loss of power in Brannon's fire magic changed things.

At least she could still use her Fireflash.

Tare remained over by the pen of strange creatures. Ever since Jace taught him that bit of magic, it seemed he wanted to connect with every creature he could find. Even hostile ones like these.

"They're not going to rip his arm off or anything, are they?"

Burgis laughed. "Possibly. But as long as he can talk to them while they do it he'll be happy."

The day passed and the sun sank into the hills in the west beyond Marlec's valley, and not a sound arose from outside the town. The

Followers huddled on the rooftop, peering out into the darkness. One of them coughed violently. The wind beyond the village walls grew to a high pitched wail.

"That's new," Allar shouted. "Burgis, you and Tare go check on the north wall. See if you can spot anything out there in this suffering dark." He quickly limped his way to the south as the two brothers hustled away.

Karanne, Mathes, Straeten and Cathlyn remained huddled over the low flames, their animal skins wrapped closely over them. "Are you okay up there?" Karanne yelled above the wind.

Nothing. Maybe they didn't hear her. She craned her neck and saw the coughing woman collapsed and the other two crouched beside her. Ash whined, his tail hanging low.

"It's all right, Ash." Karanne hurried to the rocks stacked against the hut to climb up. Her hand suddenly itched crazily but she ignored it and continued rushing up the steps. The wind screamed out against her face when she stood up on the roof. Her eyes closed beneath its blast.

She knelt beside the woman. "What happened to her?" She shook the woman's shoulders lightly. Radiating cold surged through the clothing into Karanne's fingers. "Get her something warm! Hurry!" The two men beside her stood up slowly and headed towards the others. Karanne rubbed the woman's arms and wrapped a blanket over her. "Let's get you down there."

Suddenly, the woman's eyes opened with a flash of blue light. She had no pupils, just a clear, empty eye in each socket. Karanne stumbled towards the edge of the roof but regained her footing quickly. This time the woman stood over Karanne, gazing at her with those vacant eyes. Something fluttered behind the crystal stare, something watchful.

The woman opened her mouth.

A deep, hoarse sound escaped her lips. Karanne covered her ears. A blast of ice erupted from the woman's throat towards Karanne, thrusting her backwards over the edge of the roof towards the cold, hard ground below.

Instincts honed from years as a thief kicked in and she rolled across the stony surface towards her friends. She lifted her head to see Mathes, Cathlyn, Straeten and even Ash enveloped up to their mouths in blue ice. Ash whimpered softly. She was trapped. The ice began covering her feet and then the rest of her body until the very blood within her froze. In that moment she finally realized something. The enemy wasn't coming. The cursed Followers' ice around the village wasn't meant to keep the enemy out.

It was meant to keep them in.

Fay's Followers walked between Karanne and the others wearing the same icy stares. When had this happened? Had they always been under her control, or had there been something inside waiting to awaken? Karanne's thoughts shifted to Nilen and the cursed Followers that went with them. There would be no way for them to escape.

One of the Followers ran after Burgis and Tare.

The icy cocoon constricted Karanne's chest and her breaths came short and fitful. Allar walked unknowingly into the clearing and stared at the scene. "Suffering," he uttered and raised his arm with the Soulkind. Two snaking lines of ice slithered from the Followers up his legs, body, and face, trapping him, as well. They'd been waiting for him.

The other Follower came back. "The brothers are contained as well."

Burgis and Tare, too. Karanne's vision started to slip as the coldness filled her. She wanted to yell to Cathlyn... she could do something! But Cathlyn's eyes had already drooped shut. Mathes', too, started to close. Only Straeten still fought the cold with a blazing anger in his eyes.

Her magic... she reached for her Fireflash. Her hand throbbed like it had been but then stopped suddenly. The Fireflash she usually felt was missing, somehow. Was the ice blocking it? But she'd felt it only a moment ago.

The three Followers held their hands over the dying embers in the campfire. Another wail sucked the warmth from the fire. The flames withered into the earth like a dying plant. The last light of the sun disappeared and darkness settled over them.

The wind paused, and a deep rumbling from within the earth reverberated in Karanne's bones. In a pale, silver light a shape begin to form from the ashes of the dead fire. It started as a speck, and then gathered darkness, growing until it surpassed Straeten's height. Arms and legs and a head with long, sparse, dangling hairs melded into form. Tight pale skin covered the face with no sign of eyes, a mouth, or nose. When it stopped growing, the being turned its head sideways and fixed an eyeless stare onto Karanne, unseeing but seeing. Her heart grew colder.

As it moved towards Cathlyn, the shape collapsed slightly into the ashes that formed it, and then solidified. Another shriek erupted from the Followers and the faceless creature transformed again. Black eyes grew from tiny pores. The head convulsed, the neck twisting in places it shouldn't. Karanne tried to look away from the horror of what was emerging, but the ice held her in place. A crack in the skin slit open to reveal a mouth.

A nose bulged out with a jerk and with a few more spasms a woman's visage appeared quite roughly. More hair slid out from the pale skinned scalp and hung wet in front of the being's face. It swayed back and forth in the dark, the Followers kneeling and bowing before it. What was this thing?

The creature shifted towards Allar. A low raspy sound escaped the mouth slit. "Guire will be happy to see you again. You should have left this world when you had the chance, Newell."

Fay?

Next the demon turned to Cathlyn, still unconscious. It placed its dark and twisted hand on her head and her eyes flashed open.

"My, my, my," the voice uttered. "I haven't seen someone quite like you in a long time."

Straeten struggled fiercely in the ice. The encasing on his hands started to split and loosen. A chunk of it cracked and fell from his face and he gasped in some air.

That got its attention.

The three Followers raised their heads as one towards Straeten then surrounded him. Ice crystallized over his body and sealed his mouth again. Karanne struggled to free herself, to try to call her magic while the creature approached him. Her dusty black arm seemed to caress his cheek.

"And you?" the demon breathed out with a voice like metal scraping on stone. It dragged its cracked and black fingernail across his cheek leaving a jagged cut behind. "You'll be mine as well."

The thing turned its empty eyes towards Karanne. Her heart pounded in her skull. Time to do something. She focused on the Fireflash yet she still felt nothing. Her heart raced but she couldn't do anything. For a moment she glimpsed an image of Fay, the icy Master of the Soulkind, behind the black windows of the demon's eyes.

"Now this one." Fay locked stares with her. "I can't quite figure what you're all about."

Karanne said nothing.

"I thought we took care of Marathas. Yet something is burning in you."

Karanne tried to break the stare, to avoid the gaze that peered into her very being. The icy mask around her held tight, though.

"Do you feel that cold in your heart?" Fay whispered. "I am in there with you. Now, where are the Gloves?" Black eyes scanned the village. The creature's hands curled into knotted fists and it shambled awkwardly to one of the Followers. "They are not here. You told me they were here."

The young man avoided the piercing eyes.

"No matter. They are close." It added slowly, "I can sense them." The words sank into Karanne's heart. There they kindled into a burning flame.

The creature held up its hand and moved it from side to side. The sweeping arc shortened until it stopped moving and pointed directly to the west. "Find the gloves," it said to the Followers. "And leave behind their bearer's bones."

Karanne shot a glance at Straeten whose eyes fixed on the western horizon. Why had Jace gone back that way?

Another smile stretched across the demon's face. It raised its hands above them all and a swirling frozen mist crept from the ground, slowly encasing Karanne and her friends. Karanne closed her eyes and accepted the cold.

An unfamiliar animal called out, breaking the cold silence. The ice around Karanne's body began to shake imperceptibly but constantly. In a sudden wave the beasts from the village pen burst around the corner. They streamed from the narrow streets and headed straight towards the icy shells. One threw a Follower into the air with a quick swipe of a spike on its shoulder. The young man fell to the ground, trampled under furious hooves.

The demon opened its mouth wide in an ear shattering scream, cut off by three more enraged beasts crashing into it, knocking it down. Their strong hooves struck Karanne's cage of ice, jarring it until thick shattered pieces fell to the ground. She dropped to her knees.

The female Follower stood before her and raised her hands to seal her back. Karanne closed her eyes and blocked her face but nothing happened. When she looked up, she saw an arrow piercing the Follower's throat from behind, spilling dark blood onto the ground. A thin stream of fluid poured from her eyes until the blue color broke up and faded. She fell forward, revealing Burgis and Tare, both with another arrow nocked. Tare flashed her a quick salute. She nodded once.

How had they gotten out?

A familiar light sparkled in almost excited arcs over Tare's head. The Fireflash! What was it doing out there? So that's why she'd felt it missing. Not because of the ice, but because it had in fact left. It flittered around in loops and then raced to her open palm, glowing red lines branching from where it entered. Strange that she hadn't seen it leave her hand. She'd known in the back of her mind that Burgis and Tare were trapped, but had she actually tried to free them?

Stunned and still numb from the cold, she stripped the massive ice chunks from around her legs. The stampeding beasts ran past and crashed through the icy walls of the town. Allar started to run after the last fleeing Follower then instead climbed up on another rooftop. He peered down into the bottlenecked area where the Follower had apparently forgotten about what he had helped to build.

A bolt of ice hurtled towards Allar, who casually held his shield up to block it. The frozen blast careened off the Soulkind and shot back towards the icy construction above the Follower. Three boulders shook violently and dropped along with a shower of debris. No other sounds came from below.

Karanne glanced around and almost jumped. The demon was staring right at her. Its arm snaked up to grip her throat with its leathery hand and squeezed her breath out of her. She fought to shout, ripping at her neck.

With a groan, the cursed Follower who'd been trampled by the beasts sat up as best he could. First he stared at Karanne with his blue eyes. His face contorted. He almost looked pleadingly at her, his hand raising and falling, as if unsure whether or not to attack her. Finally he turned to the demon and in a weary voice said, "Stop. Please." Swirling magic leapt from his fingertips towards the demon, but instead of sealing it in ice, the creature absorbed it, consuming the power.

A wave of energy left the Follower, shaking Karanne's body as it swept past. The man slumped to the ground and the blue in his eyes slipped away like it had with the other Follower. The thick black mark on his arm faded, too. The grip around Karanne's throat strengthened. Karanne's lungs contracted from the sudden shock of cold surrounding her body.

"No!" Cathlyn's screamed. All sound disappeared as a bubble of energy formed around her. In a rush of light, the energy burst outward and converged on the demon.

Karanne gasped for breath. The demon's arm dangled, disconnected from its body, and then disintegrated to dust. The air around Cathlyn distorted and shook. It froze momentarily and then blasted again, sending Karanne into the nearby hut. She landed beside the demon's head.

Karanne started to fade into unconsciousness. She forced her eyes open to see into the black pits in the demon's face.

"We will meet again." it uttered.

"Count on it."

With its last breath, the creature crumbled into ashes and drifted across the narrow street.

Mathes and Cathlyn hurried to Karanne's side and examined her for injuries. Tears streamed down Cathlyn's cheeks and her hands shook.

"I warned you about magic," Mathes said over a high pitched whine in Karanne's head. "It will only cause destruction. You must end it." Her vision started to fade.

Cathlyn felt Karanne's forehead and spoke through sobs. "But how?"

Mathes paused, feeling for Karanne's pulse. In a hushed whisper, he said, "I may have a way."

Karanne slipped into a dark sleep.

She awoke the next morning to gray light shining through a window in their hut. The sound of voices entered the room, Nilen's among them. Karanne strained to sit up but cringed when a sharp pain rode up her left arm into her neck. Her voice came out quiet and raspy. With her right arm, she reached for a clay container of water.

When she'd had her fill, she called out to Nilen. The young woman hurried into the hut and knelt down by Karanne's side. She rested her hand on Karanne's forehead.

"How did you make it back?" Karanne croaked.

Nilen smiled. "It was Kedan."

Karanne raised her eyebrow.

"He warned me that the Followers would turn under Fay's power. And it was all because of you and what you did for me."

Karanne remembered sending her the memories of Kedan, but could the magic account for him talking to her? "I don't understand."

"The memory you gave me became something else," she said. "He spoke, as if through a waking dream. We had time to stop them from attacking any of us." Her eyes held a deep sorrow and Karanne guessed what *stop* meant. The dark stains on her sleeves confirmed it.

"I don't believe any Darrak are coming," Karanne said. "I think Fay's plan all along was to turn her Followers against us. To get the gloves."

Nilen nodded. "Then it is time for us to move again, just in case."

Soon, Karanne's friends walked into the door one by one to check in on her. "Has anyone been affected by the Followers at all?" she said, her voice returning to normal. "Anyone with a mark?"

They shook their heads. "Wait, where's Straeten?" Cathlyn called out and ran outside.

Karanne struggled again to sit up. She groaned as the pain settled above her brow in one of the nastiest headaches she could remember. Nilen placed a cool cloth on her forehead. "You still have my necklace, to give to my mother when you see her?"

Karanne felt for it in the pouch at her side. She also instinctively reached for the white stone around her neck but then, through the fog and pain in her mind, she remembered. She had already stashed it in Straeten's pack for just this moment. When Jace saw the necklace, he would know she was with him in spirit. That she would never abandon him.

It had only been a matter of time before Straet left to follow Jace. And now that demon basically pointed him in the right direction. That's all he needed. Hungrily, she wolfed down the breakfast Nilen brought in. She could rest now. The One of Four may have kept her from following Jace, but that didn't mean she needed to stop Straeten.

Chapter 12: The Journey to Graebyrn

Jace stared at his Soulkind. The black metal had crept around the green stone a little further since the last time he'd seen it. It glinted in the moonlight. He recognized the material now from another Soulkind.

Marlec's.

He drew the gloves out of his pouch slowly to keep from making noise. Not that it really mattered much. They never seemed to make any sound when he moved them anyway. He slipped them onto his hands, the dead of night closing in. They felt cold against his skin, yet strong and welcoming. A sense of total control filled him, like when he'd used the spell to control those Darrak, yet even stronger.

There was something else. Some sort of presence. Maybe not Marlec anymore, but imprints of others who once possessed the Soulkind long before him.

He examined them more closely. On the right hand sat Marlec's black gemstone surrounded by the metal of the gloves, but on the left side there was only a small groove he hadn't noticed before. But then, he'd never really looked at them this closely. Slowly, he brought his own Soulkind next to the indentation. The metal began to hum.

He felt his thoughts expand beyond his body. Lights shone brighter around him, calling. Like a whirlpool he began to draw them nearer. Closer the lights moved, unable to resist his call. What were they?

His companions. And their minds were his to control. The burra would do as he bid, Valor would dive and attack any foe at his slightest whim. Power swelled inside him, and it felt good. Yet his hand hesitated to place his Soulkind onto Marlec's.

As he pulled the stone away, a strip of black metal reached up like an insect's leg and wrapped around it. Jace tore at it with his other hand but the thread stuck. Two more flew out of the glove and onto his rock. Their grip strengthened even as Jace tore the gloves off.

The slithering darkness enveloped the stone and then latched onto Jace's hand. One by one, more strands erupted from the gloves, moving on to his arm and shoulder. Black marks covered his skin in elaborate tracings.

Suddenly, Blue stood before him with front hooves raised high. With a powerful neigh, she stamped down onto the gloves and knocked them away from Jace's grip. The strips slithered away from him and into the earth where they fell.

Jace sat up with a start. Valor and the burra shifted upright beside him. He breathed a sigh of relief.

"Crazy dreams." He rubbed his eyes but his fingers felt cold and hard against his skin. He pulled back his hands and gaped at them.

He was wearing the gloves.

He tore them off and let them drop to the ground. Light glinted off the dark metal, drawing his eyes. He thrust them into the bottom of his pack.

Nothing seemed to be out of place in the small campsite. Nothing that he might have caused by using the gloves. He reached into the collection of stones in his pouch and each memory glistened in his mind. But they weren't his concern.

In the moonlight, the three metal corners surrounded the stone he was looking for. No change. He closed his eyes and let out a deep breath. Clasping the Soulkind tightly, he lay back down between Valor and the burra on the cold, stone valley floor and hoped for a few hours of dreamless sleep.

Jace cracked his sore neck under the gray light of another day. Valor already caught a small lizard for breakfast but the burra was nowhere to be seen. Jace reached into his pack for a bit of dried meat from Nilen's village. Three days of this was getting a little old. He missed Straeten's ability to find food anywhere they went, even if it was a little strange at times. At least it was different.

He stood up to scan the stony valley floor. "You seen Payt today?" he asked Valor. The name just seemed to fit. Name or no, the burra still wanted nothing to do with him other than to carry him around. And even that might have been pushing it. Had the leader sent him against his will? Valor cocked his head to the side and continued to tear at his breakfast.

Jace stretched his back. Riding a burra was a bit different than a horse. He was almost used to it now though and definitely knew to hold tighter when he ran.

The water in his animal skin felt low. Time to refill at a stream or spring, if he could find one. Maybe he would see the burra out this morning. Finally find out what he ate. The past two days he only saw him returning from getting water or food.

He moved quickly since the day was already getting on. He wanted to make the best use of the daylight in this rocky terrain. Around the next boulder he froze. A small group of gray hog-like creatures were drinking from a small stream. Some pulled at short yellowish grasses growing next to the water and others splashed in the rushing stream. Two stood eyeing the surroundings, although they hadn't seen Jace yet. They appeared to be the adults of the pack.

A pair of smaller ones strayed across the stream and into the shadow of the boulders towards more grass. Two soft whooshing sounds pierced the air. The hogs fell silently. A second later a great squealing arose from the others. The biggest of the beasts ran through the water to the fallen hogs.

The burra stepped out from his hiding spot, blending in with the grayness of the valley floor. The hog, probably the mother, guarded the two still bodies. Payt leaned over and quickly jerked his shoulder blades together. A foot-long spike burst out of the burra's shoulder blade with another whoosh. The spike drove clean through its head and the hog fell.

The remaining hogs screamed and ran off between rocks and crevices. Payt settled in on the three of them and began to gorge on his prey. With a sudden twist of his front legs, another short crack echoed as a pointy new spike replaced the one that had shot out. Jace gaped at the scene. Never, even in old storybooks, had he heard of such a thing. He started to walk toward Payt.

The beast started when he saw him. A loud, low growl escaped from his throat. He stamped his front hooves into the rocks and dirt.

"Whoa! It's me!" Jace called out.

Blood dripped from Payt's mouth. He took a protective stance then made a few steps towards Jace.

Jace jumped backward which spooked the burra even more. Payt bent forward, this time aiming his shoulders right at Jace.

Jace held his hands up in surrender.

The burra stamped again and growled even lower. Jace drew a deep breath. For the suffering, he couldn't die like this.

"It's just me, Payt."

Payt snorted into the air, his breath making a small cloud. Jace stood his ground. Unconsciously, he held his hands in the salute he always raised to his friends. A long silence followed. Valor swept down from the sky and with a loud flutter of wings and landed on Jace's shoulder.

Payt almost casually returned to his food and downed the remaining bites. After finishing and scouring the rocks, the burra turned around and walked towards their camp.

"Thanks, Valor," Jace whispered. Valor pulled at his hair with his beak. Jace winced. "Never mind, I take it back."

Jace followed Payt. From a distance. No more sudden moves after what he'd seen. The burra took his time. Was he full from the big breakfast? Injured? None of the food exactly fought back.

After they reached the small camp, the burra huddled next to the smoldering fire in an almost pained manner. Jace sat down to pack his things. Payt growled.

"You okay, Payt?" The burra didn't respond, his head tucked back around his shoulder. "I guess we wait then."

If it were Ash or Valor, he could've sensed something. But not with Payt. He wouldn't let Jace anywhere near him.

The waiting was killing him. The longer he sat in one place the greater the chance of bringing the Darrak right to him. He had to keep moving. That's why he'd left his friends in the first place. At least Straeten and the others were far away from him now. Turic was even farther off. Strange, Jace knew his friends were out there, but he actually *felt* them, too. Felt their direction off to the east.

He shoved his meager things into his pack one at a time—his washing towel, food, weapons. A few of his daggers would stay out in case of any unwelcome visitors. He brushed his hand past his blade with the exquisite carvings. It was still hard to believe the etchings on it were made by a Darrak.

And then there was the metal rod from Kedan's village. Where did it come from? What was it for? Staring at it now, the carvings suddenly seemed to dance in his mind. When they stopped swirling, the strange markings coalesced into sounds and words, but they made no sense to him. A name appeared: "Rushkarn." What it meant was beyond him. Perhaps Turic would know, or maybe even Graebyrn.

Graebyrn. Hopefully he would actually be talking to the old dragon soon. Graebyrn would know what to do with Marlec's Soulkind. Finally end that darkness. He had so many other questions, like how to train as a Master, and especially how to fix his newest mistake. How to remove the dark magic he'd created.

Familiar doubts crept up in him. What was he without his Soulkind? Which power came first? His being a Master, or his being able to recall memories with stones? He could use them before he found the Soulkind, couldn't he?

He felt through the pouch he always kept by his side, seeking out an old memory, something from before the time he found the Soulkind. He saw memories of Cathlyn, of Straeten and Turic, but they were all recent. What was his earliest memory? He dug deeper into the stones and the reaches of his mind.

A sudden cracking sound startled him. Payt bent his forelegs and a bulge beneath his skin at his shoulders shifted and settled. The burra stood up quickly.

"Oh, now you're ready." Payt peered down his snout at Jace almost indignantly. "I suppose this can wait."

Jace finished packing his things and threw them in a sling over his back. He approached Payt with a slow walk. Had he calmed any since his hunting earlier? Luckily the burra settled down and allowed Jace to grab a handful of hair and pull himself over to mount. Jace patted his neck. Payt reared up slightly and took off again heading south.

Jace felt a prickle at the base of his neck and kicked the burra faster. Something wasn't quite right about this area. Unfriendly eyes sought him out, followed him. Eyes unlike those of any predator he had sensed before.

Thank the light Payt ran so quickly.

As the day crept by and the winds increased, light snow began to fall. An unsettling silence masked the rocky hillsides. Giant boulders about twelve feet high towered overhead. Payt stepped quickly yet confidently among the slippery stones. Clawed toes stretched out from his hoof-like footpads to grip onto the ground. His stubby ears twitched.

A mark on his hand grew warm as he tried to feel what was bothering Payt. He stretched further towards him and collided with a sort of wall. It resisted his thoughts but he pushed harder regardless. The burra bucked him forward.

Jace sailed not quite gracefully onto the snow but was able to roll instinctively to the side. Still, he'd hit rock and his head blared with pain. Slowly he sat up, shaking his aching head, and stared at Payt, who met his look with a vicious glare. Payt crouched, his shoulder spikes shifting. A burning anger arose through Jace's clouded eyes. How dare this creature throw him? He'd make sure that never happened again. The dark mark on his arm lit with power.

Valor screeched, penetrating his heart. He took a deep breath. "Sorry, Payt."

Payt crouched on the stones, poised to dart away. Valor landed on Payt's back. The burra tilted his head to look at him and then loosened his shoulders.

A high pitched whine blasted pain into Jace's skull. Two cat-like creatures bounded off the top of a boulder and landed on Payt's back with their claws extended and their narrow, sharp teeth bared. Valor took to the skies and circled right overhead.

Payt, his ears flat against his head, reared back frantically as the cats dug their claws in further to hold on. Jace stumbled and shook the fog from his head. He grabbed the first thing he could, a fist-sized rock.

One of the gray creatures opened its large jaws and screeched the same horrible cry. Its teeth shone yellow in the afternoon light. A sharper, more intense scream threatened to burst Jace's head apart but he threw the stone anyway. The cry was silenced and replaced by a cracking sound. The creature hung its head and out fell its crushed teeth. Jace readied another stone.

A third creature clawed onto Payt's back. Payt scrambled, his thick fur turning dark with his blood. Jace tried to find a target but couldn't see one through the thrashing. Valor gave a loud cry and dove and slashed at the one attacking Payt.

Payt twisted his shoulders around to get a clear shot at his attackers. Two of the beasts clung viciously, always staying behind his shoulder spikes. Three more sprung out from behind a boulder.

"Payt! Behind you!" Jace shouted. The newcomers shrieked. Jace grimaced from the sharp pain in his ears.

Payt abruptly swerved into a sharp boulder next to him, crushing the beasts on his back. Both of the surprised creatures clambered to regain their footing. With a quick snap of Payt's shoulder blades, sharp spikes flew soundly into both of their sides. They lay motionless on the cold stony ground.

Jace's bow was too far so he unsheathed two of his knives. They would have to do. One of the creatures quickly faced him, its toothed maw slathering with spittle. The creature leapt towards Jace with two spiked claws extended fully on its forelegs.

Valor dove in front of its eyes and managed to slow it down enough for Jace to move out of its path. He swung the blade in his right hand as he jumped away from the attack, glancing off its thick hide. One of the claws slashed at his leg and it burned fiercely. The warmth of his blood ran down to his foot. Fighting the pain, he jumped atop a nearby boulder.

Payt flung the creature off his back and pinned it on the ground with one of his legs. With two quick cracks, a pair of spikes pierced it. Blood ran down Payt's hind leg, too.

A larger creature, darker than the others, jumped behind Payt and right in front of Jace. He sensed it was female, the leader of the pack. She reared up with her claws extended. He couldn't lose another friend. The power of his Soulkind called to him. The pool of magic swelled within.

He reached for the creature's thoughts.

Another scream sounded, this time right next to Jace's ear. He gripped his knives then released them. Just Valor again.

Ignoring the dark impulse, he leapt on the cat's back with incredible precision, following his old instincts instead. He plunged his knives into her back, but a bony plate cast the blows to the side. She jumped up onto her hind legs, tipping Jace off onto the stony ground. He barely avoided the jagged edges of the rocks and the beast's yellow-fanged mouth.

Another crack sounded. A foot-long spike drove into the back of her skull and through her mouth. She was dead before she hit the ground. Payt bent forward and shook heavily. The remaining creatures gathered around their leader's dead body and howled one last cry before running off.

Jace clutched his leg and limped over to Payt. Deep breathing rattled in the burra's lungs. Jace put his hand on his heaving side, staying away from the jagged claw marks. They didn't appear too deep but something was causing Payt pain, or perhaps it was only exhaustion.

"Whatever those things were, thanks for saving me."

A burning in his leg made him remember his own injuries. Part of his pants had been torn away by sharp claws, and a nasty gash lined his skin underneath. He found some of Mathes' salve and rubbed it into the wound, sending sharp pain up his leg. He winced while wrapping a clean cloth tightly around it.

Valor cried again overhead and Jace quickly opened himself to his sight. From above, he watched the escaping animals scatter into the gray landscape. They could regroup and come back, but probably wouldn't without their leader.

Jace returned to his own sight and glanced at the body of the fallen female. One of Payt's spikes stuck in the back of her skull and the other lay on the ground about twenty feet away. Jace walked over to inspect it.

What a deadly looking thing. He held it gingerly in his right hand. Sharp, solid, and balanced. Would it be weird to take it? It would certainly make a good weapon in a pinch. With what felt like honor or respect towards his companion, he strapped it carefully to his belt.

Payt meanwhile stood waiting, but Jace sensed something was wrong. No more spikes protruded from the burra's shoulders and he carried his head a little lower. Jace began to walk towards where he last sensed Graebyrn but Payt growled at him and shoved his nose into Jace's back.

"I'm not going to let you carry me now." Jace turned around. Payt's front legs wobbled and struggled with each step.

"You've got to rest." Jace raised his hand to Payt's side. Even as he said it he knew the burra would insist on pushing forward. It was just in his nature. With a sigh Jace called out to Valor. "At least let's see if we can find some water. Valor, see anything?"

The red tailed hawk circled higher and called out his sharp cry. His path pointed south so Jace led them between the large boulders in that direction, hoping they would find a bit of safety soon, and avoid any more encounters. His sight flew to Valor's eyes to spy for more creatures. Nothing.

Not for the last time did he wish Straeten and Karanne had come with him.

Chapter 13: The Fall

Jace stumbled alongside Payt on what looked to be a path. He had tended to the deep scratches on the burra's back despite constant growls and nips. Payt limped along, a deep cracking resonating from his legs every mile or so. What *was* that?

He reached out with his hand tentatively and rested it on Payt's side. He could find out one way, but he didn't want to wind up impaled by one of those spikes. Still, he had to know how serious it was. Maybe if he approached it like he would as a thief. Nice and slow and no sudden moves.

He closed his eyes, focused on his Soulkind, and took a deep breath. The familiar warmth radiated from his center to his fingertips. But this time, instead of channeling the power outward towards Payt, he held it in and examined it slowly, carefully. Something hovered just out of reach. A sensation like flowing water. He drifted closer to the flow but couldn't quite grasp it. What started as a trickle grew into a river. Its energy tugged at him, trying to pull him into its current. He shifted the stone in his palm to refocus. The flows of magic shone more clearly. The magic wasn't coming from him, instead he was a pathway for it.

Maybe he could divert a small flow, like when he played in creeks as a kid. When he sensed the stream wash over him again he nearly let the power draw him in. He backed away. Again he tried to approach, but this time, instead of letting go, he directed the flow into himself. He channeled the power through his hand and into Payt as calmly as he could. He held his breath, ready to spring into a run if needed.

But Payt didn't move. His shoulders relaxed and his breathing sounded smoother. Payt's eyes met Jace's and in that instant the burra's presence entered his thoughts. All the stumbling, his head hung over, the fighting with his spikes, no bones sticking out of his shoulders. All of it.

And then he understood.

Some spikes were still in there, but not an endless supply. And they were connected to his legs. Without them, well, this is what happened to him.

"Will they grow back?"

Payt trudged forward. Jace heard another deep crack in his legs and *saw* with his magic a spike slip into place. It would take some time but Payt would be walking normally again. He rubbed Payt's side.

Another vision appeared in his head. A memory? He saw a family of burras hunting together. Was he seeing this through Payt's eyes? The family alternated attacking their prey. After one launched a volley of spikes, another stepped in to use its own. Never did one use up all of them, they worked as a team. And when the family was done and had their food, they rested and regrew their spikes. Yet they didn't rest long since none had exhausted their supply. It all made sense now.

"I better start pulling my weight around here. Is that what you're trying to tell me?"

Payt swung his head into Jace's arm. Jace laughed. At least he still had his spirit. The fact that he could sense that spirit filled something inside him. The bond made him feel safe, like he was home. Guilt crept in, though, and his smile fell. He took a step away from Payt.

Nothing could take her place.

The landscape began to change as they headed upwards into some nearby hills. The sun, now halfway set, cast long shadows from the stunted trees covering the hillside. A fast-flowing stream of icy water bubbled down onto the floor of the valley. Cold silence fell as the winds finally ceased.

They were close to Graebyrn now, Jace was sure of it. He knelt beside the river and stared into the shallow water, its surface glowing from the setting sun. He reached in and stirred. A deep and familiar voice echoed in his ears, though he couldn't make out the words. It had to be Graebyrn, but where was it coming from?

Jace glanced in all directions, hoping for clues. Grasping his magic, he sent Valor up into the darkening skies where he could look through his eyes if needed. The dragon's voice called to him again. This time the words were clear.

"You are being followed."

Followed? Jace pulled at the burra to climb the steepening slope but Payt fought to take one last long gulp of icy mountain water.

"Come on!"

Payt finished drinking and hastened up the hill as best he could with his forelegs still wobbling. The sun finally set and in a matter of minutes the dark shadows of harsh cliffs surrounded them, blocking out the night sky.

Strange animal cries sounded in the night. More cats? Whatever they were he knew one thing. The sounds were getting closer. He kept checking behind as he stepped around boulders. He reached unconsciously for Payt's spike at his side. Out in the darkness, a stone slid and a branch cracked. His heart thudded in his chest.

He hated rushing Payt with his slow and pained walking, but what else could he do? The burra shifted a bone into place in his left leg and picked up his pace slightly. Maybe he wouldn't have to push him after all.

Valor cried out as he weaved throughout the trees. Did he see something? Jace's sight flew into the hawk's and he scanned the surroundings. The night appeared so clear though Valor's eyes. Every little rock or tree branch became visible, but it wasn't until he looked beyond the stunted forest that he saw what he was dreading. Two dark shapes slid down the rocky slope of a looming cliff wall. Not the four-legged creatures that attacked them earlier. He could've handled that a little easier.

Darrak. Here, now. At least two of them. For the suffering.

How had they tracked him here? But more important, had they seen him?

Jace felt the urge to pull out his bow, but there was no way he could face and defeat two Darrak. Not on his own. Not without…

The power of the dark mark on his arm fired into his mind, rushing up to overpower his resistance. Maybe just this once he could use it.

Payt reared back on his hind legs and butted Jace in his left shoulder. "Ow!" he said both in anger and in thanks. He tightened his pack and pulled Payt faster, this time towards the hillside. The burra yanked on Jace's grip.

Jace whispered, "Come on, Payt!" He glanced about, half expecting to see a small army of Darrak crossing the stream. Not yet. Anytime, now, though. Moonlight spilled through a break in the trees shining upon a stony hillside. His heart told him that was it. He had to reach that place. The ground flew under him as he sprinted towards it, constantly turning around to see Payt limping as fast as he could.

Move!

90

Something suddenly occurred to him. The Darrak weren't after Payt, just him. He could lead them away from Payt and catch up with him later. Hopefully. He sized up a cliff wall, half lit with the rising moon behind him. It would be a difficult climb, a hundred feet or so, but nothing he hadn't done before back in Beldan. He could make it. He glanced at Payt, who had just caught up and bowed slightly in the frigid night. Jace put his hand on Payt's back. He had to get him to a safe place.

In the corner of his eye he caught a glimpse of a small, dark opening up ahead. That could work. Unconsciously, he focused on this image and urged Payt towards it. "Go on Payt. I'll catch up with you later."

The burra started to limp off in the direction of the opening. Jace patted his side as he left. With luck, the Darrak wouldn't see him through the sparse undergrowth and darkness.

Gripping the spike tightly, he stood ready to face the Darrak. He stared into the darkness. Gradually, the outline of two shapes became visible until they stood before him. They had him cornered. He knew it. And so did they.

He took a scant step backwards as they advanced, their movements like liquid. Their dark stares locked onto Jace's eyes and he froze.

His dark thoughts swelled. If something controlled them, maybe he could too. He held up his spike, weighing his two options. He was running out of time. One of the Darrak passed a net to the other and they held it out in front of them. They wanted to capture him? They raised the net slightly as they advanced. Jace got ready to throw the spike. They snarled and took one more step.

Jace threw the spike at the attackers to knock the net out of reach. It flew straight without any spin, perfectly balanced, and into the gray one's arm. With a sound like a laugh, it yanked out the spike and threw it to the ground.

Two quick cracks sounded from behind. Both Darrak dropped to the ground, spikes embedded in their thick reptilian skulls. Jace turned to see Payt standing there. The burra's front legs buckled, unable to support his body. Not after releasing those final spikes. Jace saluted Payt as he crawled pitiably towards the shelter in the wall and turned to prepare for the next Darrak.

Bugs and other vermin swarmed up from the rocks and covered the Darrak's bodies. Jace grabbed his spike out of the decomposing Darrak and stowed it in his pack. He tightened the straps and cracked his knuckles. He jumped up to the cliff side and easily grasped onto the craggy wall. At least his days in the Guild weren't for nothing.

Ten feet, twenty. He scaled the wall quicker than he thought he could. His hand slipped and he fumbled to regain his grip. Too quick, maybe. He heard claws clicking against the rocky handholds below. A few at first, and then more. Had they seen Payt?

Payt's low growl gave him his answer. He peered down to see Payt ready his shoulders. But there were no spikes left. A cold fear grew in his heart. He could not lose another friend. The Darrak surrounded Payt and raised their claws. Dark images and burning anger swirled inside him. He could stop them all. It would be easy.

But then, Jace saw something in Payt's eyes. Something that made him hesitate. His dark thoughts subsided. There was another way.

Okay, Payt. Hope this works.

He raised his hand towards the Darrak. The calming magic he'd used on Payt grew in his mind. He directed that energy down to the valley. The Darrak jerked up to face the cliff, fixing their dark stares on Jace. The burra took this chance to creep into the safety of the cave. The Darrak wandered away from each other to the edge of the trees in a daze. Jace let out a relieved sigh.

Valor cried out. Jace leaned over the edge to see why. Another swarm of Darrak broke through the trees and pushed past their confused brethren. Jace's foot slipped on the rocks and he began to slide back down. The cliff side tore at his hands as he tried to regain his grip. A dozen feet flew by before he stopped himself. The Darrak scrambled to the wall and began to climb up like insects. Jace started back up again. His magic worked on a few, but this many? Was he ready for that? He couldn't risk taking the time to find out.

He leapt for a ledge sitting just out of reach. His already tired and bleeding fingers clutched desperately at the jagged rock. Swinging from the edge, he stole another look down. About ten of the scaly creatures were winding their way up the cliff while others had fanned out seeking another way. He pulled himself up and sprinted on the short ledge. He vaulted up through a narrow vertical gap to reach another clearing. Rocks tumbled as he climbed closer to the top.

Valor sailed beside him about forty feet above the valley floor. He certainly had it easy. Jace glanced down again in the moon's light to see the Darrak's progress. They were fast, but not nearly as fast as he was. He grinned and jumped to another rock layer above his head. He could do it. He was more than halfway there now.

Two black claws slammed down into the rock right above his head. Oh yeah, some could fly. The Darrak reached over the edge and grabbed Jace's shoulder. It lifted him off the ground, claws digging into his skin. Its reptilian fangs shone as it brought Jace closer.

A blur crashed into its head and its grip loosened.

"Valor!" Jace called out and landed back on his feet. The hawk scratched at the Darrak's eyes, dodging its swinging claws.

Jace jumped to the side and pulled himself up quickly to the ledge where the Darrak fought. Before the scaly creature could react Jace ran toward it and vaulted off of its back. The surprised Darrak flailed its arms as Jace leapt up to the next ledge, narrowly missing its claws. As Jace pulled himself up, the Darrak lost its balance and toppled off the rocks spinning awkwardly to the ground below.

Two more levels of ledges and Jace would be up to the top. He couldn't wonder what would happen once he got there. First finish up the climb, then at the top everything would be all right. The cries of the Darrak grew louder and closer now. The sharp edges of the rocks cut deeper into his hands and he slipped a couple of times in his own blood. He pulled himself to the next flatter area and knelt, breathing heavily.

A smashing on the rocks above his head snapped him out of that. Several flying Darrak dropped others without wings on the ledge. They landed skillfully and lifted the ropes they carried in their claws. Valor flapped almost frantically beside him in the air. His muscles screamed at him to rest. If he could just use his power to control on even a few, it would be over.

He had to stop them.

Suddenly, the mountain shook around his feet, shaking the very foundation of the stones within the cliff wall. He covered his ears but couldn't block out the deafening chaos. A Darrak next to him waved his arms at the two flying above. They dove quickly to grab it off the ledge.

The silver moonlight shone brightly upon a massive gray blur speeding down the cliff. Was the whole mountain dropping on him? A moment later, the mass slammed into the valley floor, rocking the cliff walls. The Darrak climbing upward toppled and fell. Jace stared in disbelief.

Graebyrn.

The ancient dragon roared, shaking the very air around him. The Darrak still clasping the cliff wall lost their grips and plummeted. Jace covered his ears again, smiling despite the pain. He leaned back against the stony wall and almost immediately, sharp claws dug into his boot threatening to pull him down. He waved his arms for something to grip onto and kicked at the Darrak. Before he could find a grip, he spun off the edge and down towards the valley floor.

A strange thought buzzed through his mind as he dropped. He fell far too often for a thief. Overhead he saw Valor dive after him.

The cliff wall flew past. A bright light filled his vision. Wings flapped and then enveloped him in a warm glow.

Chapter 14: Training

Jace woke up with Payt standing over him, his wet nose sniffing his face. Cold, hard stones pressed into his back. He brushed away the burra's furry head steering clear of his shoulders. The giant spikes had finally grown back. With a start, Jace realized he was lying on the floor of a giant cave with only a blanket covering his bare body. How long had he been out? What happened after he fell?

Flickering yellow and red lights danced across the high rocky ceiling from a nearby bonfire. His clothes and gear lay in a pile drying next to the fire. He sat up and strained his ears to hear the rain pattering outside.

His arms ached as if he'd been heavy lifting. How strange. It wasn't like he hadn't climbed that much before. At least there were no major injuries from his fall off the cliff. His right hand throbbed from gripping something tightly. He pried open his fist. The black metal protrusions covered his green stone. He stared at it, confused. How had it ended up in his hand?

Valor perched upon a granite pedestal next to the fire, glancing furtively around the vast cave. Jace scrambled to get his clothes on, and then checked the memory stones in his pouch and Marlec's Soulkind in his pack. Nothing seemed damaged from the fall. A rumbling reverberated through the air and stony floor. Something was coming. Jace fumbled to put away the tainted Soulkind.

From around a corner in the cave, Graebyrn emerged. Jace swallowed hard. His silver scales, no longer a dull gray, reflected the firelight throughout the cavern. A strong sense of his power, combined with one of peace, nearly overwhelmed Jace.

Payt bowed his head almost imperceptibly, as did Valor. The same urge to show reverence entered Jace and he instinctively knelt before the great silver dragon.

Graebyrn rumbled in what seemed like a laugh. "You may rise, Soulkind Master," he said in his deep raspy voice.

Jace smiled. "It's good to see you again." Well, that was an understatement.

"And you as well." Graebyrn stood taller and walked easier, so different from the last time they met when he could barely move.

The memory of the dragon plummeting past him at the cliff wall flashed into his mind, a brightly falling star saving him from the Darrak. How had he recovered so quickly? Jace had expected some terrible scars from the time he fended off the Darrak at his old lair. Not a scratch to be seen.

"I'm sorry I led the Darrak to you. Again."

"They were not after me, lucky for them. And not to worry. We can remain hidden from them here, at least for a time." He peered into Jace's eyes. "I see you have become stronger with your Soulkind."

Jace covered his right arm nervously. The dragon settled his huge body upon the cave floor. "I know of your dark mark."

Jace fished the Soulkind out of his pouch and held it up, showing the perversion marring its perfect green color. "Then help me get rid of it."

The dragon sighed, sending a breeze through the cave. "I cannot."

Jace drew his eyebrows together. "What do you mean? I came here to erase that mistake." Pained images of Blue passed behind his eyes and he closed them. She was gone. She was really gone.

"The magic you created is now a part of the Soulkind, as it is a part of you."

"You make it sound like a good thing."

Graebyrn gave no response.

Jace sighed. "It calls to me, and I want to use it. What do I do?"

Graebyrn motioned to the fire with his tail. "Come, you must be hungry, you have been resting for quite some time now."

"I don't want to eat, I want to know what to do." His stomach betrayed his words with a rumble that perhaps rivaled Graebyrn's roar.

The dragon raised a scaled eyebrow and showed some teeth in what might have been a smile. "Patience, young one."

Jace lowered his head. "I'm sorry. And I meant to say thank you for saving me at the cliff."

Graebyrn nodded. "There is no need to apologize. You have a need to know about your Soulkind and I will do my best to help you understand it. But first, you must eat. I apologize for not having the serving ware you are accustomed to."

96

Jace hadn't even noticed the food was just heaped onto the floor. Nor did he care. After filling himself he began to realize how hungry he had actually been. He nodded his thanks and wiped off his hands.

Tentatively he reached for his Soulkind. The metal prongs stuck out of its sides. Not making eye contact with dragon, he placed it in front of him on the bare floor. "I'm ready now."

"You are not the first to make a mistake, nor will you be the last."

"But every time I use my magic, this new part calls to me. It feels *wrong*, but it's getting harder not to use it. Please, just tell me what to do."

"I can train you to ignore its call. However the road to that peace will be a long and dangerous one. Only then will its grip upon you weaken."

"Ignore it?"

"Hmm, more like *accept*. You will see as you learn more about your Soulkind. Other paths will appear."

"Will you help me?"

Graebyrn lowered his head. "Of course. As a guardian of magic, it is my duty to guide you."

"Thank you." Relief swept over him. Finally. But learning about his powers was only one reason he'd made the journey. He swallowed hard. "I also have Marlec's gloves." That was the other.

"I know. It is they that have shown you that darker path. They call evil to them."

Jace knew that all too well. But now he could be rid of them at last. He took them gingerly out of his pack. "Destroy them quickly." He set them on the stone floor before Graebyrn.

Graebyrn drew his head back. "Are you certain? The price for such a thing is very high."

"Don't worry, I'll pay it."

"It's not something to be taken lightly. Despite how much evil is in them now, they began in a different place."

"But look at them." Jace edged away from the gloves. Their metal prongs glinted darkly. "Like I said, I'd do anything."

"Would you?" Graebyrn asked. "Well, if that is the case, then I will destroy them."

Jace let out a breath caught up inside of him for as long as he could remember and stepped further away from the gloves. He wondered briefly how the dragon would do it. Would he use fire? Just plain smash them? Jace smiled.

"In doing so, however," Graebyrn began, "I must also destroy their twin."

Chapter 15: A Trap

Turic rode out of the snowy hills and down into the valley of the Crescent River. At last. Harsh winds approached behind from the west. Hopefully the weather would be warmer than up in the mountains.

The heating spell he and his Followers cast worked well, but how much longer could they keep it going? Brannon bowed down from constantly using the spell. Even as the Soulkind's Master, Turic felt the draw on his mind and body.

Light snow still dusted the valley floor and the branches of the familiar trees on this side of the mountains. It was good to see their tall solid trunks, no longer scraggly and wind worn. The Crescent River took a turn to the east as it headed through another gorge to the coast, true to its name. The gentle curve of the river could be seen for miles. Beyond that and Turic's vision, the kingdom of Myraton sat atop the cliffs beside the great sea. Turic lingered a moment, staring off to the south towards Beldan.

Stroud followed his stare, and his thoughts. "We need to warn the king about the Darrak marching to Myraton," Stroud said with the tone of having said this many times before. "And bring the prisoner to him, as well."

Across the river, many crows sat within some leafless and dying trees at the edge of the woods, painting the treetops in their blackness. They had to be massive to be seen clearly from this distance.

Turic pulled his attention back to Stroud. "The Darrak may attack Beldan before they head to Myraton. To take this land one city at a time. We must warn them first."

"My orders are to bring the Soulkind to the King."

"Surely things have changed since we first left, do you not agree? King Reldrich would want us to protect his realm."

Stroud grunted in response and stayed his course along the riverbank.

Turic's gaze returned to the tops of the trees. He felt the crows' black eyes staring back even at this distance as they sat unmoving atop their perches. At first, one or two flapped their vast wings and leapt to lower branches. Then more. And then all of them glided on the gusting winds beside the traveling party.

"It appears we are not alone."

The large birds followed them for the next hour, advancing slowly from tree to tree. More began to appear behind them until their growing numbers filled all the branches. And yet, the normally argumentative creatures remained silent. A whisper might have caused the whole forest to collapse.

After a few hours, they found the ancient ford across the river like Jace had told them. Turic stopped the party. The crows, like huge black leaves, sat motionless.

"Here is where we must decide." Turic turned his horse to face the others.

Kal rode closer to Turic. "I'm not sure we have any time left for decisions."

Turic adjusted his spectacles. A thin wailing cry pierced the silence from the west. Like responding to a signal, the black birds took flight as one. The tremendous flapping spooked the horses, causing some to rear up. Something was coming.

"Ride!" Stroud shouted above the din. "Gerant! Make sure Dorne comes with us!"

The Guardian lashed a rope around Dorne's horse's neck to pull him along. Dorne's eyes darted to the sky. The horses splashed into the river over the ancient stonework just under the water. The massive wheeling of crows filled the sky, blocking out the sun. The horses crashed into each other as they ran. In moments, they crossed the river and came to a path heading south. A black bird dove straight at Stroud.

"Above you!" Turic shouted.

Stroud raised his sword to swing at the large swooping bird, but it spun out of range and returned to the others. A few more made dives at them, driving the horses to gallop harder to the south. Turic could now see how huge the birds actually were. At least three times the size of the largest crow he had ever seen before.

The wailing must have triggered their action, but Turic did not hear it again. Nor did he hear anything else, the cawing blocked out all other sound. Swirling feathers filled the air above the river preventing any move in that direction.

"They are herding us to the south," he shouted. Stroud didn't turn around, yet his silence told Turic he suspected the same thing.

Stroud tried to lead the horses eastward into the woods but a wall of diving birds blocked their way. Away off to his left a bright flash like lightning punctured the wall of trees. The crows spun and floundered like a huge pane of glass shattering. Stroud led the party to the break in the birds and Turic followed as fast as he could, kicking his horse repeatedly.

The flash appeared to be another signal. A dozen large wild dogs ran up the hill towards them, growling and snapping.

"Hold!" Stroud shouted. He jumped from his horse, assuming a defensive stance with his sword before him. Turic steadied himself and called upon the fires of his Soulkind. The stand would happen here. The dogs bounded even closer when the cloud of crows reached the horses. Chaos blossomed. Dogs rushed past Turic's horse and jumped at the birds.

Turic blinked in confusion. Who were the dogs here to attack?

The dark birds dodged the dogs' fangs as they gnashed at the air. A huge dog leapt upon a bird and clamped its jaws onto its large feathered body. It shook its head violently, thrashing its prey.

"Over there! Look!" Barsal pointed to a group of robed beings exiting the woods.

This was it. Turic readied himself to face the two dark Masters. He clasped his Soulkind and drew the fires into his mind. The mark around his throat burned. Before he attacked, the great flock of birds ceased their flight nearly in unison and flew to the skies in the opposite direction.

One of the robed people pulled back a hood exposing long blonde hair in the morning light. Barsal rode closer. "Lady Danelia!" He ran up to the woman and clasped her arms.

Turic approached them, as well. He took a last look at the fleeing crows and the mangy group of dogs heading toward them before turning his attention to the people. There were eight of them. Only the woman in the lead held her head up. The others looked like he felt. He recognized them from the journey from Beldan and the attack in Tilbury. Followers. The unfamiliar woman wore hunter's garb and seemed to be leading them. Her long brown hair hung in tangles below her shoulders.

"You must be Turic," the woman called out. "You're just as Jace described you."

"And you must be Ranelle." He climbed off his horse and clasped her arm in greeting. "Thank you for finding us when you did."

"Glad we could help," she said. She waved to Stroud who steered his horse closer to her.

"What of Allar?" Ranelle asked him. "Did he find his sister?"

"Not only that," Stroud said. "He saved her."

Ranelle smiled. An unexpected expression on such a hard face.

"Jace told us all about you," Turic started, "and how you knew these hills enough to guide the Followers here. You must tell us of your journey, but first, is there someplace safer? Those crows may return."

"Agreed. Follow me." Ranelle led the way into the trees. "We must move quickly. There's something else out there besides birds."

Turic led his horse and followed her through the dense forest onto what must have been a trail.

"We've been travelling on foot for weeks now," she said. "We survived on anything we could trap and pick in this freezing weather. Just two days ago we realized we couldn't avoid the Darrak any longer. We had to fight our way through a sentry tower on the mountain."

"We lost three Followers in that attack," Lady Danelia said. She reached over to Barsal and took his hand. It glowed briefly. Was she handing him some kind of light? A frown creased his face but he nodded after she let go.

"When did you get here?" he asked.

"We just crossed the ford this morning," Ranelle said. "I was glad to see my own hills."

Turic felt guilty for having made the trip on horseback. But then, walking through the mountains would have been the end of him. Clearly not for her. "How far away are the Darrak?"

"Their scouts are about a day behind, which means the army can't be much further."

"Your group looks exhausted. Do you need food? We have supplies and I could provide healing."

Ranelle smiled. "You are indeed how Jace described you. Thank you, but we have enough."

Turic kept an eye on the trees for crows. For now, anyway, their sense of purpose appeared broken.

"Lady Danelia," Turic called. The name sounded familiar, but he'd met so many Followers since they'd left Beldan. The blonde Follower walked next to him. Despite her torn and dirty clothing, she held her head high. Ah. Now he remembered. She turned to Brannon, barely visible on the other side of his horse.

"Master," she said.

Brannon hunched further behind his horse. "Not anymore," he said flatly. "Turic is your Master now."

The Followers turned their heads back to Turic. "Well," Turic started, "that is debatable. But tell us now, how did you manage to clear out those birds?"

"The Fireflash was quite helpful," Lady Danelia said.

"You have it too?" Turic asked.

She showed him her hand bearing the markings left from Karanne's spell.

"You know Karanne then."

"Is she here?" the lady asked.

Turic shook his head. "But she is all right."

"That's a relief. Hopefully our paths will cross soon." Lady Danelia glanced ahead at Ranelle. "As for the birds, we also couldn't have cleared them without Ranelle."

"Yes she does seem to be quite helpful," Turic said.

Up ahead, Ranelle led them to a wooded trail beside a creek and let out a sharp whistle. A large black dog strode to her side, wagging its tail. She scratched it behind his ears. "These dogs, I knew them from before, in a sense. They belonged to my late husband, Alid, and his clan of Seekers. They found me in the woods two nights ago at the sentry post in the mountains."

"Smart dogs." Turic reached down to brush his hand across one of their furry backs. "I thought we were trapped in a vice when they first came towards us."

"We were so lucky," Ranelle said. "I don't know how we would've gotten through without them."

Turic noticed a marking on the back of Ranelle's shoulder. He smiled. "Maybe luck had nothing to do with it."

"What do you mean?"

"I've seen a mark like that before." He gestured to her shoulder. She craned her neck to look at it. "What is it?"

"It is a pathway for magic. Someone passed you a spell."

"*I* have a spell? What does it do?"

"I believe your dogs here may hold the answer to that question," Turic said.

Wonder crossed Ranelle's face. "You think Jace passed this to me."

Turic nodded. "The marking is similar. And the magic. We are all learning about this, maybe he was unaware when he taught you. Amazing."

Ranelle smiled and pet the nearest dog. "I can't believe it." She began to lead them again through the trees.

"Where are you taking us?" Brannon asked.

Ranelle lifted her chin slightly. Jace had told Turic about Brannon abandoning them all in the wilderness. She spoke only to Turic as if he'd asked the question. "We've got a camp in the hills, but I'm afraid it won't be safe for long. We lost the Darrak scouts in the woods as we came out of the mountains, but they had some type of tracking creature with them. We barely caught a glimpse of it. It was fast and will pick up our trail again soon." She paused and then asked, "Who is that?"

Turic followed her gaze to Dorne. He wasn't as comatose. Something different lay behind his eyes. Was he thinking now? Turic shuddered with a sudden wave of cold. He made eye contact with Stroud and motioned to Dorne. Stroud nodded and took a step closer to the prisoner.

"They will be wanting him back," Turic said. "He was the vessel of their leader and can be so again."

Ranelle eyed Dorne cautiously, as if appraising a wild animal, then turned back to Turic. "Now that we've got you, we can make a run for Myraton. It is only a week's journey straight east from here. We can warn the people remaining in Tilbury along the way." She continued to lead through more winding paths Turic would never remember.

"Karanne and the others," Turic started. "They will be coming this way in a few days. By that time the whole Darrak army will have arrived."

"What are you saying?" Ranelle said.

"The Darrak knew we were coming, they may wait for the others."

Lady Danelia turned back to face Turic. "Karanne told us to go to Myraton to warn the king about this attack, and Ranelle has led us this far. We could stay one step ahead of this army of creatures if we left now, but you are right, we would risk our friends' lives."

Turic stopped where he stood. "And that is something we cannot do. I will not leave."

"My duty is to protect both you and the Soulkind," Stroud said. "If I stay to do so, I risk the Soulkind falling into the enemies hands. And Dorne as well."

Turic nodded. "Yes, but those are risks I am willing to take. When we clear whatever is waiting further south near the river, we will find a way to get him and the Soulkind to Myraton."

"Then the decision is made." Stroud nodded and turned to Ranelle. "You and I are going on a scouting mission."

Chapter 16: Training

Jace's smile fell. "What?" He unconsciously reached for his Soulkind exposed on the stone floor.

"Each Soulkind is bound to this world with a twin. The fate of one is shared by the other. If I remove the dark evil that is now in Marlec's gloves by destroying them, your Soulkind, and all of its magic, would also be destroyed." He met and held Jace's eyes.

"There has to be another way," Jace said.

"If there is one, I am not aware of it."

Jace turned his Soulkind over and stared at it. "So that's it? Either I let Marlec's magic stay in this world, or I lose my own along with his. Some choice."

"Sacrifice is a noble choice."

Jace scoffed. "But there is so much I don't know about my Soulkind. I'm sure there's more I can do with it."

Graebyrn said, "Now that is something I can help you with. I can teach you to become stronger in your own magic, and show you the secrets Lu'Calen left behind."

Jace nodded. "All right. That I can do."

"Good." Graebyrn nodded. "Let's see. How to begin?" He curled his front legs beneath him, lowering himself to the ground. "What is it that you do well?"

Jace shrugged his shoulders. "What does that have to do with my Soulkind? Can't you just tell me what to do?" Instantly he regretted the question.

"I'm afraid it is not that easy. Each Soulkind draws on separate flows from one source of magic. I can see the flows, but not the spells they contain. But if you listen to what I tell you, you may discover what they mean. So again, what is it that you do well?"

Jace clenched his Soulkind in his fist. What did he do well? He laughed without smiling. Would Graebyrn really want to know? He rubbed his arm and stared at his feet. "I was a pretty good thief."

"Thief?" Graebyrn said slowly, as if stumbling over the meaning.

"Yeah. You know, stealing, lying, cheating. I was pretty good at it all." He slumped against the cold stone wall, avoiding eye contact. "Some master, huh?"

"It is not who you were then, but who you will be that matters." Graebyrn arose from his spot in the middle of the wide cavern and strode to one of the many tunnels leaving it. His massive tail flowed smoothly and gracefully like a snake along the rocky floor. "So, who is that person?"

"You're starting to sound like Turic," Jace said under his breath.

"This Turic seems to be a highly intelligent person."

Jace's face turned bright red. "I'm sorry. I didn't mean for you to hear—"

"Reach the end of that tunnel." Graebyrn gestured with his head to a small tunnel off of the main cavern. Jace was sure he saw Graebyrn's lips pull into a smile. "If you're a skilled thief, perhaps it will be easy."

Jace twirled a blade on his palm and tossed it into the air. "I think I'm skilled enough for that." The knife then planted itself firmly into the dirt between his feet.

The dragon snorted. "I will be guarding a treasure there. Try to take it from me undetected. And doing so will require considerable stealth. I forgot to mention I have good hearing."

"All right, all right, you made your point," Jace said. "So through that tunnel then? Sounds simple enough."

Graebyrn turned his head to look back at Jace with what a raised eyebrow. A low rumbling shook the hall and the tunnel entrance sealed itself off with a thick wall of stone. The rumbling continued and another entrance slowly opened near the ceiling. About thirty feet higher than the first.

Jace whistled at the sheer wall leading to the tunnel entrance. Graebyrn left the cavern. "Huh."

Payt, lounging across the stone floor with Valor, chuffed at Jace. "What? You don't think I can do it?"

Payt and Valor glanced at each other.

"I'll be back with that treasure before you know it."

Jace dropped his pouch next to the rest of his things atop a pile of straw, tightened the straps on his leather boots, and made for the steep wall.

The climb looked difficult, unfortunately, but not entirely out of his ability. He gripped the sharp edges and hoisted himself up. Soon the stone bit into his palms. His calloused and rough hands ignored the pain.

"Easy," he breathed. But his breath soon quickened and his muscles screamed out as he neared the top. Twenty feet. His left foot slipped on the slick stone and his heart caught in his chest.

"All right. Not so easy."

Finally, with all of his muscles burning, he scrambled past the last jagged handholds to the top and pulled himself up into the tunnel to take a rest. A burst of flapping wings surrounded him.

"Suffering!"

Their screeching filled his ears. He waved to ward them off and the bats cascaded past him. He pitched backwards and fell toward the cold floor far below. The pain would soon consume him and then he'd be dead.

Nothing.

He opened his eyes and there he was, lying on the makeshift straw cot beside Payt and Valor. Payt chuffed at him again.

Jace's heart pounded in his ears. He shook his head slowly and gazed around to see what saved him from that fall.

It had to be Graebyrn, somehow, but the silver creature wasn't anywhere in sight. In fact, it felt as silent as a tomb. Only the sound of steady dripping water in the distance marked the passing of time.

"I guess I better try that again. You guys stay put, I'll be... right back."

He walked slowly to the wall and placed his hands upon the stone grips. He exhaled sharply and started up, focusing on the tunnel entrance. As he inched his way closer to the top he slowed down. Would the bats scream out at him like last time?

His already tired muscles burned fiercely as he became more cautious in his climbing. He paused at the lip of the tunnel but still nothing shot out. Hesitantly he reached up and pulled himself into the darkness, darkness so complete it seemed to penetrate his very body. In this silence he allowed his muscles to rest a bit before pressing on. What else did Graebyrn have in store for him?

He ventured into the utter blackness with his hand lightly touching the wall. The light behind him did not enter the tunnel, as if the darkness kept it at bay. The ground felt smooth, but he walked painfully slowly in case of holes.

The path, at first easy to walk upon, became alarmingly steep. He took a tentative step. A group of bats burst from the darkness around his head.

"Suffering!" He tumbled down the slope. He reached out to slow his descent but only slid faster. He lurched over another ledge and fell silently through cool, damp air. Another jolt and his body reappeared back on the hay next to Payt and Valor. This time Jace cradled his right arm. Was it broken? It sure felt like it from the bashing against the tunnel during his roll. A trickle of blood ran down his cheek. His temperature rose and heated his face.

He pounded the ground, but his body ached in response. "What do you want me to do?" he yelled out into the empty space.

Silence. He breathed in deeply before standing up again.

Did Graebyrn think he would just give up? He rubbed his sore arm, replaying the experience. What was he missing? His memory stone pouch called out to him and he reached for his green stone. The cold metal prongs bit into his palm. He clasped his Soulkind and placed it into his shirt pocket.

Up again.

His muscles shook. This time as he clambered up the wall he reached for the power of the Soulkind.

"Concentrate."

A slight tickling feeling just beyond his senses urged him forward. The closer he pushed himself to the source of power, the more energy rushed past him. He reached for the flow, not to dive in or even divert it towards himself, but to discern the streams surging from it. He could use this.

He edged closer to the tunnel and peered again into the utter blackness. A high pitched whine sounded, almost beyond his range of hearing. Through the air he could sense the creature making the sound, felt it crawling straight ahead. There were more than one. Hundreds, possibly. This was their home and he was invading it. They wanted him out.

The strong emotion he sensed from them stung his chest. He had felt it before, though. When Jace approached Payt's prey and Payt nearly attacked him. What had he done then?

He'd calmed him down. With magic.

Should he just tell them he meant no harm? It felt stupid to say the words out loud. Maybe he could just project those thoughts. A strong wave of magic flowed into him through his Soulkind. He cast the spell, sending magic and his message coursing into the tunnel before him. Seconds passed.

No more frantic whining. No more stinging calls.

He inched into the tunnel, continuing to exude calmness. Ten paces, twenty paces. He sensed them out there, just out of reach until a few flapping creatures swooped past his head. Just flitting back and forth through their home. Jace smiled. He'd really done it.

He walked forward until he met the slope again and rested his arm upon the wall. How in the suffering was he going to get down? He couldn't see a thing. All this success and still it would be the hay pile again for sure.

He gulped hard. What if Graebyrn wasn't always there to save him from the falls?

Something pulled down on his outstretched arm. Something hanging from it. Several more joined. Bats. Pitch black and yet they "saw" a perch. Turic had once explained how it worked to him. Seemed like a type of magic itself.

He almost laughed out loud. It was worth a shot. But could he use his vision with a creature he had no bond with? There was only one way to find out. He reached out again for his Soulkind.

Still holding onto the magic that calmed them, he felt haltingly, respectfully, into the darkness. He just needed a look and he could get safely through this thing and out of their home. There were a lot of them out there. He only needed one.

All he saw was darkness.

Nothingness.

But then a strange thing happened. An image formed in his brain, no colors, only the vaguest of outlines giving him a narrow slice of view. He "saw" the tunnel wall come at him and then veer away suddenly. The connection broke.

He laughed. He was getting good at this. His smile fell, though. The one image disappeared so quickly, what good did it do him? More bats swirled around him. He centered himself. If one wasn't enough...

He reached out again, broadening the push of magic. He focused on one's vision and then reached for another's. Just as the two images overlaid in his head, one slipped from his control and the whole connection failed.

He groaned but stood up straighter and reached out again. He could do this. Instead of trying to reach each individual bat, he pushed the magic into a bubble around him, calling into his own head the sight of those that entered it. Like light spilling into the tunnel, the combined vision showed the jagged rocks jutting up from the ground and knife-edged shards hanging from the ceiling. He knew the depth of the pits around him, the length of the tunnel, even the number of each drop of water dripping from the ceiling. And there *he* was, a glowing outline, arms outstretched in the blackness.

At his feet lay the sharply sloping tunnel floor. Bursts of bats entering and leaving his vision highlighted portions of the tunnel and then quickly disappeared only to show new views from another direction. He took a slow and awkward step forward, trying to maintain control of both the calming and connecting spells, to see the tunnel, and watch his feet all at once. He lost the vision at times, but crept forward with every reconnect.

The effort drained both his body and mind, but he concentrated to maintain the flow through his Soulkind. He pushed the bubble forward to get a better view of the surroundings, a steep decline peppered with occasional rocks for support. No chance he could've done this without the bats.

"Thanks, guys," he whispered, not wanting to distract them from their busy flight around him.

Slowly he made his way down the slope until he reached the very edge, a sheer drop. "That's what I fell down?" He kicked a stone over the ledge and listened for its landing. After a few seconds the stone hit the side of the wall once, twice, and then continued to fall.

Several bats flew in the chasm, giving him a view of the steep walls. A few others revealed a path, back at the top. Another tunnel filled his vision across the pit.

"So I'm supposed to jump to that thing? In the dark?"

No answer. Not that he expected one. There had to be another way. Maybe something behind him he missed.

A deep rumbling filled the tunnel. Jace stumbled slightly as the floor shifted. "You have got to be kidding." The slope seemed to be tilting towards him. Pebbles rolled into his feet.

"All right, I'm going." Jace backed up a couple of steps. He tried to hold onto the bats' vision to watch the shifting ground. With a quick burst of speed, he leapt out across the chasm.

He landed on the other side, waving his arms frantically to keep balance. The vision from the bats disappeared, like ashes blown away by wind. He stopped flailing when he realized he was on solid ground. "Well that wasn't so bad." A low growl sounded right in front of him. Warm breath blew across his face. He stepped back. With a shout he plummeted off the edge, the cold cave air billowing around his body.

"Not again."

Chapter 17: What Lies Inside

Jace reappeared a little higher above the ground. He landed with a thud right next to Payt and Valor. With a groan he pushed himself up to a sitting position and rubbed his neck. "If you're just going to sit around, could you maybe find me some more hay?"

Valor just shifted his glance around the room.

A bowl of water sat beside the hay cot. Jace drank from it heavily. This was way worse than anything Caspan Dral threw at him back in the Guild. But he would beat it. He had to. His legs shook as he struggled to his feet. He dropped to a knee and looked up at the tunnel. Had it gotten even higher?

A large cracking echoed throughout the cavern. The entrance of the tunnel collapsed.

"No more for today." Graebyrn's voice boomed from somewhere beyond the hall. "You need to rest."

Jace stood up and scanned the cave for Graebyrn. "Do you know which way he went?" he asked Payt and Valor. Payt responded with a wide yawn and stretched out like a cat on the ground.

"Comfortable?" Jace asked. "Can I get you anything?"

He limped to the center of the massive room to lean on a large stone. The smooth surface felt cold yet comforting. Up ahead across the cavern, an archway opened into a dark tunnel. He hadn't seen that before. Unlike the rest of the cave that section appeared to be carved by someone.

Forgetting the aches in his body, he walked under the arch and into the passage. Suddenly he sensed a presence close by, as if someone stood right beside him. He whipped around but was only met by the empty cave. Yet the sensation stayed.

Tiny wisps of light flickered through the air. Bits of floating dust? He fixed on them and realized they were connected to each other as if by strings. Waving his hands through them caused them to bend and twist and sometimes disappear, but they always reconnected when he pulled his hands back. What were these things?

Several of the strands surrounded him. When he took a step they trailed him like smoke. Were some attached to him? Focusing, he followed a lightly glowing strand through the air to his hand, into one of the marks from his Soulkind. He pulled back his sleeves. Tiny lines led to his other marks like pathways through the air. When he concentrated, he sensed the flows of power extending just out of reach.

Some of the lines seemed stronger, grew brighter, like the one attached to the eye-like mark on his hand. He concentrated on that line and felt the spell swelling with power. He could sense Valor's and Payt's locations as he focused.

Other pathways weren't as bright. He hesitantly glanced at a paler string of light leading to the dark mark on his right forearm. He tried to look away, but the light drew him in. Drew him back to the image he least wanted to remember. Blue falling under the Darrak's blows, crumpled and lifeless on the ground. And he was the one who caused it to happen.

He tore his mind away from the memory and dropped to the ground. The cold of the stone beneath him soothed his burning mind. He rubbed its smooth surface. Upon his left wrist a mark glowed with the faintest of lights. Connected to it was an equally faint path. He lifted his hand from the ground and the trails faded slightly. When he put it down again, the stream again glowed faintly. They glowed, but none led to any marks on his body that he could see. It had to be connected to a spell, but which?

With his hand held firmly upon the rock he pushed his thoughts into the light. Another image flickered into his head, of something large walking past. It felt vaguely like seeing a memory through his own collection, although this one was not his. Was it Graebyrn's? Whatever it was, he stood up, still aching, and followed the vision on a path across from where his companions lay.

He reached the arch leading into a branching hallway and placed his hand down upon its surface. The mark on his arm glowed again and the line of magic leading from it intensified. Another ghost-like vision of Graebyrn appeared in the air beside him. The dragon's silver claws stepped right where his hand was on the ground.

A memory that wasn't his, and he was able to see it. He smiled to himself. This wasn't the first time he'd used this spell. He'd seen Sarissa's journey to the Shadow Vale, and many more memories in Kedan's hut.

114

He just hadn't understood at the time what he was doing. The light stream connected to the mark on his wrist glowed a bit brighter than before.

Jace continued along the path to where the memory of Graebyrn led. Light flickered through the tunnel but Jace couldn't see the source. The tunnel pitched downward only slightly, though he tightened up a bit waiting for it to steepen like before. After several minutes of descending, the room opened up into a larger chamber, one strangely familiar to him. In the center of the room in front of Graebyrn's resting body sat a source of water like those below the library and in Marlec's fortress.

"Ah, so you found the pool."

Jace smiled. He sensed Graebyrn's lack of surprise.

"You have done well so far. Tomorrow, you can try again on the tunnel."

"What is this place?" Jace gestured to the room and beyond. "Ever since I walked through that arch magic feels stronger."

"Indeed. This cave was created long ago. Soulkind Masters from ages past could see the flows of power more clearly at places like this."

Was he talking about the floating lines? "I...think I've seen them."

"Have you?" Graebyrn asked.

"I see strings of light all around me, and some are attached to these marks." He gestured to a few of the Soulkind markings on his hand. "They're attached to these pools, too." Jace lingered near the pool's edge and touched its frigid surface. "You used them to talk to me, didn't you?"

"Yes."

"There was a pool in Marlec's fortress, too. That was the last place I saw Lu'Calen."

"You *saw* him?" Graebyrn asked.

"Not just there. Several times. First when he gave me the Soulkind, and then when he removed Marlec from his gauntlets. And after the awakening, I think I've seen others, like Marathas."

Graebyrn nodded slowly. "Perhaps seeing these spirits comes from something Lu'Calen created long ago."

"Maybe," Jace said. His mind raced. What else might be locked inside his Soulkind?

Unfortunately, there was no time to waste figuring it out. "They aren't the only former Masters I've encountered. There are two others. They possessed people, and are trying to get more Followers. I think they may even have the Lock." Jace shrunk at this. "I'm sorry we didn't get it back."

"Do not worry," Graebyrn said. "You will have another chance to reclaim it, I am certain. But as for the Masters, who would stay behind and to what end?" His expression hardened. "Guire and Fay, I assume."

Jace nodded. "You know them?"

"All too well. They crave power. It is that thirst which ties them to this world, corrupting them further. And others with them."

"I think they have someone already. Jervis."

"A friend of yours?"

"Hardly. It's a long story, but he and I were thieves together, and now he's a Follower. Their Follower."

"He must be powerful. Perhaps even a Deltir. They will seek out the strongest Followers to join their cause. These Deltir can learn from many different Soulkind. Guire and Fay will keep him close, train and manipulate him. I'm afraid he will be even more dangerous the next time you meet him."

"Will he be... all right?"

"That depends on how deeply he has trained with his new Masters."

"So what do I do about them?"

Graebyrn shook his head. "Avoid them, for now. You can't do anything all alone, you realize."

"But the gloves," Jace said. "Anyone that gets near me will be affected by them. I can't risk it."

"Are you sure you should decide what is right for them? Do not rob your friends of the chance to help you."

Jace shrugged off the comment. He would rob them of that chance any day if it meant keeping them safe. "I wish you could meet them. Especially Cathlyn. I need to tell you something about her."

"I know," Graebyrn said. "I've been trying to speak with her for some time, but something is interfering."

"What do you mean?" Jace said.

"I've sensed for a while that someone is alive in the world with Sarissa's powers. Once I found Cathlyn, I tried to offer her my guidance, but to no avail."

"I don't understand. I know Cathlyn. She wouldn't have missed this."

"Yes, I sensed that as well," Graebyrn said.

"How did you find her?"

Graebyrn closed his eyes and placed his massive front claw into the pool near his feet. "These waters show much. I fear she already faces great danger."

"You can see her?" Jace nearly tripped in his effort to get to the water.

Graebyrn nodded.

"Where is she?"

"Come see for yourself."

Jace peered into the water. "I can't see anything."

"Focus."

Jace opened himself to the magic and stared at the pool's surface. The waters remained clear. He stood up and kicked the side of the pool. "This isn't working."

"Patience. You will see." Graebyrn's voice above his head soothed him slightly. "Clear your mind and focus on your Soulkind. The waters of the world are all connected and you have the ability to reach them."

Did he? He'd always thought it was others who'd reached him. Jace knelt before the pool and gazed at the surface. Water. Flow. The energy just beyond the edge of his mind called to him, beckoned him. A thin stream of light drifted above his body like before. He followed it to a small mark upon his hand he had never noticed, or perhaps it hadn't fully formed yet. If he could reach that energy, will it to grow stronger. The mark on his hand glowed and the surface of the pool shifted.

"I see something! Mountains," Jace said. "I've seen them before. I think they're just outside of Beldan's valley. And there's something... dark in the trees, in the hills. Something waiting."

He stood up into Graebyrn's claws gently pressing on his shoulder. "I know you wish to help your friends."

Jace pulled himself from under Graebyrn's claw. "Then teach me something, so I can."

Graebyrn smiled. "Perhaps. After you have had some rest." Graebyrn laid his long neck across his silvery body and closed his eyes.

Graebyrn's long, low breathing reverberated in the hall as he lay motionless. Was it even night? Jace had been inside this cave so long that he had no sense of time anymore. He paced back and forth as his heart pumped wildly. How was he going to be able to help his friends if he never learned anything?

Maybe he couldn't train, but that didn't mean he had to sleep yet, either. Not that he could have slept if he'd tried. He glanced around to see if there were any other paths to explore. Several tunnels led in different directions off the main cave. He chose one.

The tunnel stretched on and on, and his steps clicked and echoed like the ticking of a great clock. After what felt like miles, the tunnel lightened. A cool breeze blew across his body. Then, a scratching noise emanated from further ahead, like claws against stone. He strained when the sound happened again. A little closer this time, a little clearer.

He stepped behind a small indentation in the cave wall and waited. He reached for his knife but he'd left everything back with Payt and Valor. A sudden fear gripped him. Should he yell out for Graebyrn?

Another scratch, a familiar scratch now. The last time he heard this was right outside Graebyrn's cave at the cliff.

From the Darrak.

A small, pale colored Darrak crept into the light in the tunnel. A tracker. It locked eyes with Jace then bolted in the opposite direction. To call others, no doubt. Without hesitation Jace tore off after him, the soreness in his body forgotten.

Pale light showed the way as the path crept steadily upward. The tunnel grew tighter, and he had to flatten himself to get past boulders. The Darrak moved quickly, but Jace matched its speed. After a few seconds, Jace's pace faltered. What was he going to do when he caught up? Ask him to go away? He suddenly felt vulnerable and alone winding up the pathway after this assailant. Or assailants.

But he couldn't stop now. If it called out to others and they raided Graebyrn's lair again … The path ended and Jace shot outside into a clearing. Trees lined one side and behind him lay the mountain. The short, gray Darrak stood waiting for him, staring at him with its beady black eyes.

There was one way to stop it. Just this once.

He felt his anger rise and held up his arm, staring at the dark mark. Blue loomed in his memory, but he pushed her aside. *Stop this Darrak.* For his sake and Graebyrn's. It was the only way.

But there was no power.

The rocks faded and the Darrak disappeared into nothingness like the passing of smoke. The trees shifted to reveal someone watching from behind their branches.

Jace hung his head.

It was Graebyrn. And he didn't say anything, which was far worse.

118

"Great. So this was all a test and you just watched me fail? I come to you for help, and you show me nothing except how weak I am?"

"You only fail when you choose not to listen."

Jace shook his head. "What are you talking about? Listen to what?"

"Your Soulkind. When you quiet your mind you will understand its true nature and power. Only then will you see past the draw of the dark mark you created."

Jace slumped down onto a rock and shrugged.

"But first, you must listen to what I suggest."

"And what is that?"

"What I've said three times now. Get some rest and try again tomorrow."

"All right, all right," Jace said. Perhaps he was getting a lesson after all.

Early the next morning, Jace began his climb up the cliff toward the reopened tunnel. Things felt different this time. He climbed faster and more confidently. The bats listened to him and showed him the way. Not because he forced them to, they just followed him like Valor or Ash.

When he landed on the other side of the chasm where the creature was lurking, he realized it wasn't trying to kill him. Like the bats, it was only defending its territory. It couldn't understand words, but emotions? Probably. Maybe he could use his Soulkind to show he wasn't going to hurt it. He reached for that power, focusing on his mark. A sense of peace emanated from the darkness. It was letting him pass. The bats stayed behind though, leaving Jace to feel his way through the remaining darkness.

Jace followed the dim light in the tunnel outside. He sensed Graebyrn's form hidden in the forest beyond the tunnel exit. A large and powerful beacon.

He deftly clung to the cliff side and worked his way down. Now to sneak up on him. No small task despite his years of training with the Guild. Graebyrn's mind stretched out like a lantern in the dark. He approached, darting silently through the trees, trying to avoid his thoughts. Still, he felt them the whole time. Finally, Graebyrn arched his neck over the stone Jace was hiding behind. Caught.

"Just because I knew you were coming doesn't mean you failed."

Maybe not. But next time he'd sneak past him for sure.

Chapter 18: Parting

Jace lowered himself down on the ground next to Graebyrn. "Last night I had a dream about the Darrak. They were trying to find me. That's only a dream, right? They can't find us here, can they?"

Graebyrn sighed. "The gloves. They still call to the Darrak. I can only slow them down for a time."

Jace said, "I need to leave. I'm leading them right to you and this place. Is there no other way to stop the power in his gloves?"

"The only way I know is to destroy them, but you have made up your mind about that."

Yes, he most definitely had. There had to be something else.

"Can you see the Darrak coming?"

"Yes." Graebyrn swept his wing over Jace and both of them reappeared in the cave with the pool in the center.

Dizzy from the sudden shift, Jace stumbled to the pool's edge. "Whoa," he said when he was able to think clearly.

Graebyrn closed his eyes and waved a clawed hand over the pool.

"Concentrate on what you seek," Graebyrn said softly. Streams of magic formed around him. Complex patterns of light entered the water.

Jace tried to follow them, to see how they flowed and soon was drawn to the pool's surface. The clear water rippled gently, reflecting the rocky ceiling. He searched for the Darrak, knowing they had to be close. If he could see the direction they came from he could make a plan for escaping without leading them right to Graebyrn. As he stared, the water grew cloudy and murky. The vision began to roil like a storm, twisting in an angry breeze, yet he caught glimpses of clearer skies beyond.

Jace needed a connection to the Darrak. He reached for Marlec's gloves in his shoulder pack. When he touched the cold metal, the vision in the water changed again like dark clouds covering the sun. The ripples settled and images of wooded hills filled the water's surface. The vision shifted, pulling away from the land just like with Valor's sight, and traced its way to the north and east.

Then it stopped. He squinted and leaned in closer. The Darrak were there, somewhere among the trees. For the suffering. There went the last bit of hope that they weren't actually out there, or at least weren't so close. No chance of that now.

He almost looked away from the water but then noticed there was something else out there tracking him. This being was familiar though. Was it someone he knew? Yes, it had to be. He focused harder. Ha! He knew who it was even without seeing him.

Straeten. An overwhelming sense of relief flooded through him. His friend was coming. A great weight on his chest lifted. He didn't have to be alone in all this. Good old Straeten, stubborn as always. Flows of light drifted into the pool's surface and centered on Straeten's form, crashing through piles of brush and dead tree limbs. A creature bounded behind him, leaping across boulders. Ash was there, too. Jace laughed. Not alone indeed!

Still smiling, Jace watched them make their way towards him. "What is that light?" He pointed to a vague blurry spot in the vision.

"He is your Follower, yes?" Graebyrn asked. "You can sense the bond tying you together."

"No. Well, yes, but that's not what I mean." Jace squinted. "There's something else there." It was like another presence, but he couldn't quite describe it. Something dark. "Can't you see that?" He tried pointing again, though its location seemed to shift.

"I'm afraid I cannot," Graebyrn said.

Jace squinted once again but no longer saw anything. "Probably just imagined it."

Graebyrn didn't respond.

Jace clenched his fist around his Soulkind and stood up. "I better go now and find him."

"And where will you two go afterwards?"

"Beldan. My friends are in trouble there."

"Right into the mouth of danger. Are you certain?"

Jace nodded.

"You have learned much in this short time," Graebyrn said. "And yet there is much more to learn. Use what you have gained, and seek more knowledge along your path."

"Why don't you come with me?"

Graebyrn laughed softly. "Someday, perhaps. Some of my former strength has returned, but I am not ready for that, yet."

Jace stood up to gather his few possessions. "Well, I hope it comes back quickly."

"So do I." The dragon stirred the water in the pool with one talon on his claw. "On your journey, remember you have ways of reaching me."

Here in Graebyrn's cave, Jace had actually felt relatively safe for once. He laughed. Having a dragon by your side could do that. Now, that relief was quickly disappearing. He shoved his meager belongings into his pack. Gingerly he held Marlec's gloves, as if some power would sense his touch.

"As I said, I can hide Marlec's power for a short time." Graebyrn breathed slowly onto the gloves Jace held up to him. Frost appeared in the air as it cooled around them. A thin layer of ice or maybe crystal collected on the black surface. Yet the gloves weren't cold. Jace buried them in the bottom of his pack and threw it over Payt's healed shoulders.

The burra stepped quickly on the stone floor after his night of rest. "You ready to run again?" Jace reached carefully between his shoulder spikes to pat him on his neck.

Valor called out sharply. He circled Graebyrn's head twice then landed on the beast's massive scaled shoulders.

Graebyrn met the hawk's eyes. Jace could swear he saw something pass between them, some unspoken thought. Valor leapt off and flapped quickly down the main tunnel leading outside.

As he packed his Soulkind, Jace brushed his fingers against the metal markings. They were permanent. He'd just have to live with them. At least now he had some tools to help. He patted his stone and then secured the straps on the pouch.

"You are further south than where we met at the stream," Graebyrn said. "Use your map, I have added to it."

"Thanks," Jace said. "I hope to see you again."

"You will." Graebyrn stretched his wings open. "Is there any way I can persuade you not to travel to your town?"

"Not likely," Jace said.

"Then be careful. Follow your heart, Soulkind Master. It is your strongest quality."

Jace walked out of the dragon's cave to the new day. Sunlight gleamed through the trees at the top of the steep hills. A young river leapt from the hillsides and plummeted through the narrow valley. Thick snow weighed down the wide evergreen branches, a fresh fall since Jace was last outside.

Payt stamped his front feet, itching to run along the path next to the water. Jace removed the map from his pouch and silently encouraged Payt to run with a slap on his flanks. He tore off nimbly along the steep banks and into the shallow but fast moving water. Valor sailed through the air above him, twisting between the low branches. Steep cliff walls towered above on both sides and huge boulders littered the narrow valley floor. There was no sign of Graebyrn's cave, it had disappeared into the trees beyond the stream.

Not that Jace needed to see it. When he faced that way he sensed Graebyrn's location, just as he sensed the sun's direction with his eyes closed. The lines of lights he had seen in Graebyrn's lair were no longer visible, but he sensed their presence as well.

Jace tipped his face towards the sun and smiled. Straeten was coming. He was drawing nearer away to his left. Not too far now. Something nagged at the back of his mind and his smile faltered. What had he seen beside Straeten in the vision? Surely, it was nothing, like he said. But then why was it creeping up again?

Jace stowed the map and urged Payt to come along. He would not let some random fleeting blur mess with his excitement. The burra leapt once more in the freezing waters and then strode ashore. Before Jace could get clear, Payt shook himself furiously.

"Thanks," Jace said, water dripping from his nose. Still, he couldn't help but smile. Soon he'd be getting the same from Ash, no doubt.

The morning sunlight slowly gave way to grayness, and the previously vibrant greens of the forest muted. The small river fed into a much larger one, flowing off this side of the mountain range and to the west. Here the area opened up much like Graebyrn's markings showed on his yellowed map. The entire valley from the path beside the river stretched to the mountain peaks in the distance. Here he would wait for his friend.

He set Payt loose along the rough greenway where he tramped confidently. Valor flew higher in the air now, circling upward in the gusts. Almost instinctively Jace slid behind Valor's eyes. The rush of power flooded his body and he scanned the landscape.

Away to the east striding along the river he saw them. First Ash leapt over some rocks, one ear flopped down and his tail wagging. Jace felt recognition swell through Valor, and wondered if the bird was excited to see his friend. Anything seemed possible now. Then, atop a familiar horse, bundled in furs himself, sat Straeten.

His friend had ventured into the wilderness alone, risking it all to find him out here. He urged Valor to descend towards them, though the hawk needed no encouragement. The distance between them quickly disappeared. Valor landed upon a dead tree next to the river.

Ash sprinted around the corner and stopped abruptly. He sniffed the air then bounded around the tree once, then twice, jumping and barking the whole time. Valor leapt off the branch and swept closely past Ash who chased him through the trees. After a minute of playing, Valor settled onto the branch again and gave a cry as Straeten's horse trotted into view.

"Valor!" Straeten held out his arm. The hawk leapt to it from the branch and peered into his face. The strain from the journey showed on his cheeks and in his eyes. A thick layer of stubble covered the lower half of his face.

As Jace watched Straeten something kept interrupting his thinking, nearly breaking his connection. He almost laughed. Straeten was using the spell he'd learned from Jace to see through Valor's eyes.

Now to use the same spell on Straet. He couldn't really talk to him, but he could *think* at him. *Follow Valor*, he urged. Jace felt Straeten's hesitant affirmation before Straet sent the hawk from his arm. Valor dove once more towards Ash, and then rose into the skies back to where Jace awaited.

124

Chapter 19: Old Friends

Payt paced at Jace's side, the spikes on his shoulders shifting and clicking. Jace put his hand on his tall back. Valor swooped through some thin fog into view. The steady clop of Straeten's horse, Rhila, grew louder against the river in the background.

And then Ash tramped through the fog. He lifted his gray ears and stopped, sniffing the air on either side until he settled in on Jace. He bounded up the path, his tail wagging furiously. Jace ran towards him and knelt. Ash ran into him, nearly knocking him over.

"Good to see you too, buddy." Jace rubbed Ash's ears. " I guess you could've made the trip with me. But I think that Straeten needed you, for sure."

Ash started in Payt's direction and released a sudden low growl.

"Whoa, Ash," Jace pet him slowly. "He's a friend. Name's Payt."

Valor called out a solemn cry and landed on Payt's back. Ash stopped his growling and pranced to Jace's side as if nothing had happened.

"Together again," Straeten said as soon as he got close enough.

"You've looked better." Jace walked to his horse, patting its side. He'd meant it as a joke, but beneath the dirt and grime, Straeten was the thinnest he'd ever been.

Straeten leapt off and steadied himself. "It has been a while since I had a proper meal. Do you know how hard it is to find—"

Jace cut him off with a giant hug. Straeten patted his friend on his back.

"What in the suffering made you come after me?" Jace punched him in his shoulder.

"Good to see you, too." Straeten pulled a water skin off of his saddle and took a long, solid drink from it. "You know I couldn't leave you out here alone. You don't even know how to start a fire properly."

Jace smiled and started to break out his camping supplies. "We've got a lot to talk about."

They sat and recounted the stories of Jace's travels and the attack on Nilen's village. The journey with Payt, and all the magic in Graebyrn's cave. And they rested. Really rested, like they hadn't done in quite some time. Even under the safety of Graebyrn, Jace still felt the call to move. But now, with his old friends, that stress just disappeared for a little while.

"Ash made the trip all right, then?" he ruffled Ash's fur as he lay down next to him.

"Yep." Straeten poked at some rocks on the ground. "You know, I don't think I could've made it this far without that little mutt."

Ash growled and Jace laughed.

"Sorry, boy," Straeten said. "I mean it though. You should've seen him running out in front of Rhila every day leading the way."

"That's my boy." Jace ruffled him again then glanced at Rhila. An unexpected pang struck his heart. How much she looked like her mother. *Blue.* He looked away. "So, just the three of you?"

"Karanne wasn't going to come along, if that's what you're wondering. Not after you wrote that letter."

"How'd she take it?"

"The *One of Four*? You know she'd never go back on one of those. But she sure didn't stop me. In fact, she planted this in my bag before I left. Like she knew I was going. I didn't even know she did it until I was on my way."

Straeten handed over Karanne's necklace.

Jace took the white stone and silver chain. "I bet you didn't." He laughed quietly. "She never took this thing off."

"Where did she get it?"

Straeten's voice faded. The world closed off as Jace held the necklace. A strangely familiar song tickled the back of his mind. As his hand touched the cool white surface a vision began to unfold like with his stones. The strange thing was, this wasn't one of them.

He was climbing a great stone wall into some building, perhaps a house. An expensive house. And not like any style he had ever seen in Beldan. Two, maybe three floors? Whatever it was, it was a long way down.

Now he remembered. The house belonged to some speaker, a representative of the King, and it was bound to hold enough loot for him to get out of this stinking city. He finished nimbly scaling the wall to peek in one of the back rooms of the estate. He lightly jumped in.

Observe, observe, observe. This was going to be easy.

A sharp, acrid smell of smoke filled his nose. He heard the harsh sound of voices arguing in the next room and crouched beside the wall.

Maybe not.

He listened closely. From the sound of it all, there were four people—three men and a woman. The woman was crying. Good, they were distracted. Clean out this room and get out. A sharp crack sounded followed by a scream. Smoke poured into the room from the top of the doorway. A fire? This was starting to be more work than it was worth. Maybe the next house. He backed slowly to the window.

A woman burst into the room and fell face first on the floor. She was bleeding from her forehead. Badly. Between sobs, she pulled herself along the rug towards him. He started to turn around but the dying woman's eyes found his. She froze, holding out her shaking, clenched fist.

She was trying to get him to move closer. Although he knew it was time to bail he ran to her side. With much effort, she opened her fist and turned it over. He held out his hand and into it fell a necklace with a white stone, covered in her blood. The sound of yelling grew louder in the other room, and closer. There was no more time.

"Why do you want me to have this?" His voice sounded different, higher.

The woman convulsed. Her green eyes locked again onto his. She pointed past him towards the corner of the room. A soft melody played, as if from a music box. And there in the back of the room beyond the window lay what appeared to be a basket.

But it was no basket. It was a cradle. He was in a nursery. In it was a young child, curly haired and just under a year old, sleeping soundly. He looked back at the woman lying nearly still on the floor.

Over the strangely familiar bell-like music, she breathed her last word.

"Jace."

He desperately scooped up the child and wrapped him under his cloak. The baby's eyes opened, as green as the woman's. As green as his own.

As he turned to finally leave this mistake of a house, a short man dressed in dark clothes rushed into the room. He swept out a long knife and stepped over the fallen mother's body.

"There's no way out," he uttered.

"I always have a way out." And with that, he leapt out the window, the baby in his arms.

"Where did she get it?" Straeten said.

Jace blinked his eyes. "What?"

"Wake up. I said *where did she get it?*"

"I...don't know. At least, I don't think I do."

Straeten lifted an eyebrow and shrugged his shoulders. "Well, she wanted you to have it for some reason."

The white stone glistened in the daylight, deeper colors swirling inside as Jace turned it over. What just happened? Part of some magic he learned in the cave? The images kept flashing into his head. The high voice he spoke with. He knew that voice. The woman and the baby. Strangers and yet so familiar. All the images rushed together. He dropped his head into his hands. How had he missed it?

"She got it from my mother."

"What?"

"The necklace." Jace found himself choking up and cleared his throat. "It came from my real mom."

"Are you serious? Wait, how do you know?"

"I saw something, something from my past, and Karanne's. When I touched the necklace. I think I used a new spell." He tried to tell Straeten everything he saw but many of the details slipped away. A few things burned there still. His mother's eyes. The way she called out his name. The fact that she hadn't just thrown him away.

"You actually saw your mom?" Straeten said.

"Yeah." Jace closed his fist around the necklace. Why hadn't Karanne told him about her before? He understood saving a helpless baby, but keeping him? Her voice sounded so young in the vision. What was she thinking? A teenage thief raising a baby. He chuckled . Almost as crazy as jumping out a window with one.

His smile faded. If she hadn't done both... "You sure Karanne was okay when you left?"

Straeten scoffed. "You think I'd have gone if she wasn't?"

"Thanks." Jace noticed Straeten scratching furiously behind his shoulder blade. "Did your horse give you fleas?"

"Nice." Straeten pulled his cloak down over his shoulder to try to get a look at it. "Well, maybe."

Upon his neck wound a Soulkind mark darker than the others. A pit grew in Jace's stomach. What was that from? The vision in the cave came up unbidden.

"What are you looking at?" Straeten asked.

"You've got a mark back there."

"So?"

"Do you know what spell it's from?"

Straeten shrugged. "I've learned a few, maybe Turic gave it to me." Straeten shot the mark some uneasy glances.

Jace threw one of his knives into the log at his feet and it stuck deeply. "After the villagers turned, did they use the magic?"

Straeten stopped scratching. "Well yeah, to block us in."

"Did they do anything else?"

"Like what?"

Jace sighed. "Are you sure none of them gave *you* any of their magic?"

Straeten scratched the area slowly. His head slumped forward. "It must have happened right after the Followers attacked us at the village. The... demon... touched my face when they had me trapped." He swallowed. "They just did what that thing told them to do. Their eyes froze over." He stood up and paced. "I don't want to end up like them."

"Hey, you're going to be all right," Jace said.

Straeten sat down again. "What do they even want with me?"

Jace thought back to what Graebyrn said about Guire and Fay. About them gathering Followers to join their cause. It all made sense now. "You can use different kinds of magic, right?"

Straeten looked at the marks on his hands. "Yeah."

"Guire and Fay want to build an army, and they want really powerful Followers. Ones who can do what you can. Deltirs."

"*Deltirs?*"

Jace nodded. "That's what Graebyrn called them."

"Me? I guess I always knew I was pretty amazing."

"Seriously Straet," Jace said. "They're going to be after you. And they already have one on their side."

Straeten groaned. "Jervis, right?"

Jace nodded again. "They're just using him, like they did the villagers. And they'll use you, too, if they get the chance."

Straeten rubbed his temple. "Maybe if I don't use the magic she gave me I won't turn out like those Followers."

"It might be hard to ignore it." Jace unconsciously rubbed the mark on his arm.

"Is there a way I can get rid of it?"

Jace shrugged. "I don't know. This is new to me, too. Maybe Cathlyn can help. I'm still trying to figure out what to do with Marlec's gloves."

Straeten began to stuff things into his pack. "Wait, you still have them?" He fumbled a bit with a knife.

Jace opened his bag and showed him the crystal covering the Soulkind. "Don't worry. Graebyrn said this should help keep us hidden for now."

"If you say so." Straeten stood up. "Let's get going. I can't stand all this sitting around."

Jace got up, too. "We'll figure this out. For now, we need to find the quickest way back to Cathlyn. As far as we know she's heading to Beldan too. Graebyrn gave me a map to show us a way around the Darrak and back home." He placed a hand on Straeten's shoulder. "Come on. You're still you."

Straeten smiled a bit but it faded. He stroked his horse's neck. "For a bit, anyway."

"Hey, I mean it." Jace peeked into his bag and carefully stowed Karanne's necklace. He touched it one more time to relive that moment.

Something rattled as he shifted the contents of the pack. He moved some things aside and found what looked like ice or glass. Or crystal. A small portion of Graebyrn's covering must have fallen off the gloves. The crystal crumbled into dust and he let it fall to the ground. He closed the bag without a word and mounted Payt quickly to begin the next part of the journey.

Chapter 20: A Conspiracy

Karanne travelled for a few days before admitting to herself that the pain in her head wasn't going away. Every jog and bump as she rode through the hills reminded her of it. She wasn't about to ask Mathes for help, though. Or for anything else.

Mathes rode close to Cathlyn ever since they left Varkran. Karanne's memory was a bit fuzzy about the attack there. Had they been talking about magic right before she passed out? She hadn't been able to get a word out of Cathlyn about it.

Frigid winds gusted through the looming rocks. Karanne pulled the thick fur over her face to block their sting. She patted down the pouch at her side to feel for the golden necklace Nilen sent with her. It would mean a lot to Nilen's mother, Lunara.

It would mean a lot if Jace came back with hers.

That boy. Ever since he was a baby he'd been a handful. But always a good kid. She'd have to yell at him for getting lost in the middle of nowhere. Someday he would run out of those suffering "One of Four" promises he made her keep. Another sharp pain shot through her skull. Perhaps it was for the best that her condition didn't slow Straeten down now. He'd find Jace. And if he couldn't do it himself, that dog surely could.

Burgis and Tare rode alongside Allar on the path behind her. She felt something small, maybe a pinecone, strike her back. Now wasn't the time for this. She shot him back a cold expression.

"Hey, sorry," Burgis said. "I was just checking in on you. You seemed to be getting a little loopy looking in your saddle there. Everything all right?"

She forced a smile. "I'm doing okay. Thanks again."

He nodded briefly. She had thanked him repeatedly for saving her life back at the village. Hopefully she wasn't overdoing it.

"It was your magic that freed us first," Burgis said. "And you'd have done the same for one of us."

It was true. Though he and his brother had initially come to deal out revenge for their parents, they'd become a part of this group. Almost like family now. Would they return to their town once they got out of the mountains? She watched Tare concentrating on his horse much like Jace did with Valor and Ash at times. Allar and Burgis were talking about hunting out in the wild, joking like old friends.

No, the two boys wouldn't be leaving anytime soon.

Mathes glanced at her over his shoulder and then returned his focus to Cathlyn. What had they talked about back in the village?

The pain felt like a spike of ice driving through her spine. Her head flopped forward and she felt herself slipping out of consciousness. When she opened her eyes again, both Cathlyn and Mathes were riding next to her nudging her awake.

"Are you all right?" Mathes gripped her horse's reins.

Cathlyn reached over hesitantly towards Karanne's forehead but withdrew her hand slightly.

"Why are you stopping, Cath?" Allar asked suddenly from behind. "You can help her."

"I..." she started.

"If you can do anything, do it," he insisted.

Mathes shot Cathlyn a stare and shook his head. "I've got something in here for her." He fumbled in his bag.

Before Cathlyn could pull her hand back completely, Karanne gently grabbed onto her wrist. "You don't have to be afraid of it."

Cathlyn pulled sharply to release her grip. She gave an apologetic glance and nudged her horse into a quick gallop.

"I'm sorry," Allar said quietly. "She isn't herself lately."

Karanne shook her head, both to acknowledge what he said and to clear the fogginess in her mind. Allar rode up ahead to his sister's side and spoke to her in hushed tones, too quiet for Karanne to hear.

"We could really use magic like hers," Burgis said to Karanne. "I mean, think of what she could do."

"I think that's what she's worried about," Karanne murmured.

Mathes opened his pack wider and several vials spilled out onto the ground. Quickly he stopped his horse to pick them up. "Who could blame her?" Mathes handed Karanne a bottle of red liquid. "Now take this."

Well, maybe she would accept his help this once. Anything to end the pain and fog. She downed it quickly and shook her head from the intense rush. "Whoa, that's better." She sat up on her horse straighter.

She could hear Allar up ahead now, though the glistening light reflecting off the Crescent River prevented her from seeing him. Cathlyn jabbed her horse sharply with her heels and galloped ahead to the water. Allar glanced back and forth between his sister and the others.

He leapt off Chase and limped his way back to Karanne.

"What is it?" she asked.

"There's something wrong with her." Allar grabbed her reins and everyone stopped. He flexed his right fist slightly and Newell's Soulkind twisted in the light. "I can see things with this Soulkind. When Newell lets me."

"What do you mean?" Burgis said.

"I can see how things are built. I can tell if they're rotten, or falling apart. People, too."

Mathes threw his pack over his shoulder and began to quickly walk towards his horse.

"I can see if they're sick or injured." His eyes locked onto Mathes. "Or drugged."

Karanne shook her head to clear some of the fogginess. "Drugged?" She looked ahead at Cathlyn then at Mathes. Her heart started pounding. "How could you?" The cold surged again in her mind and she wobbled in her saddle. She winced and reached for her temples. "Is that what's wrong with me, too?"

"You're crazy," Mathes said, turning to face her. "Are you listening to yourself?"

Allar placed his hand on Karanne's and a ripple of light flashed across his eyes. "It's not the same as Cathlyn, but something is definitely weakening her."

Burgis drew an arrow and centered it on Mathes' chest.

"I didn't do anything to her. She's just sick and needs some sleep," Mathes said taking a step toward Karanne. Burgis pulled back further on his bowstring and Mathes froze.

A sudden scream pierced the air.

"It's Cathlyn!" Allar jumped onto his horse and tore off into the woods after his sister.

The sound of cracking, as if a tree were being splintered, rung in the air. Karanne kicked her horse and sprang forward after Cathlyn and Allar. Burgis and Tare rode beside her. She vaguely noticed no other hooves followed behind.

Chapter 21: Taken

Another scream cut through the woods.

Trees flew past Karanne as she rode hard towards the source. Funny, it didn't sound like Cathlyn.

The forest opened suddenly. A huge expanse of gray rock covered the riverbank. Allar sat atop his horse in the clearing, staring intently at the trees. Karanne and the others halted their mounts next to his. Allar tilted his head as if listening for something. "I should've seen this coming," he uttered.

"What do you mean? Where is Cathlyn?"

He shook his head. "They were waiting for us."

Karanne glanced around quickly. A lone figure stood on the edge of the forest a few hundred feet away, slowly walking towards them.

"I don't see anyone else. Where are they?" Karanne asked.

Allar gestured all around them. He took in the entire landscape in one sweeping glance, seeming to calculate all the possibilities. Karanne still saw no one else in the area, but she didn't doubt Allar. Several large black birds circled above the tree tops to their right. Really large birds.

"We better get out of here," Karanne said.

Allar held up the hand with his shield strapped to it. "She is coming to ask us something."

"But we've got to leave. We've got to find Cathlyn."

Allar flashed Karanne a stare that told her not to question it.

"All right then," Karanne said. With a flick of her hand, the circular marks on her palm glowed like fire and the pulsating little flame shot out into the air. "Just don't expect me to wait quietly." The Fireflash arced around the horses in a tight loop.

The woman walking across the rocky terrain nearly reached them. She wore the clothing of a peasant or a farmer. Probably someone who lived nearby. She was older, perhaps fifty or so.

What struck Karanne were her eyes.

Instead of irises and pupils, lifeless pale crystals stared back at them. Similar to the icy glare they encountered from Fay's Followers back in the village, only more intense. The pain in Karanne's head deepened as the woman approached. She shook her head to push away the pain. It wasn't Mathes' herbs that caused this. It was something planted by Fay when they last met.

Sorry, Mathes.

She glanced around for any sign of attackers, the ones that Allar clearly sensed, or knew would be coming. Her heart raced and pounded loudly in her head. A host of the large birds perched in the upper branches of the trees on her right. The river blocked them on their left. How had she let herself be trapped? She turned her head to see behind, catching a glimpse of shadows passing between the trees. Where was Mathes? Hopefully he was all right.

"You better know what you're doing," she whispered to Allar.

The Follower moved only her mouth when she spoke. "We have your friend and will take her to your town." Her empty voice matched her dead eyes. "She will be of great use to Fay."

Karanne squinted hard at her and said under her breath, "She's bluffing. They don't have your sister."

She glanced back at Burgis. He took off his bow and nocked an arrow.

The Follower's hands began to glow with a pale white light. Moisture in the air turned into thick fog around her fingers. She turned to Burgis, though her eyes didn't meet his. "My lady has no use for you. You are dead to magic and so you may leave."

Burgis pulled back his arrow further and aimed it at the Follower's throat. "No thanks," he said. Allar gave a warning glare and Burgis lowered the arrow slightly.

A slight breeze radiated from Allar, his shield raised. Karanne felt safer afterwards. Her Fireflash continued to revolve around them, as well.

More frost emanated from the Follower's arms and mouth. Karanne noticed movement from within the woods. The Fireflash intensified its arcing. "If you've got a plan, now would be the time to share it," she said.

Burgis released the arrow upon the woman with a sharp twang. The arrow pierced her throat and she dropped to the ground.

An uneasy silence fell over everyone. Allar rode to Burgis' side, grabbed him by the furs around his neck, and shook him.

"I thought I made it clear not to do that," he said.

Karanne felt the fear in Burgis' face. "Let him go," she said. Behind her, she heard Tare jumping from his horse.

Allar gripped Burgis more tightly then cast him to the stones below. "I had this under control." He leapt from his horse and picked Burgis up by his neck with both hands now.

"Allar!" Karanne shouted. "What are you doing? This is crazy!" Her mind went again to Mathes and the accusations made against him by this mad man.

Allar kept his eyes on Burgis and spoke through gritted teeth. "Stay out of this!"

From behind, Tare cracked him on the back of his head with a club. Allar dropped as quickly as the Follower had.

Tare helped up his brother and then lifted Allar up and onto his horse, lying him face down on his saddle. He saluted to Karanne and then climbed up onto his own horse.

"All right, let's get out of here. Back the way we just came." She yanked on her reins then grabbed Allar's horse's to lead him away.

The shadows beyond the trees shifted. Dark creatures hung between the branches. Were they what Allar was talking about? Could they be the Darrak that came down from the mountainside? She had hoped they would beat them here. Whatever they were, they didn't leave the edge of the woods. They held their shadowy ground all around the clearing. The huge black birds leapt from the tree tops and began to circle above.

Suddenly, there was a silence so complete it startled her. Their horses came to an abrupt stop and no manner of nudging or prodding could get them to move.

"Come on!" Karanne yelled, her voice sounding offensive in the unnatural stillness. A sudden and cold chill ran across her neck as she glanced over at Tare and Burgis, both motionless and with bewildered expressions on their faces.

She slowly turned around. The Follower stood before them again. Her head hung at an awkward angle, resting on the arrow feathers sticking from her neck. Karanne tried to summon the magical fires she'd learned from Brannon, but the power was not the same. A weak flame issued from her palm, barely bursting five feet as it dispersed into the cold air. "Suffering."

A storm broke and the woods erupted with the chaos of Darrak and large cat-like creatures running towards them. The swarms of birds grew in number like an encroaching wave.

136

"Don't move," Cathlyn's voice echoed in Karanne's head.

The light around them bent in a sickly swirl, like it was being squeezed and pulled and then suddenly plucked upward. Her mind spun wildly. The lights folded back to normal, and the momentary disorientation slipped away. She was in a different place, air surrounding her, and moving quickly. The sensation of dropping took over. Her horse screamed. She watched in horror as the ground, nearly twenty feet below, rushed up to meet them. Rocks and soil from their previous location floated at their feet.

The bones of her horse cracked, breaking her fall, as she landed on top of the river rocks. Luckily, she had the sense to leap and roll free before being crushed by the horse's writhing. Only Chase landed on his hooves safely, stumbling just a few steps. Allar fell off the saddle and to the ground.

Karanne heard sobbing in the distance. Cathlyn again.

"I'm sorry!" she called softly, sounding far away. "One of them came with you! Run, *now!*"

One of them? Karanne rushed to Allar's side and shook him. He appeared groggy and looked at her blankly.

"Get up!" she yelled. "We're not alone here."

Tare and Burgis stood above their fallen and broken horses as well, looks of bewilderment on their faces.

"Behind you!" Allar pointed weakly.

Karanne spun to see a lone Darrak perched awkwardly in a nearby tree crouching to leap at her. She flicked her wrist and cast the Fireflash into its face with a powerful blast of light. Half in its leap already, it snarled with yellowed teeth and clawed at its eyes, falling headlong through the thick branches.

When it hit the ground, Burgis pinned it down with arrows as fast as he could draw them. Several missed, but two planted into his chest. Tare ran quickly to finish him with his club. Karanne grabbed Allar by his arm and helped him onto Chase. She shot a pitying glance at the horses on the ground as she led Chase south. "Hold on."

"What happened?" Allar mumbled.

"Your sister," Karanne said. "She moved us somehow."

"Not very far," Burgis said, taking in the trees. "I still recognize these woods. That means the Darrak can't be too far behind."

"How did she do it?" Allar asked. "Where is she?"

"I don't know," Karanne said, "But let's move quickly." A quarter of a mile into the woods, she felt Chase's tension rise. His eyes flashed and his nostrils flared rapidly. She listened intently, but only heard her own heartbeat thumping in her head.

Allar struggled to dismount when Burgis came alongside him. He started to say something but stopped himself. A few seconds later, he managed to say, "I'm sorry, I didn't mean—"

"That wasn't you," Burgis replied.

Allar rested back onto the saddle as best he could as the horse stamped through the trees. After a minute, Burgis fell behind. Tare went to his side, gesturing intently, but Burgis waved him off. Tare persisted and sweat beaded on Burgis' forehead. Finally, Burgis said, "I just killed someone."

Karanne nodded to herself and fell back beside them. "She wasn't really human anymore, not after Fay did that to her." She placed her hand on his shoulder.

Burgis wiped his brow with the back of his sleeve. "I guess."

Killing a person was different than killing one of those mindless Darrak. She knew that all too well.

A few hundred yards down the slope they reached a dirt path. The way to the right led back up the mountains to the Shadow Vale. Karanne turned and headed left which she hoped would eventually lead them to the river and back home.

Tare veered off into the woods and Burgis took off after him.

"Where are you going?" Karanne shouted between panting breaths. "For the suffering." She followed them in and nearly ran into Tare just standing there like a tree.

Burgis spoke in a low voice, attempting to pull Tare toward the river. Tare shook his head emphatically then began to run headlong further into the woods.

Burgis shrugged at Karanne. "I've only seen him like this a few times." He dashed after his brother through the thick trees.

There was only one thing she could do. She sighed and followed.

Chapter 22: Across the Crescent River

The two brothers led the way, jumping nimbly and silently despite the brush in their path. Must have been an useful skill in their hunting days. Back before this whole thing started.

An outcropping of rock cut through the trees exposing the foothills of the great mountain range to the west. With luck, they could reach it without being spotted by any patrols. She didn't know how far Cathlyn managed to move them, but she did sense that danger wasn't far away enough.

A minute into the woods, Karanne heard something and ducked down. She motioned for the others to do the same. Through the trees about a hundred feet back on the path they'd just left, a group of about ten black creatures moved steadily to the east. More Darrak? Were these the ones they'd just left?

The patrol passed. They appeared smaller and thinner than the others. Possibly trackers? One Darrak slowed to examine the ground near the edge of the path. Karanne held her breath. Another Darrak ran beside the crouched over one and pulled him along. They spoke in their harsh language for a moment then ran up towards the others.

Karanne let out her breath. She nodded her thanks to Tare.

"Anyone want to ride Chase for a while?" Allar asked. "I think I can run now."

No one spoke up. Karanne felt too guilty to ride before anyone else. She was tired, but not that tired.

"Hey, how did Tare know to get us off that path?" Karanne asked. "We would've been spotted for sure."

Burgis shrugged. Tare tapped his forehead with a forefinger and smiled.

"Where is Cathlyn? It doesn't make any sense," Allar said.

"I heard her voice after she moved us," Karanne said. "I couldn't tell where it came from, but she didn't sound scared for herself, just for us."

"I heard her, too." Allar pried intently at the strap on his shield. It wouldn't budge. "Why can't I do anything right?" He hammered on it with his fist. "First I lose my sister, then I'm attacking Burgis. It's this thing." He finally unlatched the shield from his arm and yanked it off. "I'm done." He held out the Soulkind to Karanne. She reached for it but he quickly seized it back.

Burgis put a hand on his shoulder, his grip supportive but also firm. Allar spun to him and knocked his hand off. "Get back!"

"Allar," Karanne said calmly. She'd dealt with desperate before. No need to mix it up even more. "We need *you* now. Your sister needs *you*. We have to get out of here. Quietly."

Allar slowly strapped the Soulkind back onto his forearm. The metal shield fit snugly. He rubbed his other hand over its cool surface. "I'm fine."

Right. "We've got to get across the river," she said to Burgis quietly. "You know these woods?"

"Our pa ran us over here to hunt," Burgis said. "We spent more time on our side of the water to the east, but I've been here before."

"Can you get us further south?" she asked.

"You sure? It's a straight shot to the river that way." Burgis pointed east.

"Yeah, but something is telling me to go south." It just felt like the way to go, somehow.

"To the south then." Burgis signaled to his brother.

Tare rode Chase into the trees and Karanne followed. Three large birds circled above the tree top. Karanne wished there were more cover.

Another mile through the woods, the outcroppings of rock grew higher. Great mounds of it formed column-like shapes straight up the sides. They passed quickly through them, always taking the lower paths.

"It isn't far off now," Burgis said. "If we're lucky, the river will be running low enough that we can cross. Otherwise, we might need a change of clothing. Tare, did you bring my sweater?"

Tare shook his head and gave him a shove.

A high ridge line rose to their right, obscuring the sun as it dropped in its path to the west. Karanne was exhausted and their stores of food were getting pretty low. She was no survivalist, but she didn't need Burgis to tell her that camping here was a bad idea. Not with Darrak so close. At least the birds no longer circled overhead. That was a good sign. Hopefully.

Burgis rode on the horse now, his head bowed over. Karanne knew exactly how he felt. Tare gently stroked Chase's nose. The horse relaxed once the Darrak had passed by. Allar, however, had not. His eyes darted continuously to the hillside and through the trees. No one spoke or even breathed loudly. The gray cliff wall loomed overhead, strange shadows shifting across its top. Ahead, the river appeared, and with it, thoughts of the road home.

Home. Such a distant memory.

Luckily, the waters were low enough to expose some sand bars and stones for crossing, although the second half of the river seemed a bit deeper. Burgis jogged ahead and bent down to fill his water skin. Chase, too, drank from the slow moving currents.

"We'll rest for a bit after we cross." Karanne rubbed her sore calf muscles. "It will be safer there."

Tare nodded and pulled on Chase's reins to lead him into the river, but the horse resisted. Tare stroked him gently across his jaw, keeping eye contact. Step by step, he slowly followed Tare into the water.

Karanne took a step in and bit back the cold that chilled her whole body. Halfway across they reached a sand bar. The silence seemed to grow. Upriver, huge chunks of ice floes piled up with logs and other debris jammed up the path. They could now see the far side of the river. It was deeper than they'd thought and moved with a greater speed. They would have to find a different way across.

A slight burning emanated from Karanne's palm. It was itching like mad again. What was with all the itching? The circular symbol created by the Fireflash glowed and then slowly faded. She halted and scanned the area. A shadow caught her eye up on the cliff high above the river. She squinted to see two silhouettes, both human-shaped.

The words, "Be careful," echoed in her head.

"Up there!" she said. Everyone shifted their gazes until they landed on two figures on the cliff.

"Cathlyn!" Allar shouted.

Karanne's eyes then fell to the line of creatures emerging from the woods. Scrawny but large cat-like animals stepped towards them onto the riverbank, cutting off their retreat. The group of nearly thirty stopped as one. Karanne's hand pulsed with the heat of her spell.

An ear splitting shriek filled the air. Karanne staggered trying to keep her footing. The pain receded as their cries paused yet her mind went blank. Chase let out a pained whinny. Tare rested his hand on Chase's neck with one hand, and drew out his club with the other.

Karanne quickly glanced up the cliff and no longer saw either shadow. Why hadn't Cathlyn moved them this time?

"Cathlyn?" Allar called out again.

"Hey, we have to cross here!" Karanne shouted. The swift current threatened to drag them under, but what choice did they have?

Burgis yanked on his brother's sleeve to get him moving. They both cringed as they stepped into the frigid waters. Two light-colored Darrak emerged from the cover of the cliff wall. Bursts of ice leapt from their upturned claws and raced towards Burgis, now waist deep.

"Watch out!" Karanne yelled.

Instantly the water around his legs froze, locking him in place. He vainly smashed at the ice with his fist. Tare shattered the surface of with his club, but the rest remained frozen solid.

Allar stepped in front of the others and raised his shield. "Get him out!" he urged Karanne.

The cat creatures reached the river and stepped into the water. They opened their mouths in unison and filled the air with their screams again. This time Chase added his own cries and Karanne uselessly covered her ears. By the time the screaming stopped and Karanne was able to focus again, several creatures had waded out to Burgis.

Karanne held up her hand and closed her eyes. The Fireflash burst out of her palm and spun around Burgis' legs in brilliant tight arcs. Thick slush formed in the wake of the spell. Burgis pulled himself out while holding onto his brother's strong arm. When he got his feet steady he reached for his bow and strung an arrow to aim at the large stalking cats.

The Darrak waited beneath the cliff wall. Another Darrak launched ice crackling through the air. This time Allar leapt in front of the spell with his arm upraised. The blast hit the shield and careened away from them, its impact shaking the very air. The frosty orb of energy spun towards the creatures on the shore. With a shattering sound, the spell bounced off the surface of the shallow water and hit one of the cats. A white shell coated the stringy haired beast in an icy cocoon, its own cry stopping abruptly as ice filled its mouth.

"We can't hold them off forever." Burgis dropped another one. "I'm running low on arrows."

Karanne eyed the deep water again and then gave a half-smile. The next time an ice-wielding Darrak lofted a blast at them, she grabbed Allar's shield arm and directed it at the behind them. The shield recoiled from the icy spell, but sent the blast skimming across the surface to the other side of the river.

Allar gripped her wrist sharply. "Don't."

Karanne said in a slow, firm voice, "Let go of me." Her free hand hovered over the knife strapped to her belt.

"Look!" Burgis shouted.

Allar released his grip. Karanne let out a breath and relaxed her hand. Would she have actually used the knife if he hadn't?

A path of ice nearly five feet wide had formed on the water in the spell's wake.

"Go!" Karanne shouted but Burgis was already running. Allar shot the bridge a glance and followed him with a strong limp. Karanne's heart raced.

Chase refused to walk onto the pathway.

Burgis and Allar nearly crossed the span, but she could not leave Tare and Chase. The cat creatures approached the bridge, claws extended. One opened its mouth to scream but Karanne was ready. The Fireflash, already pulsing in the air, awaited the sudden flick from her wrist and shot into the cat's mouth.

A quick burst of light and smoke escaped its neck as the Fireflash shot out the other side and returned to Karanne's hand. The cat's lifeless body hit the ground like a rock.

"Get him moving!" she yelled to Tare, who yanked on Chase's reins.

Tare stopped yanking and closed his eyes, sighing deeply. When he opened them again he gazed straight into Chase's and held his hand up in the signal Jace taught him. Chase stepped onto the bridge.

A flash of white light burst from the closest Darrak. Karanne held up her hands to shield herself from the incoming ice. The Fireflash darted in front of her, weaving a barrier of fire. The spell hit the flames and instantly spattered and steamed. Shards of ice pelted her hands and a ball of frost began to envelop them. She cried out in pain as the ice continued to build over her hands and up her arms. The pulsing of the Fireflash slowed as the pain in her head consumed her. With a grunt she struggled to cross the bridge, the ice almost to her shoulders.

She knew the ice would cover her face soon. She turned back to the cat creatures, baring their teeth as they followed her onto the ice bridge. Her Fireflash nearly faded from sight in front of her. She dropped to her knees.

"Come on Karanne!" Burgis shouted from the bank of the river, his bow singing with arrows.

His cry rekindled her determination. Her heart flared out in a pulse like the Fireflash and the flame raced back to her in a burst of light. The flash hit the icy surface of her arms like a hammer. Bits of ice flew across her face. She stumbled along the ice bridge towards her friends. The ice, warmed from the blast that freed her, formed a slick surface and she slipped.

A sudden deep crack resounded in her body when she hit the ice. The bridge split into several pieces, sending the ice beneath her and the cats in a spiral downstream. Fatigue and pain overwhelmed her and she toppled into the water. The strong current pulled her under.

As she bobbed up to the surface she heard the screams of the cats as the river's cold grasp carried them downstream. Weakly, she pushed herself towards the shore and flailed for some branches jutting into the water.

She gripped one, but it strained under her weight and snapped off. Her vision began to fade. She saw one last branch in the cluster and reached for it. The rough bark tore into her numbed fingers as she struggled to keep her grip. The water pounded past her.

She let go of the branch and slipped below the surface.

Chapter 23: Reunion

A strong hand pierced the surface of the water, gripped Karanne's forearm, and wrenched her from the iciness of the river.

"We've been looking for you," a voice said.

She could barely make out the hard features of a familiar man. The grizzled and scarred face of the Guardian leader came into focus in the dying light. Stroud plunged his sword into the hide of a cat creature trying to scramble ashore out of the freezing water.

A blast of fire, bright as the sun, twisted through the air and into the chest of an ice-casting Darrak, incinerating it instantly. The force of the impact knocked the one behind it into the rocky surface of the cliff. Its neck snapped and it dropped, lifeless, into the river.

Other less bright blasts of light erupted from beyond the riverbank, piercing the ranks of the attacking cats. The beasts crashed into each other to avoid the bursts of fire, causing the magic to leap between them and set their coats aflame. The pack dispersed into the woods, their screams fading. All that remained were scattered smoldering bodies in the river and on the bank.

Karanne shook uncontrollably, her cold drenched clothing clinging tightly to her body. She wasn't sure if the night had grown darker or if her eyes dimmed from the pain of the cold. Still shivering, she watched an aged figure come towards her in the dark.

"This will not do." The old man placed his hands on her forehead. The air around her warmed like the sun on a summer's day. The weight of the water in her clothes lifted. She smiled, her eyes closing heavily.

"Thanks, Turic," she mumbled. She barely managed to reach Turic and wrap her arms around him in a hug. "If not for you…"

"You would have managed something, I am sure." He returned the hug. "You always do."

Someone lifted her up to a saddle and began leading her along a path into the forest.

"No time for sleeping now," Turic said lightly. "They have surely been watching for this. We have to make it to our camp." He offered her a small flask. "How long has it been since you had some sleep?"

She weakly grabbed the flask and took a deep drink. The medicine coursed hotly through her head and body. Her fingertips tingled. "That did it." Karanne noticed the others walking beside her. Stroud, Brannon Co'lere, Barsal... She almost laughed.

"Danelia!" She dismounted and nearly fell off her horse in the process. She stumbled to the blonde lady's side and clasped her tightly.

"It is good to see you again," Danelia said.

Karanne and Danelia held their palms up to each other as they walked. A bright glow emitted from their hands and a burning light grew in Karanne's chest. Images flew in and out of her memory. Memories of the people she had seen fall, and others of people she hadn't. Those were from Danelia.

They smiled a bit sadly and let their hands drop.

Karanne asked the group. "How did you find us?" Stroud waved her voice down and continued ahead silently. "And where are we heading?" Daylight had now completely faded and the trees felt a bit closer in the darkness. Stroud disappeared up on their path.

"He's an odd one," Danelia whispered. "But I guess it's for the best that we don't make too much sound. At the camp, we can rest and talk freely. I've been so anxious to find you. For a while now I knew you were close, and then those animal cries just now drew us to you."

"What do you mean, you *knew* I was close?"

Danelia shrugged. "I don't know, I just... knew."

Had Karanne known, as well? Something had drawn her to this place. Perhaps she'd been too distracted to notice.

"Luckily, we had someone familiar enough with these woods to keep us hidden and moving in the right direction."

"Who?" Karanne asked.

A woman appeared up ahead through the trees. Several large dogs stood at her side, tongues hanging out and tails wagging. Long brown hair pulled back into a ponytail draped over her shoulder. Karanne didn't know her, but she had heard stories from Jace. Tare and Burgis jogged to her side and clasped her arm like old friends. Allar also followed and soon they were in a deep conversation.

"That is Ranelle," Danelia said. "They know her?"

"They seem to." Ranelle. A tracker of some sort. That would be helpful getting past the Darrak in these woods. The group followed Ranelle under deeper cover into some dense thickets.

Karanne pushed aside some branches in her path. "So why didn't you head to Beldan already?"

"We are surrounded by the Darrak army that poured out of the Shadow Vale. The very beginnings of that army are here now. Some in our party suggested leaving two days ago, but others were more convincing."

Turic. Of course he was. "And what about the Soulkind and the prisoner?"

"Dorne is yet with us. He is still quiet, but there's something alive in him. Gerant watches him. They are both at the makeshift camp up ahead." Danelia paused. "Now that you and Allar are back with us, Turic says we can bring all the Soulkind to Myraton to safety."

Ranelle continued leading them up a hill, twisting through trees and steep rock faces. Past the next effacement, they turned abruptly to see the path drop into a clearing with a dark stone in the center.

"We are safe here," Ranelle said and nodded to Allar who led Chase to a small spring for a drink. "This was one of Alid's camps. No one will find us here." Allar placed his hand on her shoulder. Karanne remembered Jace saying her husband had been killed.

In the clearing Karanne recognized the man watching over Dorne. "Gerant." She saluted the Guardian.

He nodded, his sword trained on Dorne's throat.

The dark, silent man's eyes flashed up at her as she drew near. Hmm. That was a change.

Turic waved his arm and cast a glowing ball of light into the clearing. The flaming globe throbbed in the frigid night air, enveloping the companions with its warmth. "Tell us of your journey here."

Karanne told how Fay and Guire turned the prisoners rescued from the Darrak, of Jace and Straeten's escape to the wastelands, and about Mathes' and Cathlyn's separation from the group.

Allar kicked the dirt.

"She'll be all right," Karanne said. "She and Mathes will get each other home. Seems like the Darrak were more interested in us for some reason."

Allar slowly twisted the Soulkind shield on his arm. "I need to find her and make sure she's okay."

"We need to get to Myraton." Stroud stood up. "That army is fast approaching, if not already here."

Turic nodded slowly. "The King does need to be warned now that we know Guire and Fay are close. It is a shame your sister is not here, Allar. I am sure she will be instrumental to how this all plays out."

Allar laughed dryly. "She doesn't use her magic, not unless she's forced to."

"No?" Turic asked. "Mathes is a convincing teacher, perhaps he is close with her now."

"I thought he might be persuading her, as well," Karanne said. "Newell claimed Mathes was drugging people to do his will. I'm still not sure what to think."

Allar said nothing and kept prodding the ground with a stick.

"*Newell?*" Turic asked as he sat down next to Allar. "So it is as we suspected."

Allar nodded and held the Soulkind up for Turic. "It's a part of me now."

Turic nodded. "We must investigate when we have the chance. As for Mathes, his beliefs are strong, yet to betray magic that way by hurting people? I do not believe he is capable."

Brannon coughed. Everyone turned to face him.

"Something to say, Brannon?"

"You may feel differently if you knew everything." Brannon fidgeted with a stone he had picked up. "Those ten years ago, when you were denied the research in Myraton, it was Mathes who convinced the Hall Council to send me instead of you."

Turic turned his back to everyone. Karanne remembered Jace talking about Turic's embarrassing dismissal from healing studies in the Hall. He went almost mad from his obsession with the Soulkind and the denial of the research position. Poor Turic.

"We thought he was drugging me, too," Karanne said. "But I was only reacting to Fay's magic."

Turic glanced up and squinted over his spectacles. "What do you mean?"

"I've been getting freezing pains in my head for the past week, and I was sure Mathes was behind it." A familiar burning sensation in her hand made her arm twitch.

"When have these pains occurred?" Turic walked slowly to Karanne and placed his hands on her head.

She scratched at the itch in her palm. What was it? Her Fireflash? "Well, when Fay's Follower met us by the river." Her eyes widened. It wasn't just a coincidence that the Darrak found them by the cliff side.

"It must be something Fay placed in your head." Turic placed his hand on her forehead. "You were being tracked."

Her hand itched again. It always seemed to itch just before… She stood up. Sharp pain pierced her head.

"Not *were*," a voice called out somewhere above them.

A shadow fell thickly over the clearing. They scrambled for their weapons. Karanne's vision faded. She heard swords being drawn and others shouting in confusion.

That voice. She knew it well. She ran towards the sound of familiar laughter, but then it came from behind. She turned and tripped over someone's leg and stumbled to the ground.

"That's not like you, Karanne," Jervis said. His voice now surrounded her.

"Why are you doing this?" Karanne knelt on the hard ground, rubbing her knee. Her leggings were damp, probably with her blood. Several blows sounded harshly in her ears. She barely heard her companions cry out in pain above the Darrak clicking their claws on the stony ground.

"Search her. Fay said it would be on her."

Karanne whipped her head around, still trying to locate him, but couldn't see through the thick blackness. This was the same magic that he used back in the tower. Marlec's magic. Rough hands grabbed and pawed at her. She flailed her arms but they were quickly held down.

"Jervis, what is going on? Are they making you do this?" He was a despicable person, but this seemed beyond even him.

She heard Darrak shuffling past her. She kicked out at the nearest sound but got slammed to the ground because of it. Her chest burned with pain.

"I said not to hurt her!" Jervis cried out and a crackling sound emanated from her right side. A blast of cold air hit rushed past her face. If only she could see what was going on.

"I keep forgetting about you," Karanne muttered to her palm. She raised her hands and willed Fireflash to clear the darkness and find where Jervis stood. A blast of light ripped through the shadows around her.

The light revealed a Darrak enveloped in ice. Its yellow reptilian eyes moved frantically back and forth. Jervis did this? Several of her friends knelt in pain, but none appeared dead. Several creatures ran out of the camp clumsily, clawing at their eyes from the burst of light. A cloaked figure, in gray and black, stood at the top of the path. Her Fireflash pulsated in the air in front of Jervis' form.

"Don't take the Soulkind." Karanne fell back to the ground, still reeling from the hit she took.

Jervis held up his arm and pointed to her. "Don't follow me, Karanne. You won't want to be there when my new friends and our old gang meet."

Old gang? The guild back in Beldan?

He raised his arms and the cloak slid down, exposing several dark marks running up his forearms. The last of the Darrak ran past him. A wall of ice grew from the rocky ground in earth-shaking jolts forming a solid dome over them all. Interspersed within the ice were huge bulbous thorns, sickly and dripping with thick green ooze. What else had Jervis learned?

Stroud stood first and strode to the wall with his sword drawn. He hacked at it furiously. A spray of ice covered him with every stroke. Allar cradled his shield arm, Tare stood rubbing his forehead, and Lady Danelia tried to stand, but stumbled.

"Are the Soulkind still with us?" Turic called out sharply.

Barsal checked in the center of the clearing but came up with nothing. He then reached under his robe lying on the ground and held up a heavy pack triumphantly. "They're still here."

Turic scrunched up his eyes and the many wrinkles stood out sharply. "Then why did they even come?"

"He's gone!" Gerant called out.

Stroud stopped pounding on the icy prison. "Who's gone?"

Gerant rubbed the giant purple bruise growing on the side of his head and pointed to Dorne's lone cloak resting on a stone bench.

Stroud turned and resumed his pounding on the wall. "Get us out of here!"

"He's heading to Beldan," Karanne said.

"Are you sure?" Turic asked.

"Pretty sure." Jervis' words echoed in her head.

Allar joined Stroud in hammering on the wall.

"What did he take?" Turic asked. "He said there was something on you, Karanne."

Karanne patted herself down. What could she possibly have that Fay would want? Her heart dropped when she felt her bare neck. Almost instantly, she sighed in relief. Her necklace was with Straeten. But where was the other one? The one from Nilen? She searched through her pouch and pockets.

It was gone.

What could Fay possibly want with that?

Mathes looked over the edge of the cliff with Cathlyn at his side. It had been an hour since Karanne met up with Turic and the others and rode off into the woods. He and Cathlyn decided to make camp for the night up on the safety of the hilltop. The wind howled below the cliff just past the cover of the boulders at its edge.

"You didn't try that spell again, to move them."

Cathlyn sat atop her horse. Her long brown hair blew in her face and she tucked it into a fur-lined hood. "I killed three horses last time."

"I thought you weren't going to use magic again in the first place."

Cathlyn shifted in her saddle. "I told you, they were going to be captured or killed by that… creature, or whatever you would call that woman with the frozen eyes."

"How did you even know? You weren't there."

"I just saw them, somehow. I see things, and hear things, all the time. I just cannot—"

"Control it? It will be *your* undoing as well as everyone else's, unless you do something about it."

"You say that."

Mathes shuffled towards his horse to reach his pouch. "It is getting late. I'm sure it will be safe for a few more hours before that army is due to reach here."

Cathlyn's eyes went out of focus. "What was I just saying?" She put her hand to her head as she slid to the ground from her horse. "I'm so tired."

Mathes rushed to her side. "Whenever you use the magic it takes its toll on you. We've got to get you better or you'll be in no shape when we find those dark Masters."

"They're going to Beldan. That I know." Cathlyn stood up suddenly and faced south where the Khalad mountains came together leading back home. "There is something there they need, or are waiting for." She waved at the air near her ears as if warding something off.

Mathes put his hand on her shoulder. "We will be there, to stop it all from getting any worse. Now here, drink this. It will make that pain and those voices go away."

Cathlyn smiled and reached for the cup he handed to her. Good. Cathlyn still believed in him, even if Karanne and Allar didn't.

Cathlyn downed the liquid he gave her without pause. He pawed through his pouch. The herbs he was using on Cathlyn were running low, and there still were many days until they reached Beldan. They needed to hurry.

His hand brushed against the Lock he had taken in Marlec's tower. He recoiled. The white material felt cold and lifeless to his touch and he loathed it. But Cathlyn could use it, to finish it all. He had come too far now for this not to work. Sacrificed so much.

"You will use Sarissa's Lock to stop the magic."

Cathlyn smiled as her eyes glazed over in the deepening dark. "Sarissa's Lock to stop the magic."

Chapter 24: The Call

The young deer crept through the sparse branches of the trees, placing every step carefully so as not to make a noise. Her mother had taught her that before being killed by a tarn, one of those large screaming cats.

Images like this continued flitting through Jace's mind as he sat behind a stand of tall grass with his bow pulled taut and an arrow aimed at the deer's heart. He could drop the deer easily from this distance. His stomach grumbled loudly.

"What are you waiting for?" Straeten whispered from beside him as they watched the deer moving closer. "Shoot!"

Jace pulled back further on the bow. *You're all right. Just a little closer.*

"We need to eat," Straeten urged.

The deer's life shone in Jace's head. It felt safe.

He'd made it feel safe.

He let up on the string.

"What are you doing?"

Jace stared at the deer. "I can't."

"Well then I'll do it," Straeten said angrily and quickly lifted his bow to take aim.

"Straet, don't!" Jace let go of his connection. The deer abruptly jerked its head before crashing off and disappearing into the woods. Straeten's arrow sailed wide and buried itself into a tree.

"For the suffering, Jace! We're going to starve out here!"

"We're not going to starve. At least not yet."

Straeten threw his bow to the ground and it clattered on some rocks. "You know, there's going to be a time when one of those mushrooms I find is going to be poisonous. And those dried, rotten berries? I'm not so into them anymore."

Jace put his bow away. They had to eat and it wasn't like he was against eating a deer. He tracked it down using stones to read where it had been, just like he had with Graebyrn.

But he'd made it feel safe.

"I miss Burgis and Tare," Jace said.

"We don't need them. Well, not if you'd just let your arrows fly."

Ash crept by Jace's side and Jace scratched him behind his ears. "It's this magic." He pointed to his dark mark on his arm.

"What about it?"

Jace's chest tightened. He hadn't told Straeten about his part in Blue's death. He took a deep breath. It was time.

He told him everything.

"So you've been keeping that from me?" Straeten crossed his arms. "Worried that *I* was going to do something terrible with Fay's magic?" Anger rose off Straeten like heat waves.

"What's wrong with you?" Jace said. "This has been killing me. I finally tell you, and you yell at me?"

Straeten closed his eyes and rubbed his temples.

Jace put his hand on his shoulder. "Hey, are you all right?"

Straeten shook his head. "I'm sorry. I'm having trouble thinking straight. Just tired, I guess. Haven't slept in a real bed forever."

Jace nodded. Maybe it was just that. Jace could certainly relate. "So, do you have any poisonous mushrooms or rotten berries left?"

Straeten didn't respond but Jace was pretty sure he saw a small smile on his face.

Jace walked beside his horse and rubbed the white stone of Karanne's necklace. He watched her again, little more than a child jumping from a burning building with him in her arms. Now he knew why it was so important to her. It held the memory of him coming into her life. And yet there was something beyond the memory that called to him. What was it? He slipped it back under his cloak.

"How's Rhila doing?" Jace asked Straeten. "We've been riding pretty hard lately."

Straeten patted Rhila's side. "She's doing all right. I'm worried a little about Ash, though. He's gotten even scrawnier, if that's possible."

"You hear that, Ash? Big old Straeten says you're getting scrawny. I wouldn't worry. He's always got a mouse he caught or something from Valor."

Straeten nodded and stared off into the woods.

154

"And how about you? Any better?" Jace asked.

"I'm fine. Just need a little waking up." Straeten slapped his cheeks a few times and shook his head.

"So nothing from Fay?"

Confusion flashed on Straeten's face, but left quickly. "There's nothing going on in here." Straeten tapped his head. "Well, maybe a little of my old genius. But no ice spells."

"That might not last long." Jace pulled out the gloves. "Look." As if to make his point, another piece of the crystal covering chipped off the black surface. "I think when this is all gone, we might have problems."

"Yeah, because things are going just great right now."

Jace forced a laugh and returned the gloves to his pack. They seemed heavier than before. Things were far from great, but did they have to be? He tried to ignore the question, but another popped up. Would things be different if he'd just let Graebyrn destroy the gloves? He clutched his own Soulkind so tight it hurt. There had to be another way.

"What is it?"

"Nothing." Straet hadn't exactly taken to his last confession.

"You know, we can fix this," Straeten said. "We're going to get back to Beldan, together. We'll figure it out when we get there. Like we always do."

Jace nodded. There was the Straeten he knew. He wanted to believe it. And he almost did. Yet the knot in his chest remained.

Jace took out his map and placed it upon a flat rock. Straeten examined it over his shoulder. The yellowed paper had seen its share of scrawling since the whole adventure started. There was his valley home in Beldan where it all began. What started out as empty spots were now filled in with things he never imagined he would see.

Further to the south he spotted a path that led along the outer reaches of the Shadow Vale and then wound its way to Beldan and the Crescent River again. A wave of longing for home passed over him. He hadn't realized how much he missed it.

"What's that song you're always humming, by the way?" Straeten asked.

"What song?"

"The last few days, you've been humming the same tune whenever we stop."

Jace's hand instinctively went to Karanne's necklace at his throat. "I don't know. Must've heard it in Nilen's village." Had he really been humming?

"What are those scratches on there?" Straeten said.

"Scratches?" Graebyrn's scrawls on the map. Jace had forgotten others couldn't read other languages like he could. "Graebyrn wrote some things to help us out along the way. This says there's a camping place in these caves by the mountainside."

"Wouldn't a different way to Beldan be a lot faster?" Straeten asked.

"It sure looks like it. Why would he want us to go this way? It'll lead us right off a cliff."

"Well, do you trust him?" Straeten walked back to his horse.

"Pretty much. He is a dragon, after all."

Straeten laughed. "Well then, what are we waiting for?"

Jace rolled up the map and put it in his pack. He turned to Straeten and gasped.

"What's the matter?" Straeten asked.

"Your eyes, they..." Jace blinked. Had they been blue? Impossible. They were just as brown as they always were. He must've imagined it.

"They what? Drew you in with their beauty?"

Jace tossed a small stick at him and Straeten ducked quickly to avoid it.

"It was nothing. Come on, let's get moving." Imagined, not seen, he told himself again.

Chapter 25: The Map

For two more days they marched south, keeping the twin mountains to their left. After they climbed the foothills of a smaller range, the pass grew almost too difficult for Rhila. Payt's flanks heaved from the exertion of the climb. Valor cried out high above, wheeling in the air with what appeared to be another hawk. Too bad they didn't all have wings.

"You sure Graebyrn said to go this way?" Straeten said when Rhila slipped again.

Jace pulled the map out. "Pretty sure."

Straeten peered over his shoulder and pointed to some markings. "What does that say?"

"Darrak encampments."

Jace casually glanced over at his best friend. Had he really just *imagined* his eyes turning blue? At least it hadn't happened again. If Straet's draw to the dark power was anything like his own, he'd eventually want to use it. Was he strong enough to resist? Jace furrowed his brows. Maybe he didn't have to be.

"Hey, Straet," he said.

Straeten raised an eyebrow. "I know that tone."

"I want to try something, get into your head like I do with Valor to see what's going on in there."

"Oh, is that all? No problem."

"No really. Maybe I can undo what Fay did. Or at least understand it better. It might help, you know, if you get the urge to freeze me or something."

"Not likely." Straeten's tone turned serious. "Just don't mess with my brain too much."

"What brain?"

Straeten pretended to blast him with a spell.

Jace laughed and then cleared his mind. He focused on the river of magic just beyond the borders of his thoughts. The spell pathways felt

157

solid, supportive and strong. The warmth of the power surged through him, encouraged him, and he nudged forward into Straeten's mind.

A storm of thoughts raged inside forcing Jace out. The shock of it caused a sharp pain in his skull and he nearly disconnected from the spell. There was no way he could maneuver through this. He needed to calm whatever this was so he could concentrate. He thought back on Payt blocking him in a similar way. Maybe using what he tried with him would work here with Straeten.

"There's a lot going on in there, actually," Jace said. Straeten rolled his eyes. "I'm going to try to settle your thoughts a bit."

The right pathways clicked into place, like the tumblers in a complex lock. Jace felt energy flow through them. The air around him lightened and he breathed in the fragrant hillside. His muscles loosened.

Ash circled several times slowly and lay down with a yawn at Payt's hooves. Straeten sat down and faced the cloudy sky with a small smile. Jace continued directing his thoughts to Straeten's and soon his friend's eyes began to close.

"That's pretty good," Straeten said calmly.

Jace too, felt at peace. Time to try again. Nothing would go wrong. He walked over to Straeten, laid his hand on top of his head, and drifted slowly behind Straet's eyes.

This time no chaos thwarted him. Still, it was quite different than when he entered an animal's mind. Instead of Straeten's thoughts merging with Jace's like Ash's and Valor's, they bounced past him. His concentration faltered amidst the stream of them.

Jace sought to sift through them without looking too closely. Even the calm couldn't make him comfortable invading his friend's private thoughts, though they were hard to ignore. Where was Fay's magic? There were far too many places to look. He sensed hints of frustration and impatience. Great. The calm was starting to wear off. Should he give up? Just then, something in the center of it all summoned him. Something strong. Something cold. He drew closer.

There it was. It had to be. A pulsating orb of ice shedding waves of cold energy. It was in there, growing. Now to do something about it. But what? He only knew that the orb, like a weed taking deep root, needed to be removed.

"I've got this," Jace started, confident. The orb withdrew, but then suddenly pulsed out, tendrils reaching for him across Straeten's mind. A few latched onto his own. So cold. More veins of ice reached for him. He couldn't move. His thoughts slowed.

158

He was trapped.

He felt his awareness slipping, like falling into a dream. Silently yet insistently, something called to him from outside, jarring him to consciousness. His own magic. The calming spell. He had not yet let go. He forced himself to focus on the flows of magic, to draw on them as deeply as he could. The calm grew once more.

The creeping tendrils slowed, loosening their grasp ever so slightly. Jace took that momentary lapse to pull completely out of Straeten's mind, ripping his thoughts from the clinging ice. He collapsed with a splitting headache unlike any he'd ever known.

Straeten rushed to his side. "Are you all right?"

He held up his hand for a moment until he could speak. "I'm fine." He shook his head and the pain began to dissipate. "That could have gone better."

"What happened? What did you see?" Straeten rubbed his temples.

"It's in there," Jace said. "In there pretty good."

Straeten nodded slowly.

The image of Fay's magic inside Straeten, festering and reaching, burned in his memory.

He had to get that out.

The trek up the mountain proved as hard as Jace expected. Piles of fallen rock often blocked their path. Even Payt slipped across some loose stones. Ash splashed through rushing torrents as he led the way. Soon the trail cut through a narrow valley of tall scraggy trees.

"When you were in my head, could you tell what I was thinking?" Straeten said.

"I could've, but I tried not to. I kept my focus on finding Fay's magic."

"Thanks. I mean, I could tell were trying not to, I just didn't know if it worked."

"What do you mean *you could tell*? How?"

"I don't know, from your magic. I guess it works both ways."

"Huh." That could get him into trouble if he wasn't careful. "Glad I didn't think about how I took some of your breakfast."

"Nice." Straeten said. "So, are we going the right way?"

"I think so," Jace said. "This valley cut is one of Graebyrn's marks on the map. Says it leads to Beldan's mines after a few days. It sure is dark, though." Even though the sun was near its peak, the light failed to reach the path.

They rode deeper into the nearly hidden way along the mountain. The nearness of the rock walls deadened all sound except for the loud scuffling of hooves. Valor soared above them and then disappeared quickly over the rocky cliff wall. Had something spooked him? Jace reached out for Valor's sight.

"Are you sure there's a way through all this?" Straeten shouted, breaking Jace's concentration.

"Graebyrn wouldn't have sent us here if there wasn't." Up ahead, the sound of water rushing across rocks filled the air, somewhere past the standing stones and twisting paths.

In about a hundred feet they crept down a short ledge above a shimmering mountain-fed pool. Sweet smelling plants and sudden warmth filled Jace with peace he had not felt in a long time. Valor swooped down low over the pool's surface just up ahead.

Right over the top of a group of Darrak.

It was too late to hide. The Darrak stared at the invaders. Ash growled and Payt clicked his shoulder spikes into place.

Why had Graebyrn sent them through this way? Jace fumbled for his knives but stopped. The only way out of this was to use the magic from his dark mark. Hopefully it would be strong enough to affect them all. The power of the darkness surged through his body.

He glanced at Valor, alit calmly in a tree right above the group of Darrak. The huddling Darrak. The hunched over and clothed in tattered rags Darrak.

He reluctantly let go of the magic.

They weren't here to kill him and Straeten. They were running from something. The fear in their eyes made Jace want to run too.

Chapter 26: The Refugees

"Straeten, no!"

Straeten held back an arrow on the large bow he took from Nilen's village.

"What? Are you crazy?" Straeten drew back further on the bow but didn't shoot.

"Just look at them." Jace placed his hand on Payt's quivering shoulders to calm him.

The ten Darrak stood back to back, holding makeshift weapons, some merely walking staves. Never before had Jace seen them this close. At least not this close and not trying to kill him. He could even see differences in their appearances, varying color and height. Lighter scales covered some of the smaller Darrak, and gray scales covered one who stooped, possibly an elder.

The two groups stood silently for a minute. No one made a move. Straeten glanced back a few times at the sharp climb that would prevent a hasty retreat.

Finally Valor leapt off a branch, glided gently through the air and landed gracefully on Jace's outstretched arm. One of the Darrak gestured to the hawk. Their weapons dropped slightly.

Jace made a pointed glance at Straeten's bow. Straeten slowly lowered it. Jace spoke soothing words to Ash and he stopped growling.

"Just stay back here for a minute," Jace whispered to Straeten. "Don't worry."

Jace raised his right hand in his salute and took a few tentative steps towards the Darrak. Instantly they raised their weapons again. One of the creatures stepped in front of the others. It wasn't the largest of the group, but Jace sensed its determination and protective nature. The leader.

He drew a deep breath and let it out slowly, pushing all his fear of these beasts out of his mind. Something compelled him to take another step and sit cross-legged before them. Valor shifted on his shoulder.

"What are you doing?" Straeten hissed.

Jace waved him off and waited quietly in front of the Darrak.

Another Darrak stepped cautiously towards Jace, still gripping its spear tightly with both hands. Yellow spikes in its elbows popped out as its arms flexed.

Quiet, rasping snarls and harsh whispers of "Sephintal!" filled the air from the cluster of scaled creatures. It's name? Had to be. Sephintal slowed and turned back. Jace couldn't quite hear what they were talking about, but when it resumed its approach, it held the wicked-looking spear even tighter.

Valor kneaded his talons into Jace's shoulder. Jace resisted an urge to push him off. "We mean you no harm," he called out.

The group of creatures stopped their murmuring.

"What are you saying to them?" Straeten asked. "Your voice, you sound like… one of them." The bonelike spikes on the Darrak slowly retracted into its elbows.

The spear made a small clattering sound on the stony ground by Sephintal's feet. "How did you find us?" Sephintal said with a raspy voice and then sat across from Jace. The Darrak language and its meaning blended in Jace's mind.

How *did* they end up walking right into them? Jace thought about his map and the curious path Graebyrn sent them on. He chuckled and shook his head. The dragon knew exactly where he was sending him. "A friend led us here." This time, he noticed his voice. He did indeed sound as harsh and raspy as the Darrak.

Sephintal's claws flexed. "This place is hidden, there are no humans, no one knows but us."

The Darrak behind Sephintal shifted and murmured again.

"Don't worry, our friend won't tell anyone else about this place," Jace said.

Sephintal waved for them to calm down. "They are afraid. Afraid they will be found."

"Who are they hiding from?"

"They are hiding from the others. From the Call."

"The *Call?*"

"How can you speak like one of us?" Sephintal scanned Jace's hands and exposed forearms. "You are one with the Soulkind."

"I am. But I don't want to hurt you."

Sephintal frowned.

162

How could he prove that he meant them no harm? Straeten said the magic went both ways. Maybe he could show them. "I have an idea." He raised his hand and stared into the creature's black eyes. The magic began to course through him.

Sephintal flinched and reached for the spear on the ground. Jace released the flows and grunted out an apology.

Sephintal slowly lowered the spear but still held it tightly. "Stay out of my mind. *That* is what they are afraid of."

"Bad idea, sorry."

The silence in the clearing grew awkward. "Can I show you something different?" Jace asked. "Something that doesn't involve magic?"

Sephintal squinted with suspicion but at least didn't refuse. Jace reached into his pouch slowly and laid its contents on the flat stone in front of the Darrak. Kedan's metal artifact, covered in Darrak markings, sat among the items.

Sephintal's eyes widened slightly. "Where did you find this?"

"It was given to me by someone north of here."

"Then it was not a gift given lightly." Sephintal reached for the silvery metal rod and held it up. The rest of the Darrak crept in, weapons drawn. The lead Darrak's eyes stayed on Jace.

One of the Darrak snarled and pointed his spear at Jace. "He stole it!"

Jace tried to stay calm. "No, it was a gift." The Darrak took another step closer, his spear raised.

Abruptly, Payt leapt forward, his shoulder blades cracking.

"Payt, no!" Jace shouted. A sharp splitting sound told him it was too late. The Darrak stumbled backward, two spikes protruding from his arm and shoulder.

Jace whirled around. Even Straeten had his bow drawn and centered on the Darrak. "Stop!"

Behind him, Sephintal tried to do the same with the others. The Darrak Payt had attacked dug at the spikes imbedded in its scaly flesh. Payt stamped his hooves on the rocks furiously. Two more shoulder spikes stuck out and locked into place with a click. Jace reached out with his magic, this time his calming spell. The power flowed through him readily, as if it were just waiting for this moment. A breeze blew in off the mountain, cool and quiet. Weapons lowered. Ash sat beside Jace.

An unpleasant thought occurred to Jace. This magic felt dangerously close to the controlling spell. Were they just two edges of a single blade?

"That was a good save," Straeten whispered as he stood close to Jace . "They were going to kill you."

"They weren't."

Straeten scoffed. "That's not what it looked like to me."

"They're just scared."

Straeten shook his head. "I can relate to that." If only he understood what they were saying. Jace smiled to himself. Maybe there was a way he could.

"Come here, quick." Jace gestured. The mark on the back of his neck warmed as he thought of the spell. He held Straeten by the wrist and willed the magic to him. The spell passed readily. Straeten twitched then nodded as glowing lines wrapped around his wrist like a serpent. He marveled as they changed into a solid black mark.

"What was that?"

"Just wait."

Jace turned to see Sephintal showing the metal rod again to the group of Darrak. The eldest Darrak, a grayish creature with cloudy scales, took the rod and turned it over in its clawed hands. An awed whispering erupted. Jace noticed the skillfully crafted necklaces around the elder's neck and wondered if they signified rank.

The Darrak stood a little more comfortably. Even the injured one seemed a little less hostile. They spoke to each other quietly as they passed the metal rod among themselves.

"What is it?" Jace said.

Several spun around and lifted their weapons. They had nearly forgotten he was even there.

The elder placed his hand on one of the Darrak's shoulder and approached Jace. "I am sorry about this. It is not often that we meet allies here in the wild."

Straeten gasped. Jace tried not to laugh. Looked like the spell had worked.

"We were once free from the Call of the Dark Magic. Free to live where we wanted, and to be our own people. Even then, before the Call, many wars were fought between us and humans. This gift was a peace offering."

"It says 'Rushkarn' on it," Jace said. "Do you know what that means?"

164

"So, you can read our language, too?" The Darrak turned the artifact over, exposing the symbols beneath. "This is from a once great tribe far in the north called the Kra'rath. Rushkarn was their leader. And very wise. But that was many years old ago."

"And what is your tribe?"

The old one appeared both surprised and saddened by this question. "We have none. We come from many different groups. We found each other two moons ago and united to fight the Call."

"Sephintal spoke of the *Call*, too. What is it?"

"It is the voice that guides Darrak warriors. Long have we heard and heeded it. Few can hear and not listen. Luckily, the voice has been quieter as of late and we are not tempted."

The gloves. They caused this. Had Graebyrn's magic been what quieted the Call? Last time he checked there were only a few crystals remaining. He thought better of checking now.

He sat back down on the ground now that things seemed calmer. The injured Darrak rested, a few green herbs pressed into its wounds. "I'm sorry about what happened to you. He was just protecting me." He gestured to Payt.

The Darrak responded with a sound like a hacking cough. Jace knew there were some words in that as well but couldn't quite make them out.

"Ignore Harkra, he does not speak for our group. Still, we thought that attack was young Sephintal's fault."

"No," Jace started. "He is an excellent ambassador."

Another strange sound arose. This time, a type of gurgling that Jace thought might actually be laughter. Each of the Darrak was making it, even Sephintal.

"I mean it. He did nothing wrong."

The sound grew louder.

The old Darrak pulled back his dark lips into what was definitely a smile. "I'm afraid you don't understand. If you are to lead your people in talks with the Darrak, there is one thing you must learn."

"And what is that?"

"How to tell the difference between a male and female Darrak."

Chapter 27: No Rest

"So, you used magic to connect with this creature?" Sephintal walked closer to Payt. But not too close.

"And others." Valor sat on Jace's shoulder and Ash stood alert by his side.

Darrak walked passed him around the camp as if it were the most normal thing. Without the Call, he supposed it was. And yet every fluid movement from their reptilian bodies caused fear to creep up in his chest. How long before he could shake his past fears? Before he could see them without remembering every wrong or evil their brothers had done?

Jace watched Sephintal while she observed the burra. What identified her as female? Was it her tail? Was it slightly more tapered than a male's? He glanced at the injured Harkra to compare, but Harkra narrowed his eyes so Jace looked away. Did they have differently shaped heads? He resisted the instinct to start drawing them in his journal. There was no time for that now.

"That magic you tried with me requires a great deal of trust." Sephintal tentatively put her hand on Payt's back. "And I don't trust you yet."

"Because you're such a trustworthy bunch yourselves, right?" Straeten said, surprising Jace from behind Payt.

Sephintal stared at him for a moment and then shifted to Jace. "What does the large one say?"

"What do you mean?"

"He speaks in the slurred sounds of your tongue. Not like you."

"Straet, she can't understand you," Jace said in the human tongue. "Luckily." Hadn't he taught him? Perhaps there was more to passing along spells than he knew.

Straeten approached Harkra and leaned over to carefully inspect the type of herb he was using on his wounds. The injured Darrak glowered at the weapon in Straeten's hands. From this distance Jace couldn't really tell how they were communicating but at least they weren't trying to kill each other.

"How long have you been running from the Call?" Jace asked.

Sephintal stepped away from Payt. "Ten years. My clan was summoned to war far to the west. I resisted."

"Ten years?" Had they really been around that long without anyone knowing about them? "How did you avoid capture? I'm sure they didn't just let you go."

"No, they did not. My own family could not avoid the Call. My brothers left me with these." Sephintal lifted her scaled and sinewy arm to expose painful looking scars. "Chran, the elder, found me in the mountains near our tribe."

"And you've all been running since then?"

"Running. And falling. The Call still comes for us, and the weak still follow it."

"And that's why we need to leave as soon as we can," Jace said abruptly.

"The Call is not here now. We'll not harm you."

"We have to get to our town and warn them before an army of Darrak reaches its borders. Even if you won't harm them, there are others who will."

"It is late. You can stay here with us, restock your supplies, and then continue to the east."

Jace smiled and nodded.

"You see? We are not all evil."

"I always knew that," Jace said. "Now I believe it."

Night settled in and the Darrak began to set up their fires. Chran still had not returned the relic. What was he doing with it? The old Darrak passed it around again and Jace tried to keep an eye on its silvery metal glinting in the firelight.

"Should I help them with the fire?" Straeten asked. "Although maybe we shouldn't let them know everything we can do. What if they try to force us to teach them magic?"

"I don't think it will come to that. We just need to keep them away from the gloves. I don't think they'd understand."

Straeten nodded.

Sephintal and Harkra arrived back at camp with some fresh kill. Several Darrak sat around the fire skinning and cleaning the large deer with their extended claws. Soon, the smells of roasting meat drifted through the small glade. It had been so long since they had something besides dried meat. Jace's stomach growled. Ash crept closer to the campfire.

A few Darrak glanced at Jace and Straeten standing away from the fire and murmured to each other. Chran stood and invited them to the gathering. Slowly they joined the others upon rough hewn logs. It still felt a little strange joining mortal enemies for a meal. Ash, however, had no problems sitting among them and begging for scraps of food, which the Darrak doled out readily.

The Darrak were still wary of Payt, though. Two of the braver Darrak approached the burra with a chunk of raw meat and tossed it to him. Slowly Payt lowered his head to the ground to sniff the food and then rapidly devoured it.

"How long have you been at this camp?" Jace asked Sephintal.

"We never stay in one camp too long. You happened to find us on our way out to search for other Darrak to join us."

"I'll be right back." Straeten shuffled off around the edge of the fire to Harkra and handed him something, which he ate. Harkra gave Straeten something in return. What was that all about?

Jace was able to tell who some of the Darrak were now by subtle differences in their appearance. Harkra wore metal bands on his forearms, Chran had lighter scales and walked with a hunch, and Sephintal... It was more than appearance, Jace sensed something inside of her that told him who she was.

"I'd like to help with the Call."

Sephintal paused between bites of deer. "How could you do that?"

"I just mean that I'd like to, not that I know a way."

Sephintal touched Jace's shoulder and turned him to face her. "I know there is something you won't tell us, but I sense that you want to help. Trust us."

Jace stared into her round black eyes. "Then you must trust me."

Sephintal nodded briefly and Jace took that as a sign to proceed. He continued staring into her eyes, sensing her thoughts as he pressed forward. The rush of his Soulkind's power filled him. He was now in control. His own mind entered the Darrak's and the two merged.

Her mind was different than the beings he'd merged with before. Even Straeten's wasn't quite as varied as hers. Thoughts, memories, pain... all flooded into him. He prepared to explore, although he wasn't really sure what to expect.

Suddenly a dark fog swirled like a vortex. What was that? Unlike the river he tapped into, this sought *him* out. Black tendrils crept into his body. He tried to resist but drifted further and further. He stopped fighting. Time to let go...

"What is it?" Chran shouted, holding onto his head. The two Darrak who had been feeding Payt yanked Jace to his feet, breaking his link with Sephintal. One handled him roughly. Was he searching him for something?

"Do you see how hard it is to resist?" Sephintal asked quietly.

Dazed, Jace nodded.

So *that* was the Call.

Chapter 28: The Betrayal

Jace hung between the two Darrak, slumping to the ground. Straeten hurried towards his side.

Harkra held Straeten back with a shaking arm. "The Call is stronger now, why?"

Jace clutched his pouch. The gloves were still inside.

Harkra's gaze followed the movement. "What are you carrying?" The Darrak yanked Jace's pack and dumped its contents onto the ground.

Marlec's gloves clanged against the rocks. With a grimace, Jace noticed that the last of the crystal had disappeared completely.

"Who are you?" Sephintal shouted. "The Master who commands the Call?" Her dark eyes narrowed to mere slits, still drawn to the gloves on the ground. She clenched her fists and a thick yellow talon slid out of her elbow.

Harkra grabbed him tightly from behind, holding his arms back. Another Darrak hit him over the skull with a clawed fist. Jace's vision spun..

Chran held Jace's chin and glared at him. Jace stared into the Darrak's unwavering black eyes, felt his hate. Not hate. This was the Call. The power of it was so close to them, they could no longer fight it.

Pain shot through Jace's knees as someone shoved him to the rocky ground. Valor's cries and Ash's barking reached his foggy mind through the chaos. He tried to grasp onto anything in his head, anything that might help. And there it was. The right thing, the only thing that could stop them all. With a burning throb, he drew in power and darkness.

Flames flew through the air at the Darrak but bounced off harmlessly. Straeten. That magic wasn't working. But he had another kind. Jace crawled towards him with a hand raised in protest. "Don't let her in!" But it was too late.

170

A blast of ice flew from Straeten's palms covering everything in frost. In seconds, the Darrak were fully trapped in the grip of Fay's magic. Sephintal barely managed to clench and unclench her claws under the layer of ice. The glade rested in an uneasy stillness. Frost clung to the branches of the trees like on a winter's morning.

"What did you do?" Jace struggled to his feet and raced to Straeten's side. He peered into his eyes. A faint glow of blue light slowly faded until brown returned.

"I'm sorry, it was all I could think of."

"Just help me free their heads so they can breathe." Jace quickly and carefully hammered away at the nearest Darrak with a rock to chip away at the ice.

"What are you doing? They're going to kill us!"

"It was the gloves. It wasn't their fault."

Jace cracked the ice covering Sephintal's reptilian head and pulled a sheet off. "I'm not what you think I am."

She said nothing. Jace ignored the pang in his heart and moved quickly to another Darrak.

A bolt of light spun from Straeten's fist. Karanne's Fireflash melted away the ice around Chran's and Harkra's heads. Luckily, all the Darrak were still alive by the time they finished. A sudden image struck him… of Darrak hibernating in chambers deep under the ground, waiting to be awakened. He ran to the gloves and shoved them in his pack.

"I'm sorry," he said as he and Straeten quickly packed their mounts. "We didn't want any of this to happen."

The Darrak remained silent.

"We have to hurry. Others will be drawn here." Not to mention Fay, who could probably now sense her power in Straeten. "Don't follow us. You're not safe with us near. Not anymore."

Many of the Darrak strained against their bonds, eyes like wild animals. Chran, however, stared at the ground. Jace rode over to him on Payt before leaving.

"One Master cannot control two Soulkind," Chran said. "There must be another to balance the power."

"But I can do something about those gloves. I can stop the Call. I'm sorry, Chran."

"Take this with you."

Jace followed Chran's stare to the familiar metal glint of the artifact on the ground. He jumped off of Payt to retrieve it. Something was different about it.

"It has the symbols for our new tribe. Use it when you find others like us, they will allow you to pass."

Jace nodded in thanks. Perhaps they understood more than he realized.

Jace rushed toward Sephintal. Her eyes flashed back and forth between anger and relative calm. The Call. He waited until her head stopped twitching and her eyes flashing, then placed his hands upon her. Sephintal's eyes widened when he lifted his hands.

He jumped back upon Payt's back in one swift motion and headed east. Ash sprinted alongside. High above the ridge line through the trees, Valor followed from above. The darkness of the sky ahead matched the feeling of dread in his gut. They had to reach the city before it was too late. Before Straet turned into one of Fay's Followers.

"What did you do to her?" Straeten asked, struggling to keep up with Payt's pace. "What was that look she gave you after you touched her?"

Jace stroked Payt's rough fur along his back. "I needed her to know she could trust me. I taught her a spell."

Chapter 29: The Way Through

Jace and Straeten rode the rest of the night without speaking. Exhaustion almost overtook them. Only Payt's careful strides prevented Jace from falling off. Further and further they rode along the south ridge of the mountains, closer to home.

"I can't believe that happened," Jace said after being awakened by a jostle.

"Which part? The gloves or me?"

"Everything. You know she's going to take over your mind now, right?"

Straeten stared straight ahead. "You're welcome."

Jace dropped his head and let out a sigh. "I didn't mean it that way. You saved me, you saved both of us. I just wish I could've done something then. To stop you from letting her in."

"I'm going to be okay. I don't even feel any different."

"Look, I can figure something out with my Soulkind. Maybe go in your mind again?"

"No thanks. Don't worry about me. Let's just get to Beldan."

"Just let me try one thing," Jace said. "My calming spell helped when I tried to find Fay's magic before. I could teach it to you. You could use it to help keep her away."

"I said no thanks, all right?" Straeten kicked Rhila sharply in the sides. The exhausted horse barely responded. Straeten rubbed his forehead intensely. "Look, I'm sorry. I'll be all right. Let's just hurry." He stroked the side of Rhila's neck.

Jace rode quietly and fought to keep his eyes open. And on his friend.

They headed eastward while the sun rose over a shorter range of mountains straight ahead. Shorter, but just as hard to cross. Jagged peaks and piles of boulders around the bases of the slopes threatened to twist an ankle or ensnare a leg.

Valor circled high in the gray skies. Jace wondered if he too could sense the nearness of home.

In the morning glimmer of light, Jace held up the map to search for any clues about how to proceed. Graebyrn's last mark, the glade of refugee Darrak, stung his heart. He had almost befriended those creatures, only to betray them with Marlec's gloves. And Straeten's ice attack.

But what would've happened if Straet hadn't used Fay's magic? The dark mark on his arm tingled at the thought.

A few of Graebyrn's marks on the map showed a path over the mountains. Where could it be? There was nothing but lots of brush and loose rocks, nothing that resembled a path.

Rhila and Payt grunted as they ascended the hills. Even Ash slowed his near constant bounding. Jace frowned to think of anything breaking the dog's spirit.

After a short rest and the last few strips of dried meat, they made their way up the rocky slope again looking for a rounded peak they had seen on the map. Jace squinted at the hills. He and Straeten shrugged at each other.

"It's got to be around here somewhere."

Tall, familiar pine trees lined the hillsides. Jace smiled at the memory of running through these woods as a kid. Valor kneaded his shoulder and took to circling the skies high above. Perhaps he could help spot any landmarks. How seamless it was now to shift behind the hawk's eyes, yet no less thrilling.

Valor soared over the tops of the mountains but storm clouds blocked his view beyond them. Amidst stone and tree he spied a glint of light off of water. That could be it. Jace pulled his sight back to his own and focused on steering Payt through the maze of sliding stones towards the water.

"This suffering hillside!" Straeten shouted and drove his heels into Rhila's sides.

"Take it easy, we're almost at the top here."

"Yeah, right."

Straeten's anger came off him like heat from a stove. His fingers twitched. Was Fay's influence finally taking over? Straeten apologized quietly to his horse and stroked her neck again. Maybe it was just the anticipation of nearing the end.

Hours passed while they tried to find their way through the shifting rock piles. Fortunately no one lost their footing, or worse. The sun sank behind them as they climbed the cloud-covered hills and the air soon became damp with the fog. The coldness chilled Jace to his core. Darkness settled in.

The clinging dampness plastered Straeten's hair to his cheek, yet he never so much as shivered.

An hour after sundown they reached the stream. It flowed to the east. To Beldan. They were finally heading downhill.

The animals lowered their heads to the cold mountain water. Straeten and Jace joined them, though Jace could only take a few gulps before it grew too cold for him. Straeten drank heavily.

"Do you think the others have made it to Beldan by now?" Straeten asked. "Or maybe they went to Myraton."

Something tugged at Jace's mind as he tried to focus on the others. Specifically when he thought of Karanne. He took off her white stone necklace and held it up to the failing light. Something continued to bug him, telling him there was more to this necklace than the memories. What was it?

"She's close to Beldan, or already there."

"Who? Karanne?" Straeten stared at the necklace. "How do you know?"

Jace closed his fist around the necklace and pocketed it. "I just know."

He led Payt along the creek. Smoother stones sat neatly ordered next to the water. Was it evidence of an old road? If so, that could mean miners.

"I think we're almost there."

"We've got to stop." Straeten trudged alongside dragging Rhila along.

"Not yet. We're close." Something inside told him to keep pushing on.

The stream babbled along its stony course. The smooth path beside the water made their trek a little easier. Was this actually the way home though? It might only get them lost within the mountains, tangled amidst the old mining tunnels.

Jace noticed on Straeten the same depressed expression that he felt. They plodded on for several hundred paces until they reached the wall.

"What do we do now?" Straeten asked through a yawn.

"This is the way, I'm sure of it," Jace said despite his doubts. He took out his map and strained his eyes trying to look at it in the darkness. "Suffering."

Straeten raised his palm up and the Fireflash burst out in shards of light. Jace smiled his thanks. The stream was undoubtedly the same one that Graebyrn drew on the map. But how were they supposed to get through?

Ash's bark echoed from up ahead in the darkness, barely audible over the sounds of the churning water. "What is it, Ash?"

A few seconds passed and then he barked again. Jace reached out for the dog with his mind, to see through his eyes. At first only darkness filled his sight, but then Ash's sensitive eyesight showed him thin outlines of surrounding rocks. He was inside something.

Straeten raised the Fireflash from Jace's map over to the wall at the end of their path. The pathway next to the stream burrowed into the cliff wall.

Ash popped out of the tunnel entrance and wagged his tail with a rapid spin. Jace clapped Straeten on his back. "Keep that light burning, we're going through this and back home."

"You think Rhila and Payt will be able to get through there?"

Jace sensed Rhila's hesitation about being led into the darkness of the mountain tunnel. He placed a calming hand on her head. "They'll have to, we can't leave them back here." The horse took a second then strode in with ease next to Payt.

Straeten rubbed at his temples with his hands.

"You okay, Straet?"

"Let's just keep moving."

As soon as they entered the tunnel, Straeten's Fireflash sped around, casting long shadows onto the floor. The sounds of the water faded as they went further down the path. After an hour of steady walking, Straeten began to waver a bit on his feet.

"You all right?"

"I feel like I've been running for miles, to tell you the truth." The Fireflash began to fade slightly.

"You've been holding onto that spell all this time. Have you ever held it for so long before?"

Straeten shrugged. "Not this long." He staggered.

Jace rushed to his side to stop him from falling over. The light from the spell flickered until it faded completely.

176

"We better get some light or we'll never get to the other side." Jace scrapped around for a loose stick or anything to make a torch but the tunnel was clear of debris, at least in range of his blind eyes.

With a sigh he felt Payt breathing down onto his forehead. "What, boy? You got something to tell me?" Payt's long narrow head brushed gently against his own. "I don't know, the last couple of times you kind of shoved me out." His temples ached at the thought of trying to connect. Softly again Payt's snout brushed over his neck. With a sigh, Jace tentatively reached out with his mind.

He felt the familiar floating. The connection he had with his dog and hawk both emanated from their locations. Ash at his side and Valor gripping onto Payt's back. Payt was a little tougher to sense, but he pushed on. Slowly.

He met no resistance this time. His sight slipped behind Payt's eyes and like a fog lifting, the walls of the tunnel appeared in his mind. They didn't appear exactly like they had with Straeten's Fireflash. In fact there was no color at all. But with each step a finer detail of the stone walls blossomed into his perception. He stamped his foot and the image rippled clearer with every echo.

"I wish you could see what I'm seeing right now."

Jace heard Straeten shuffle into the wall and moan. "I wish I could see anything right now."

Stifling a laugh, Jace *saw* Straeten's voice bounce off the rough rock texture. Rhila's hooves clopped onto the ground, further adding depth to the tunnel.

"That's pretty amazing." Jace scratched Payt's head behind his ears. "Hey, can you get up on Rhila?"

Straeten mumbled "I guess so, why?"

"Just do it. You need a rest and I can lead the way."

"In this darkness?"

"I'll show you this later. You need to rest. Now are you going to get up there yourself?"

Straeten grumbled again but reluctantly climbed atop Rhila. Jace smiled. No better way to get him moving than to suggest help.

He double-checked the ceiling height. "As long as you don't stand up on her you're going to be all right."

"I'll try not to."

Straeten's words bounced off the ceiling to Payt's ears and into Jace's mind showing it to be smooth, perhaps carved by some mason from another time. It was an odd sensation trying to see out of Payt's head and feeling his own body move differently. Eventually he heard Straeten get off his horse. His footsteps sounded slow.

"You sure you're okay?"

"I'm all right. My head is better and I don't feel like I'm going to fall over."

"If you say so," Jace said. "Just hold onto Rhila."

An hour or so later, an area opened alongside the flowing water. The two tunnels merged and continued on but Jace's aching feet could carry him no further. He and Straeten lay down on the hard, rocky floor, falling asleep almost instantly.

The morning sunlight streamed into the tunnel entrance up ahead, waking Jace and revealing intricate carvings on the stone walls. Familiar walls. He bolted upright off the floor and shook Straeten. When he didn't wake, Jace splashed him with some of the ice cold water.

Straeten sputtered and cursed then opened his eyes wide as he took in their surroundings. Rushing to the tunnel entrance, Jace watched as the waters fell through the air into the Soulwash hundreds of feet beneath them.

Beldan.

Home.

Chapter 30: Beldan

"Did you see the wall here?" Straeten called out.

Jace had barely glanced at it before running outside. "Has it changed again?"

"You could say that."

Jace tore his gaze away from the fog covered town and headed back inside. The sun cast its brightness onto the wall as if the cave were a grand stage. Jace stepped through the freezing water to get a closer look. Such amazing detail. He ran his fingers over the intricate drawings, over the place that started their whole adventure. How long ago it seemed.

This time, the picture showed Darrak in fields to the north preparing to siege the city. He stepped back into the freezing waters to get a better look.

A strong voice called out to him. He shot Straeten a questioning glance but his friend only shrugged. He hadn't heard it. Jace knelt down by the water's edge and placed his hand into its depths. He sensed the great river of magic coursing through his Soulkind. A great power welled up inside of him, filling him with its warmth despite the frigid water.

The quiet in his head soon gave way to a resonating hum matching the pitch of the mountain stream. He shut out all other thoughts and focused on that sound.

Jace. Your friend, Cathlyn, is on a dark path.

Jace pushed in his mind for the dragon to continue. Graebyrn's words were known to him again.

She seeks to silence magic again. This time forever. You must stop her.

The connection weakened and his voice sounded scattered.

Undo the evil that binds the Call. You must go where the magic is strongest to see its pathways.

The voice faded into the sound of the rushing water. Jace felt a wave of exhaustion hit him as he strained to revive the connection. It was gone.

So now in addition to preventing an attack on Beldan, he had to stop Cathlyn. And sever the Call. But how?

With his back to the wall, he carefully opened his pack and pulled out the gloves. He peered into the dark stone. He could sense the Call, see the magic that caused it. And he could stop it.

Suddenly, darkness surrounded his mind like a whirlpool and held him there. He could not break his stare.

From a great distance, he sensed a shaking. It had to be the Call. Another great shake. Blaring pain ripped through his skull.

"Drop them!" Straeten shouted, seemingly from a great distance. Jace glanced up from the gloves to Straeten's raised fist. He dropped the gloves onto the ground and winced at a different pain in his shoulder.

"Did you have to hit me?"

Straeten raised his eyebrows. "I did, actually. Now just put those things away."

Jace snatched them and hid them in his pouch once again.

"What are we doing, Jace? We're bringing those things right where the Darrak are going, if this wall has anything to say about it. They're just going to make things worse."

"But I know I can do something about them. I can figure out the Call, cut it off somehow. Graebyrn said to bring them to a strong magical place."

"Any idea where?"

"Maybe." Under the Library? One of those pools lay underneath it. Maybe Turic would know. Whatever the case, he had to head to Beldan now.

Valor broke out of the tunnel entrance with a sharp cry and spread his wings to glide over the town so far below. Jace felt the pull to follow him. He went back out and peered over the cliff edge. A thick shroud of fog covered the city, enveloping all of the towers he knew so well. Soft glowing lit the fog in places, only to fade and reappear elsewhere. He needed to get down there as soon as possible.

"I… I think I can *see* the two dark Soulkind down there."

Straeten gave him a sideways glance.

"No really, they're down there." Jace turned to face him. "And Graebyrn told me that Cathlyn's here somewhere, too."

"Well that's a relief. She can help us."

Jace tried to peer through the thick fog. He didn't know how to tell him what the dragon had really said about her. Few things were clear, but he did know one thing.

He couldn't fail.

They packed up quickly and started the descent. Valor swooped over their heads and into the valley. The fog broke suddenly to expose the city towers shrouded in black smoke. No doubt now. Something had already started. He quickened his pace and climbed the last mile without speaking.

"Let's head to the Tower of Law," Jace said. "Let them know what happened out there. I think this time they'll believe us."

They reached the bottom of the giant hill and mounted their rides to approach the city. The thick cloud cover still hung heavy in the sky, the city towers barely visible once more. Valor flew low in the air now, as if the oppressive fog kept him down.

They followed the trail past Turic's cottage and across one of the lesser bridges to the south of the city. The great stone walls stood empty. Even with fewer guards, there should have been at least a couple.

Jace got off of Payt and removed the packs he needed. "I don't think it's a good idea to bring you into town now." The burra stared unblinkingly down at him. "We're trying *not* to be noticed if there's any trouble. I'm not sure bringing you in would help the cause."

Payt stomped on the stony path. Jace put his hand onto his head and locked eyes with him. Before he thought of how to tell Payt to wait for him here, the beast turned towards the woods and wandered into the trees. "I'll be back for you." Payt chuffed as if to say be quick about it. Ash ran out a few steps to watch the burra until he disappeared and then returned to Jace's side.

A month ago at this time of day the town would have been bustling with merchants lining the streets and boats upon the river. Now it was silent and empty. Some people shifted behind closed windows but not one came outside.

Rhila's hooves hitting the cobblestone streets made more noise than Jace wanted. They took to side alleyways to avoid the stares of any townsfolk. Valor's talons kneaded into Jace's shoulder.

Straeten's pace picked up slightly when they got closer to his home. He handed Rhila off to Jace.

"I want to check on my parents. Get her stabled, could you?"

Jace nodded and led the horse to the stables. Not another horse in sight. The stalls stood clean and empty. Jace took off Rhila's saddle and made sure she had enough food and water.

In a few minutes, Straeten hurried into the stables. "They're not here."

"What do you mean?"

"I mean all their stuff is gone. It's like they packed up and just left."

Straeten ran off to the next house and rapped on the door impatiently. An old lady opened the door and held up her hands to hush him.

From this distance Jace could barely hear their conversation of hushed whispers. "Rin? Rin Ver Straeten?" the lady said and gave him a quick hug. "What is this?" She reached up and pulled at the scraggly starting of a beard.

"I've been busy, I guess. Do you know where my parents are?"

"They've been gone for a week now, ever since *they* came." The lady motioned for Straeten and Jace to come in off the streets. She raised her eyebrow at Valor perched on Jace's shoulder but still hustled them and Ash into the house. "Strange times are here, for sure."

"Where did they go, Rashnah?"

The old woman shut the door behind them quickly, leaving a dark interior. She pulled out plates from the cupboards, but kept her eyes on the streets outside the window. "Here, eat. You two look like you haven't had a meal in a month. And you, too, I suppose." Rashnah tossed Ash a scrap of meat. Valor cocked his head at her and she handed him a morsel as well. He quickly plucked it from her fingers with his beak.

"What's going on?" Jace asked as he stuffed warm bread and cheese into his mouth. It did seem like a month. Maybe longer. "We barely saw anyone on the street."

"A short while ago, two came to Beldan from the north."

"Just two?" Straeten asked.

Rashnah nodded. "They had… magic." Her face showed that she still could not quite believe that it had returned. Or that she didn't want to. "That's when people began to get sick." She motioned to another room where an old man lay sleeping restlessly. Jace saw beads of sweat lining his brow and flushed skin.

"I'm sorry." Straeten checked in on the man. "We've seen this before. How did it happen?"

"Those that gathered by NorBridge to hear what the man and woman had to say were affected."

Guire and Fay. It had to be.

"Some got sick, the ones that refused to listen to them, that is." Rashnah's jaw quivered a bit. "He came back home and fell into this stupor. Your parents offered to bring us with them before the city closed off, but he couldn't be moved."

Jace frowned. "What do you mean *closed off?*"

"No one in or out. They have guards posted at all the entrances."

All the entrances? Why hadn't they seen anybody? How had he gotten through so easily?

"Rumor says they have taken over the Hall."

"Did my parents say where they were going?" Straeten stood up and began to pace around the room.

"They headed south. Took their horses with them, too, and a few of the other neighbors." Rashnah sat at the table and buried her face in her palms.

Jace stood up. "If Fay and Guire are in the Hall, that's where Cathlyn will be heading as well."

Rashnah kept her face hidden in her hands. "Notices are up asking others to join them. They speak throughout the day, looking for people. They say the sickness will go away if we do." She turned toward the other room where her husband lay. She got up slowly, walked to him and rested her hand on his fevered forehead.

"They'll be like those people back at Nilen's," Straeten said.

"And with enough to form an army," Jace said. "We've got to get in there and stop them somehow." He peered out the window into the streets. A group of four soldiers walked past the house and hammered a parchment onto a building. "But it's not like we can just blend in with people. There's no one out there. And I don't know how to get into the Hall except by the main entrance." Well, he did know of another way, but he didn't think swimming under the Soulwash was a good idea.

"Maybe your 'friends' could help."

Jace turned to Straeten. "Good idea. It's worth a try. We'll head to the Guild, but I've got to do something else first."

"Don't walk around in the daytime," Rashnah said. "They will bring you in."

"Don't worry, we know a few of the back ways, right Straet?"

Straeten nodded slowly.

"Your parents are all right. They made it out of town. They're safe." If only he were as sure as he sounded.

Rashnah packed them with some food, despite Straeten's protests, and gave Straeten a hug. Jace wondered if that was what having a grandmother was like. They crept out behind the small cottage and towards the dark alley ahead.

Once in the alley, Jace could've walked to Karanne's and his place blindfolded. The buildings squeezed together closely, the walkways used mainly as sewer and storm drains. Houses and other structures rested upon the solid foundation built ages ago. His mind raced for ways to get into the Hall undetected. Did any of these sewers open up on the other side of the Crescent River?

Ash led the way even though he had never been here before, anticipating every turn and running a little faster if Jace got close to his tail. Soon they reached the back entrance to their house. Jace fiddled with the lock for only a moment before the door creaked open.

"I'll be right back, I've got to do something," Jace called as he ran inside the dark home. He almost expected her to be there waiting for him as she was countless times. Not too long ago, he and his friends had all sat together in this front room, so excited and hopeful about magic awakening. How naïve they all were. He lit a small candle. Time to focus on his task.

He scribbled onto a piece of parchment on the table to let Karanne know he was heading to the Guild for help. If only they were all here together, they could end this. He laughed dryly. To think that almost everyone he knew was now able to control some form of magic. They'd all been worried they would be left out.

Karanne's necklace felt cold in his hands. She risked everything she had to save his life, and spent her life taking care of him. He went into her room to hide the letter and necklace. When he came back out, Straeten startled him.

"Took you long enough." Straeten leaned his head over to look behind Jace.

"Come on, we've got to go." Jace pulled the door closed behind him.

"To the Guild, right?"

Jace shrugged. "They're not going to like me bringing an outsider there. But it's the best idea we've got." He locked the door to the silent, empty house and disappeared into the alley.

Chapter 31: The Guild

Guard patrols swept by frequently now through the main streets. Jace made his way unseen, even in the daylight and with Straeten in tow.

"You see their eyes?" Jace asked. "They're all a bright blue. Like what you saw back in Nilen's village."

Straeten squinted as he clung to the building beside them. "She must have spread her power here, and quickly. They'll be looking for us."

"Jervis has probably told her all about me. Could be he knows I might try to get to the Guild for their help."

"You don't think he'd go there himself, do you?" Straeten asked.

"He didn't leave on good terms, so they probably wouldn't let him in. But seeing as though he might have learned some new tricks along the way I don't know if they could stop him."

Straeten stumbled when they started walking again, knocking over a bucket into the street. Jace grabbed onto his cloak and pulled him back into the darkness. Ash growled low in his throat. "You trying to get us killed?"

"Sorry, I'm just a big clumsy oaf is all. I thought you knew that."

"Good point. Come on, we're almost there."

Jace led them to a spot beside the city wall with a small opening at its base. Through it he heard the sound of rushing water from a sewer draining into the river. He bent over and took one step into it.

"We're going through there?" Straeten asked ducking down. "Don't you see the river right next to it?"

Jace gingerly stepped into the water. The sewer flowed a short distance past the wall into the fast flowing Crescent River. "Yeah, and the sharp rocks, too. Here, Ash!" He whistled and tried to pull Ash through. Ash backed up abruptly then wouldn't move.

"He doesn't seem to think being smashed against some rocks is a good idea either."

Valor flitted to the top of the stone wall. Straeten stepped into the tunnel, promptly slipped on the mud, and reached out for help. Jace managed to keep his footing as he yanked Straeten up onto a precarious path. "Careful, oaf." He patted Straeten on the back and tried again with Ash. "Come on, boy!" Despite his efforts, the dog wouldn't budge. Jace sighed. "Ok, Valor, you'll have to get him out of the city. Bring him to the south gate."

High above, Valor responded to his request without hesitation. Jace made a silent vow never to take that ability for granted. Marlec forced the Darrak to do his will. With Valor, all Jace had to do was ask. The hawk instantly landed at Ash's paws and nudged him gently until he turned around and trotted off.

"All right, let's go." Jace jumped off the edge of the bedrock foundation next to the rushing river. The sewer flow poured off the wall next to them creating a little waterfall. They walked under it to the south.

Straeten stumbled again and stopped to rub his eyes.

"You've been falling all over the place. I mean, even more than normal. Are you okay?"

"I..." Straeten looked around, confused. "I don't even remember us coming here. I feel like I've been sleep walking."

Jace patted him on the shoulder. "You've got me worried. Come on, we'll rest some up ahead, hopefully. And then figure out what to do about the town."

"Do you think the Council is okay?" Straeten pointed to the Tower of Law back behind them.

Jace just shrugged in response. Had Brannon's father given himself over to Fay and Guire's rule, or was he wasting away, sick from Guire's power, in one of the cells?

"The Guild will be in their backup caves, now, no doubt," Jace said as he walked along the edge of the river. "Maybe they can tell us what's going on." Fresh rain raised the level of the river a bit. Hopefully it wouldn't wash them both away. "Not much further." He turned his head to his left, reaching out to sense Valor and Ash. Still within the walls of the city. They'd be out soon though. He kept climbing over the large river rocks.

After a few hundred steps down the river Jace paused where the water thrashed the bank. A singular white stone, about Straeten's height, leaned against the gray bedrock at the water level. "Never thought I'd get to show you this. Come on."

Jace led Straeten past the white stone and a hidden entrance appeared leading further under the escarpment. The bottom of the pathway was filled with water, soaking their feet and shins.

186

"This fills up at different times of the day but we found some carved out spots that lead underground to some drier places. Karanne's old place, before the Guild made her the house, used to be in one of these tunnels."

"That's interesting. Why don't you go ahead and make sure it's all safe. I'll hang back here." Straeten rubbed at his forehead.

Jace peered back at him. "You sure you'll be all right?"

Straeten turned away abruptly. He dropped his hands to his sides and just stood there. "I'm fine." His voice sounded empty. Perhaps he really was scared.

"Don't worry, only a few thieves have gotten washed away who didn't know how the river flows."

"I'm fine," he said again. "Now go."

"Whatever you say. I'll be back soon." Jace crept forward, ducking his head to avoid hitting it on the low ceiling. The light of day quickly faded as he walked further in and slowly upward. He remembered as a child being afraid of the waters creeping into the tunnels. Plenty of stories about young thieves who didn't pay attention to the time of day, the season, or the weather who ended up washed downriver. But he knew it well now and Straeten would be safe for a few hours.

Up ahead through the dark he saw the flickering light of an oil lamp mounted on the wall. He whistled a quick trill and soon heard a voice call out.

"Been a while since we used that call."

"It's me, Jace. I need help." He rounded the corner after a narrow tunnel and the path opened up. Two men held their bows drawn and pointed right at him.

"Are you alone?"

Jace paused. "A friend of mine is out at the entrance. Let me go back and get him. I just wanted to check ahead first."

"Dral ain't going be thrilled to have you back now."

"I just need his help to get into the Hall."

The two thieves laughed at this. "Why do you want to get close to what's going on in there?"

"Let me talk to Dral. Are you going to lower those bows?" A familiar old face came around the bend of the tunnel. "Picks!"

The old locks expert stared at Jace in amazement. "You can't be here, boy. They're looking for you in the city. If they find you here…" The strings of the bows creaked as the guards slowly released the tension on them.

"What do you mean *looking for me?*" Jace sensed movement next to him and a sudden chill in the air. "Hey Straet, I thought you…" A sharp pain blared in Jace's neck. He dropped to the ground. As his fingers touched the stones beside him, a hazy image flashed through his mind, a memory in the rocks. Straeten, watching the river. Almost as if he were waiting for somebody.

Through his fading vision he saw icy blasts strike the two thieves, knocking them to the ground. Picks ran back in the tunnels, avoiding the burst of magic aimed for him.

With his hands still on the rocks, Jace saw another vision of Straeten, this time beckoning hooded men into the tunnel.

Jace tried to reach out to anything, any magic he could think of, but nothing worked. The pain spread across his head and the world spun. Several people pushed past him into the cave, shouting orders.

With his last wits he turned his eyes upward into Straeten's face. His eyes shone blue. No one would listen now, his world narrowed. Straeten raised a stick and struck Jace's face. He faded into darkness.

Chapter 32: The Return to the Valley

"Don't move!" Turic urged.

Karanne tried to hold her head still while Turic stared into her eyes. His hands wavered in front of her face. "I'm trying! You've just been doing this for a long time."

"We do not want to be followed again, nor do you want to wake up screaming like you did last night, so I must find what Fay placed in your head."

A warmth brushed against her skull and she withdrew. She flashed him her best "I'm sorry" glance put her head back in position. He raised an eyebrow at her. She took a slow breath to calm herself.

"I think I am almost there," he whispered. "Well, here is something."

A sudden pain seared her brain. It felt like her head would split. Yet this time, she barely moved. "Hurry up!" she uttered with gritted teeth.

"Yes, yes, I have it now."

A soothing warmth filled her. She let out a long breath. "Did you get it?"

Turic laid her head back against a small blanket. "From what I saw, she planted an ice crystal in your brain. I used something I created earlier on this trip plus some of my brain research."

She shot him a questioning look.

"I used to examine pig brains back in Beldan."

Her eyes widened. "Pig brains. Great."

"Oh you were a much better patient," Turic said with a smile. "And yes, I believe I melted away whatever she imbedded in your head. That should help you sleep better, and keep us all alive longer."

"Well, looks like I owe you for yet another thing. Thanks."

"Of course." Turic stood silently for a moment.

"What's the matter?"

"It is just something that I have been wondering about for a time now. How did the Fireflash come about?"

She thought back to its inception and traced the lines on her palm. The dark fortress. Images of being trapped. Images of the Darrak. How many Followers had she lost in there? The memories she gathered from them stung her mind. "It came at great need."

"Yet it did not come from my Soulkind," Turic said. "I cannot wield that magic."

A space of awkward silence followed. Karanne fidgeted with her knife.

"You are not like Cathlyn," Turic said. "She is a rarity and can wield power without any artifact." Turic drew out his fiery red Soulkind. "You're not wielding a Soulkind, are you?"

Karanne furrowed her brows. "Of course not."

"Well, you have your Fireflash. That has been helpful so far."

"You'll find a way to stop Fay," Karanne said. "She has your Soulkind's *twin*. That's what you call it, right?"

"We balance each other," Turic said. "That is how I was able to find her ice crystal in your skull, I presume. But I am worried about what might happen if they reach Beldan. Their magic together is far too powerful."

"Your magic is powerful, too."

"Quite powerful. But I don't have the experience they do."

"Just keep at it until we're out of time."

Turic held up his arm and pulled back his sleeve to reveal a glowing mark. "Well, I've got one more spell, thanks to you!"

"Glad I could help."

Suddenly, she felt an emptiness when she thought about her Fireflash and the mark on her palm.

It was still there, but something was missing.

"This does not feel right," Danelia told Karanne as they packed their horses for the final ride home. "After you burnt the other Follower's remains and passed the memory to us back in the fortress, I can think of nothing else. And now the pain is growing stronger."

Vivid images of the dead flashed in Karanne's head. She knew that pain well. "We're coming closer to the families they left behind. I think the burden we carry can only be lifted one way."

Lady Danelia shrugged her shoulders uncomfortably. "I don't know…"

190

"We've got to pass the memories on. I'm not exactly thrilled to tell them that their wives, husbands—"

"Or children."

"Yes. That they died." Karanne said. Every family member glowed in her mind like a beacon in the distance. When they could, she knew she would have to find them. Even Blue's light pushed into her thoughts now. Jace might not be ready to hear about his horse, but he would need to someday. That much was clear.

She glanced around at the party as they travelled. Stroud had left the main group and taken several others, including Kal, Gerant, and Barsal, with him to Myraton. He struggled with whether to chase after Dorne or bring the Soulkind to the King. Yet he was still a Guardian, charged first with protecting the Soulkind.

There was much debate as to where Turic needed to go, but the old Master felt his calling drew him to his Soulkind's twin, despite his guilt at having lost Dorne.

Finally they rode their horses into familiar territory. The Citadel tower rose up in the distance, welcoming Karanne home into the valley. She would have relished that feeling if it weren't for a sense of foreboding about what awaited them further on in the city. She squinted for a moment at the massive bridge spanning the river. Something wasn't right. Where were the look-outs?

Allar kicked Chase into a gallop. He must've sensed something as well. A thin black substance stained the stony road leading to the bridge and an acrid smell wafted through the air. Smashed and crumbling masonry lined the bases of the stone walls, their tops deteriorated as if something was eating away at the stone from the inside. Stony bits and dust drifted down from the parapets as they rode under the wide arch.

Karanne urged her horse faster.

Allar rode onto the bridge a few steps and then dismounted. He held his hand up to the others to stop them from following. "Hello!"

Karanne listened for any reply from the guards who would normally patrol the Citadel but heard only the flow of water and the crumbling of the rocks.

"Do you think they ran?" she asked.

Allar kept walking, a slight limp in his step. He tapped at the bridge with his boots. "This is Guire's doing. Trying to undo Newell's magic from long ago."

"They are just trying to slow us down, Allar," Turic said. "To prevent us from getting Dorne. We need to hurry, to make certain he does not reclaim the gloves."

Allar continued to feel out the integrity of the bridge. "I need to fix this."

"Allar, we have to go." Ranelle put her hand on his shoulder.

For a moment his expression appeared to soften. But then a section of the citadel wall collapsed into the river raising a huge spray of water.

"I said I must stay!" Allar pushed Ranelle away abruptly.

Ranelle cradled her arm. Must've been extreme force to make Ranelle flinch. They all took a few steps away from him when he turned back to examine the bridge.

"His mind is fading," Turic said quietly as he assessed Ranelle's arm. "Newell's soul has stayed too long in this world, in Allar's body. If Newell continues this path, he will fall further into insanity."

"Can you do anything to prevent it?"

"I am not sure. All I know is that he is needed to fight against Guire. *His* Soulkind twin."

Allar knelt and put his hand onto the stonework of the bridge. Karanne felt a throb of energy course through her as Newell summoned a spell to begin mending the failing structure.

"I need to finish this," he said in a deep voice.

Turic pulled himself back onto his horse. "We need your help in Beldan. We cannot do this without you."

Allar focused on the bridge and bit by bit, the cracks and missing pieces began to fill in. Slowly.

"This will take too long!" Burgis shouted, but still kept his distance from Allar.

"And we do not have the time." Turic turned to the south. "This is exactly what Guire wanted. He counted on Newell's pride to distract him. This does not bode well for us."

Turic drew out his Soulkind. The fiery red gem and golden chain sparkled in the sunlight. As he spoke, all other sounds seemed to fade. "You took an oath, Newell."

Allar silently continued to work on the bridge.

"To protect the true path of the Soulkind. To uphold the laws and virtues of the land." Turic paused.

"To stand against the darkness," Allar finished. He sighed as if a great weight lifted. Everyone let out a collective breath as well. Allar

192

walked quickly to Ranelle's side to inspect her arm and apologized. "I can see what's happening around me when he takes over, but I can do little to fight it."

"I'll be all right," Ranelle said. "You've got to listen to us when we try to help you. Can you not take off that shield?"

"But we need it."

"It is a pity he does not give you mastery over it," Turic said. "We do indeed need its powers. And someone sane controlling them." Turic watched Allar for his reaction.

He gave none.

Karanne urged her horse alongside Turic's. "What was that you said to him?"

"I have studied the Soulkind longer than you have been alive, Karanne." Turic smiled under his beard. "Each ancient Master had to swear the Oaths and were thus bound to uphold them."

"We're lucky that he listened."

"I would say that Allar was lucky that Newell listened. I fear his grasp on his own mind is slipping too."

Chapter 33: Fire in the City

A few more hours of riding and still Karanne saw nothing on the road. No one leaving the city. No one on the river casting nets. The fog clung heavily to the valley floor blocking any view of Beldan's towers. The vast fields north of the city stretched out before them.

"I don't like this," Karanne said. "I see no one, yet I know we're being watched."

Turic turned around. "What do you suggest we do?"

Karanne shrugged. "They already know we're coming, so there's no use sneaking around. Not with eight of us."

"The guards have probably been captured by Guire and Fay," Allar said. "More than likely they're being held in the Hall. We need to free them somehow. Get control back of the city."

"But they have magic, and the guards don't." Karanne said. The city walls slowly began appearing through the fog.

"You could free the guards to draw their focus away from us," Allar said. "That way Newell could face Guire unhindered."

"I'll do what I can about the guards." Karanne stared at Allar. "Can't you stop him from taking control of you again?"

"Letting him in is the best way to stop Guire. Now hurry, they'll be looking for us."

Karanne hesitated. "I know how to get by without being seen. But what about you all? You're not the most inconspicuous bunch."

"I see your point. We'll wait at my house until the guards are released," Turic said. "It is out of the way."

"All right," Karanne said. "Just lay low until dark."

Ranelle spoke up. "Some of my friends followed us from the woods around Tilbury. I'll see if they'll help us, too."

Karanne listened carefully and heard dogs in the distance howling to each other. Or to Ranelle. They could use all the help they could get.

She saw something wheeling above them and glanced up. She squinted her eyes and gasped. "Are you all seeing this?" She pointed to the sky. "Isn't that Jace's hawk?" Her horse started stepping in her excitement

Valor circled and descended towards them. Tare lifted his arm up as he got closer. With a flurry of flapping Valor slowed and landed on the silent boy's arm. They stared into each other's eyes.

Valor leapt off into the air and flapped to perch on the top of the city wall.

"What does this mean?" Karanne asked. "Is he here somewhere?"

"That's his hawk, so he has to be." Ranelle nodded at Tare. "It looks like he wants to lead you somewhere." She turned to Karanne, "Tare can help guide you. Send word if you find him." She clasped Tare's arm before leaving to join her wild dogs across the field.

Tare saluted Ranelle and faced Valor upon the wall. Karanne watched his eyes to see the two make a connection. Just as Jace had done so many times before he left the village. That all seemed so long ago now.

Sudden howling and baying jolted her into action. She and Tare crouched facing the city wall under the cover of the fog. From here she still couldn't see anyone at the city gates and was tempted to walk right through but her instincts made her wait.

Just before she accepted that no one was coming, a small group of guards bearing the city colors hurried out the gates and into the fields. Karanne nudged Tare to go, and followed him under the towering archway.

Valor jumped off the wall just as they passed through. At first she didn't notice anyone manning the wall, but as she looked closer at the openings in the stonework she saw people beyond it staring out into the fog towards the unnerving barking.

She grabbed Tare by the arm and pulled him into an alleyway. He didn't possess her skill for blending into the shadows, but he could move quickly and quietly if needed. Hopefully Ranelle's distraction would do the rest. Valor kept disappearing beyond the towers, but Tare's quick eyes and connection to the bird seemed to keep them on track.

Soon she was able to tell where the hawk was leading them—towards the southern part of the city, away from the bigger buildings, and closer to the edge of the woods and plains. Towards her home.

Across the street from her house she almost gave a relieved shout. Tare held up his hand to stop her. Valor flew in circles above the simple dwelling nestled among several others.

"Why stop now? What's the matter?" Karanne nearly stumbled over a rough, gray furred mutt at her feet.

"Ash!"

With a laugh she reached over to pet him. Her laugh quickly dropped as several soldiers left her house. The first one out kicked the front door open roughly and threw several papers into the street.

She held her breath as the last of the soldiers walked out. No Jace. She let out the breath with a big sigh. Why were they there in the first place? And why did the hawk lead them here? Valor landed upon the rooftop and sat perfectly still. She watched the soldiers until they all disappeared.

"What now?" Karanne asked. Tare shrugged. Ash nuzzled against her legs and she scratched his head. "Well, he led us here for a reason."

Karanne made sure to watch the house an extra hour after the guards all left. She wasn't about to make a mistake now. Afternoon drew to an end, yet the usual tolling of the city bells was silent. Motioning to Tare to stay with Ash, she stole her way across the street to the back of her house.

At the back door, her hand started to tingle and she held herself back, although she could barely stand to do so. "All right, I told you I wouldn't ignore you anymore," she said to the markings on her hand. "I'll be ready."

Her Fireflash symbols glowed brightly on her palm for a moment and then the spinning ball of light came forth. It hovered in the air right next to her head as she slowly opened the door and slipped into her home.

"Straeten?" Karanne uttered in disbelief. She ran over to grab him in a tight hug. "I can't believe you're here. How did you get here?" She held his shoulders. "Where's Jace?" The Fireflash bobbed around the room illuminating her things strewn about the floor.

"I don't know." Straeten stared at the floor. "He was captured after we came here." He didn't look up.

"He what?" Karanne said and stepped back. "What do you mean? Where is he now?"

Straeten just stared at the floor.

"Hey, what's the matter with you? Look, it's not your fault. We'll find him, okay?"

Karanne ran to her room. "I can ask some of my old friends if they know anything, don't worry. We're all here now. Turic, Allar, and I think even Cathlyn and Mathes. Did Jace say why he came to our house?"

From the other room Straeten said, "He left something for you. I couldn't find it, though."

Karanne turned to see Straeten standing in her room entrance. "My necklace? You gave it to him, right?" She went back to searching through her things.

"Yes."

"I sure hope he left it here somewhere." She combed through her desk drawers.

"I hope so too."

Karanne paused. "You feeling all right?"

"I'm just tired."

Her hand almost burst from the Fireflash pulsing around inside. Something had to be wrong. "Hey, I have a feeling something is coming, something dangerous. Can you go keep an eye out? It would make me feel better."

Straeten walked from the room without a word.

One more place to look. Jace probably didn't even know about it since she never showed him. But then again, he always seemed to know about every gift before she gave it. She got on the floor and slid under her bed. Under the third bed board she pressed in one of the knots and a small panel popped open.

Out slid a note and her necklace. She let out a great sigh of relief. She pulled herself out from under her bed and opened up Jace's note.

Karanne, I'm here in Beldan, what's left of it. I knew you'd find this, I just wish I could have given it to you myself. I'll be at the Guild, hope to see you there soon. Jace. P.S. I need to talk to you about this necklace.

Karanne read it over again and rubbed her necklace in her palm. It felt so good to have it back. What did he want to ask about it? She got up and started. Straeten stood quietly in the doorway. A sudden flapping of wings outside her bedroom window made her jump again.

"Did you find anything?" Straeten asked coolly.

How long had he been standing there? His eyes... Were they *blue*? Her Fireflash pulsed right over his head. The hairs on the back of her neck raised slightly. How had she not seen it?

"Yes, I found a note. Must've been what he meant." She clenched her necklace and walked calmly to the window again. The flapping repeated. "It's Valor." Outside the hawk flitted from one rooftop to another. "I'll be right out, okay? I need to get a few things I'm going to need. I could use a change of clothes." Was she talking too quickly?

Karanne turned and saw Straeten had already left. This wasn't the first time she had to figure her way out of a plan gone wrong, but this was the worst. Her mind shifted to the strange blue eyes of the Followers back in Varkran. Not Straeten. Please, not him.

She closed the door and bolted it shut. She changed into some old thieving gear and then tapped the back of the closet. The wall gave way to a small, dark crevice in the house's siding allowing her to slink into its darkness. In moments she was crawling under her house through a tunnel the thieves had helped her build in case she needed to run from soldiers someday. Never had she imagined she'd use it like this.

The tunnel forced her to crawl. A claustrophobic wave passed through her, something she had never been proud of and spent hours trying to get over. Getting through dark uncomfortable places was pretty much what thieves did on a daily basis.

Twenty, thirty feet she crawled towards the back alley away from any peering eyes. Breathing deeply, she tried to quell the thudding of her heart. Would this ever end? Finally sunlight streamed in from up ahead through a grate. She pushed up on the metal bars, a little too harshly, and slid the grate to the side to pull herself out. She replaced the cover and brushed herself off.

"Never thought you'd get chance to use that exit, did you?"

She knew that voice all too well.

"Dral."

She turned to face him, knowing not to make any sudden moves. She might be faster than him on her good days, but today wasn't turning out to be one of those.

There he was, the leader of the thieves. All in black. Hands as twitchy as ever. "What are you doing here?"

"Your boy, Jace, came into our back entrance just yesterday. That big 'friend' of his followed him. Straeten? Knocked Jace out, never saw it coming. Straeten brought in two people we were hoping not to meet. That's why we were hiding out in the caves. I suppose we couldn't stay hidden forever."

Karanne glanced up and down the alleyway. No sign of Straeten. Yet. She could tell when she was being stalled. "So you're one of them, too, are you?"

"What do you mean?"

"Just let me go."

"I can't do that, girl." Dral licked his lips, his eyes never leaving hers. "Their magic didn't take with me. But they have their ways."

"What are you going to do?" Karanne slowly took a few steps backwards.

"Listen, Karanne. They just want your necklace. They said they wouldn't hurt you. Just give it to me and I'll bring it to them." Dral matched her steps like a cat stalking a mouse.

My *necklace?* "And where might they be?"

"Same place they're holding Jace. He's all right. You'll be, too. Just give me the necklace."

Karanne heard a fearful tone in his voice. Something she'd never heard before, and it made her a bit more nervous. "Just tell me where he is. You owe me that."

Dral motioned to the street through the alley. "They have something special planned for him. In a place where they can see the whole valley."

"The Tower of Law?" Karanne said.

"The very place we could never get into, huh? Right at the top." The sound of shuffling feet quickly approached and he glanced behind him. "I'm sorry, Karanne. I really am."

"Me too."

Her Fireflash leapt out of her palm and danced in front of Dral's face. His eyes followed its light. "Well, that's awfully pretty. You're not going to hurt me with it, are you?" His voice clearly implied he knew she wouldn't.

"Not me."

A large shadow emerged from a corner of the alley and landed a sharp blow onto Dral's head. The master thief dropped without even seeing the attacker. Tare lifted his club again but Karanne grabbed him by the wrist. "I know where they've got Jace. Let's go."

They ran through the alley, the soft scurrying of Ash's paws beside them. The Tower of Law broke over the tops of the houses and Dral's words echoed in her head. *They just want your necklace.* What in the suffering for?

Chapter 34: The Lock

Cathlyn strode quietly and carefully through the empty streets of Beldan towards Mathes' dwelling. Her constant headaches had started to fade on the journey here, and now they were practically gone. Was it really just from using less magic like Mathes said?

The powers she possessed were so far out of her control. That was proved many times, like when she killed those horses after "moving" her brother and the others. Like Mathes said, magic would turn everything evil.

And now they had a way to stop the evil from rising further. Sarissa's lock. Good thing Mathes had managed to take it off of Dorne's body back in the Shadow Vale. She frowned. Or was it? Yes, she wanted to stop the evil in the world, but was destroying magic the only way? Here she was, after all these years of study, able to touch the very fabric of magic in the world. Without even a Soulkind. How could she give up her childhood dreams? And force so many others to do the same?

"Are you sure we're doing the right thing?" she asked Mathes who lead the way. He peered back at her with a surprised then worried expression.

"You must not be feeling well. You've known what needed to be done for weeks now." Mathes wrapped his red robes, worn and dirty, about him and picked up his pace.

"I'm actually feeling better now and thinking clearly as well." She left off that she'd started to hear strange voices in the wind. "Where are we going again?" So strange that she couldn't remember.

"To my school. There are some students that I would like you to meet. I have worked with them their whole lives. They can help us."

"Didn't Karanne teach there, as well?"

Mathes didn't answer.

They moved quickly through the darkening streets, merging with other groups of people, careful to avoid notice from the soldiers with blue eyes.

The river and the lights of the massive torches on NorBridge came into view. It seemed like only yesterday Cathlyn was crossing that bridge with the Followers, encouraged by *Aeril* to lie to her friends. Marlec somehow knew her weakness, and forced her to be dishonest. No, not forced. Just nudged. Mathes was right. Magic corrupted even good people do bad things.

Just like Jace. Even he couldn't fight the dark path. But now, according to Mathes, she could help him. By using the Lock. She glanced up at the Hall on the other side of the river. Up to the rooftops of those buildings in which she studied the forgotten magic with Turic.

Even he would turn to darkness. Perhaps it had already started, as it did with Brannon and Marathas before him.

Finally Mathes reached a darkened building with a large courtyard in front. His school. Cathlyn had never known much about it other than Karanne's few words about taking care of the youngest students. Some of the children were from the richest families in Beldan.

From the upper level of the building, several people stared back out at her from dark rooms. Mathes walked up to the front door and rapidly knocked while glancing back through the streets. A tall boy, roughly Cathlyn's age with narrow features, opened it partially and let Mathes and her through.

"Ralanor." Mathes greeted him with a curt nod. "This is the one."

Ralanor took an involuntary step backwards when he looked at Cathlyn. He stumbled into several other students holed up in the school, all holding weapons. They seemed to have closed themselves off from the town, and judging by their careworn expressions, things had been rough.

Both fear and respect showed in the students' faces as they saw her. They lowered their knives and thin swords.

"Why haven't they gone home?" she asked. "Don't they have families?"

"This is their home now," Mathes said. "And they protect it."

"What kind of school is this?" she asked, but Mathes had already pushed his way past the students into the back and disappeared.

A younger female led her further inside the building. "Are you going to save us?"

Cathlyn scanned her scared face, she couldn't have been more than ten years old. "If I can." She rubbed her temples.

Ralanor spoke from behind. "There has been so much death here since the magic came. Surely you must."

Cathlyn turned to meet his pleading stare. "What is it you think I must do?"

Several students cocked their heads. Others furrowed their brows. Ralanor wore a half-amused smile. "Mathes would only be back here now if he had both you and the artifact."

"Did Mathes tell you that before he left?" Cathlyn asked.

"That is what we learn here. Mathes taught us the evils of magic and how to extricate it from the world."

Another student continued. "He spent much of his time researching how to end magic in the Hall and in Myraton. You are the key to sealing the magic away again."

Cathlyn shifted under the gaze of the thirty or so students, both young and old, who had entered the room. She silently wondered how many of them were here, and how many different families they had influence over with Mathes' teachings. The room seemed to shrink. She looked for a window or door. The only exit was the door she came through, behind the many students.

The crowd parted for Mathes, who came back with a tray of hot food and drink. He placed it in front of her next to a small round table with two chairs at it. He gestured for the others to go. She joined him, sitting down for the first time in a long while, hungrily eating the soup and drinking his strange tea. Her head started to spin. The journey must've taxed her more than she realized.

With a startling clang, Mathes set the severed Lock on the wooden table. So pure and white. She longed to touch the sleek curved band, to hold it on her arm again. So much power. Power to help her friends, to help everyone.

"All the pieces are set now," Mathes began. "The Masters of the Soulkind are in Beldan. The Darrak armies are marching here from the north. All you need to do is seal all magic back into this artifact and you will save the town from the attack."

His words echoed in her head. She nodded as they sank in. Yes, she would save the town. "What about the other Soulkind?"

"If you reach a high enough place, you can lock them all. Now, you must focus and call upon Sarissa's spells to save us."

Cathlyn reached for the white metal Lock. The last time she held it she had released the souls from the Soulkind and awakened their magic. She hesitated and withdrew her hands. The headache was back. Had just thinking about using magic triggered it?

Mathes sighed. "This is your fault. We would not be in this predicament if not for you. Now, accept responsibility for this mistake and correct it." Mathes' words swam in her mind.

Reluctantly she reached for the Lock again and this time held the cool metal, trying to feel Sarissa's thoughts and the magic within. All voices in her mind numbed to a dull hum.

Mathes' voice rose above the humming as he kept repeating what needed to be done. "You can do this."

She *would* do this.

She would silence magic. Forever.

Chapter 35: Returned

Jace awoke from a cold dream, his fingertips raw from scraping through ice and darkness.

Straeten. He was theirs now, their slave. He'd known it was coming, known she could take over his mind. And yet, he'd held on to the hope that he could help him first. He lifted his head from the hard stone. Some help he'd been.

A single barred window lit the empty cell. Fumbling slowly for balance, he tried to stand but slid down the stony wall. His head ached with a dull throbbing. His mouth and throat were so dry he could barely draw a breath.

How long had he been out?

He leaned against the wall, listening to the sounds of shouting and fighting drifting through the open window. He put his hands over his ears to block out the thudding.

That was when he felt them.

Stones of some sort were embedded in his temples. He felt the smooth facets. Crystal? Ice? Their cold emanated into his skull. He tried to pull them off, making his head feel as if it were ripping in half. Numbness shot through his arms from where he touched them. His anguished cry rang through the small cell.

His breathing slowed as he tried to focus and figure out what was happening. Something was different, something was missing. He quickly felt around his waist for his pouch. It had to be there. He rifled through the stones, each memory jarring his thoughts like a hammer blow. They'd taken it. Why wouldn't they?

But no, there it was, his green stone. He felt its familiar smooth texture, the lines on its surface, the unfortunate metal prongs attached to its back and sides. He let out a deep sigh. His heart slowly stopped pounding through his body.

204

And yet, the difference, the hole he sensed, remained. His heartbeat resumed thudding in his ears. The Soulkind felt just like any of his other stones. He reached for the magic, any magic.

Nothing. He pushed again and felt a cold void and the clenching grip of the ice on the sides of his head. He instinctively reached for them and sharp pain brought spasms throughout his body.

They left the stone to torture him.

He moaned and stared out the window into the dark night. What had Fay done to him? He had to get out and fix it. But where was he? The area felt vaguely like the Hall. The sounds of fighting faded but a red light flickered against the outer walls. Someone was coming. Jace kneeled down and swept his hands over the rough stone floor to search for anything to protect him from whatever approached. He hadn't felt this helpless for... he could not even remember. Was he that dependent on his Soulkind?

Shuffling footsteps and quiet murmuring stopped outside of his cell door. A metal lock clicked. Two shadows outlined by the light from outside stood in the doorway staring at him.

"Awake at last," a lady's voice whispered. Jace squinted at her as she walked into the small room. Her companion removed his lamp from a stick and hung it on a ceiling hook. The rocking of the light shifted the shadows around the floor. Something in the woman's right hand glinted when the light hit it.

Jace blinked at the piercing brightness. What was it? He swallowed hard. She wasn't holding anything. On her right hand sat a crystal ring. A Soulkind.

Fay's Soulkind.

He recognized it from Marlec's fortress. This wasn't exactly how he'd hoped to be meeting her. How strange to see Nilen's sharp features on her face. Yet her eyes spoke from another time. A man stood beside her, undoubtedly Guire. He had abandoned the furs of Varkran for the finery of Beldan. A corroded weapon sat upon his forearm, clearly the twin to Allar's shield.

Jace tried to talk but his voice failed him.

"No, you need not speak," Fay said. "We merely wanted to see you at last. It has been some time since we last saw the former master of your Soulkind."

Guire stepped forward and flourished a mocking bow to him. "Lu'Calen?" he asked. "Are you still in there? Of course not. I am sure he took the opportunity to leave you when he had the chance."

Fay laughed softly. "My dear, you look confused." Her steel blue eyes bored into Jace's, seeing more than he wanted her to.

He glanced past them. The tall turrets from the Hall barracks stood plainly beyond his prison door. The bodies of several lay motionless on the courtyard ground.

"Why am I still alive?" Jace croaked finally.

Fay raised her eyebrow and inspected him as if appraising a farm animal or a slave.

"I suppose you would not know." She tapped her fingers on her crossed arms, showcasing the icy ring. "We cannot risk your precious Soulkind falling into another's possession. If you die it can find another. It's more convenient having you here where we can keep an eye on you."

Guire walked along the edge of the cell scraping the pointed edge of his Soulkind on the rough stone walls. A corrosive trail hissed and smoked quietly in its wake.

Jace's anger burned. He awaited the familiar temptation to bend their will. Yet it never came. He felt nothing. It was almost a relief.

"You have made something new with your Soulkind, it seems," Guire said. "Something beautiful. I don't think Lu'Calen would have approved though." He laughed. "A pity you will never use it. I do believe it could even have stopped us. Such a beautiful thing, indeed."

Jace changed his mind. He'd do anything to wipe that look off Guire's face.

"Thirsty?" Fay held out her hand to Jace. A fine shower of frost escaped from her fingertips and formed into a lump of ice upon the floor.

Jace's breath turned to mist in the quickly cooling air. He resisted the urge to grab the ice and eat it.

"You had some interesting items on you," Guire said, producing Jace's pack. He pulled out his dagger, the one with the Darrak engravings on it, followed by the metal rod. "Why so interested in those beasts? They would kill you sooner than listen to you."

"We can use this, don't you think?" Fay said, taking the rod and turning it over in her hands. Guire smiled. How would they twist it to their own perverse purposes?

Someone appeared in the doorway. Jace blinked. Jervis? The former thief drew breaths as if he'd run for miles. Marks snaked around his neck and forearms. So he, too, was collecting magic as a Deltir.

Jervis stood from a deep bow. His eyes widened when he saw Jace.

206

"How did you capture him?"

Fay laughed. "His *friend* helped us, the large one. He probably could have taken Jace earlier, but we wanted to use him to rout your little thieves from their holes in the ground. You were right. Your friends were hiding from you, but they still trusted Jace."

Jace's heart dropped again. He'd brought Straeten and the gloves closer to Fay and Guire, and led them right to the Guild. This was all his fault. He glanced up at Jervis, half expecting to see some well-earned sneer on his face. Instead, he looked ragged and exhausted, thick with dirt and grime. And there was no sneer.

"I have news." Jervis turned his attention to Fay and Guire. He backed out of the room but the two stood waiting for him to speak. Apparently, they didn't care what Jace overheard.

"I brought Dorne here, like you wanted."

Dorne? Here? Could it get any worse? The gloves that Jace so conveniently brought to them would now be in his possession. He would reclaim them and they would have their Master back. The dark Soulkind would take over the land. And if Dorne was here, that could mean only one thing. The finality of it all crushed his heart.

"Where is he?" Guire said with no emotion.

"In the tower," Jervis said. "And I brought this as well. I found it on her, just like you said it would be." Jervis glanced over at Jace then quickly away.

Jace squinted to see Jervis pull out a shiny golden necklace. A mere blur of a shadow formed behind Fay as she gazed at it. Fay nodded solemnly at the necklace with deep brown eyes, the same as her daughter's. Not a trace of blue. In a softer voice he barely heard her whisper, "Nilen."

The shadow behind Nilen's mother wavered. He had seen shadows like that before with Marathas. Was he still able to perceive the souls attached to the Soulkind? Could it be that his magic was only being blocked?

A moment later, the shadow merged forcefully back into Nilen's mother's body with a sickening spasm. His connection to the Soulkind vanished. With disgust, Fay held the necklace out to Guire and strung it onto the tip of his outstretched Soulkind. The gold slipped down the chipped, rusted metal of his weapon. He spun it around several times.

"What is this?" he mused. "Not what you were looking for, I gather."

"It is something that belonged to *her*. Now destroy it." Fay spun on her heel, only to stop next to a cowering Jervis. She raised her hand as if to strike him.

Jervis bowed, apologizing profusely.

"Do not fail me again." She lowered her hand to smooth her dress and spared one last look back at the locket.

Guire gave Jace a half-smile. "Women and their jewelry." He lifted the simple locket with his Soulkind so Jace could see the painted image of a small girl. Nilen? But why? Where had he gotten it? The chain began to turn a sickly green and then turned to dust. The locket hit the ground near Jace's legs, smashing into bits.

Guire turned and left the room. Jervis stood at the door for a moment looking at Jace.

"Why are you doing this?" Jace asked. "You'd sell us all for them? They're just using you!"

Jervis clenched his fists, flexing the many marks upon them. He closed the door and a solid click locked it behind him.

A frigid gust of air blew the dust of the corroded necklace across the floor. Jace opened up his fist to see the one piece of it he'd been able to catch without being seen. A single small gemstone that resisted Guire's poison. He gripped it tightly.

Chapter 36: Vision

Jace stood up to warm his frozen fingertips in the timid warmth of Fay's lamp, though it was too high to do much. He could reach it if he tried. He had to. Ignoring the ache of his mind and body, he leapt up and kicked off one wall. In midair he clasped the metal chain of the lamp, lifted it up quickly and cradled it gently as he crouched for a landing. At least his old thief skills weren't gone.

Warmth.

He covered his hand with the thick material of his sleeve, picked up the chunk of ice Fay had so graciously left for him, and held it beside the lamp. The ice started to slowly drip as it melted. Jace held his other shaking hand under it to catch every drop of the water. Soon his cupped palm filled enough to at least moisten his dry, cracked lips.

A small puddle had collected from the water that leaked out of his fingers. He struggled not to lick it off the stones. Something moved within the puddle. He stooped down to see. An image of a rooftop appeared.

"Graebyrn?" he asked. He heard only a string of hissing and grating sounds. He tried to focus his mind into the water but a sudden pain in his temples made him cry out.

Grim understanding hit him. It had to be Graebyrn reaching out to him, but without magic, he could not understand his words. But maybe he could still get his message. He melted more ice and formed several small pools. Bit by bit, more images appeared. The smaller sections pooled together until one large scene coalesced. It appeared much like the ones he saw in the cave above the valley.

The image continued to grow until it became familiar. The parapets, the low roof barrier surrounding its edges. It was the Library. The vision shifted to two people overlooking the large field to the north of Beldan. The moon split the clouds and shone onto an army of Darrak marching onto his town.

What were the people doing on the roof? The vision drew close to their faces, yet only darkness appeared under their hoods. The person near the edge of the rooftop held something up to the skies, something powerful.

The image shifted to the Darrak again. They were clawing painfully at their faces and ears. It had to be Fay up there, but why would she be doing this to her soldiers? And how could she manage to kill so many?

In a fluid motion, the water revealed the face of the woman on the roof. The image shimmered, but the details were unmistakable. Long hair, smooth and calm features. And she held something in her hands, though he couldn't make it out.

The image faded leaving nothing but the normal stone block beneath his feet. All the ice had melted and the water now seeped into the cracks and pores of the rock. In the last waning reflection, wings flapped within the moonlight. Why that last image? None of it made sense without words. With a groan he hit the floor with his palm.

He rested his head back upon the stone wall and looked out the small window. His heart jumped. Up on the roof of the nearby building a bird flapped its wings as it landed. Perhaps the last image hadn't been a vision.

Jace stood up quickly. No doubt now. His old red-tailed friend stood only yards away. The chips of ice in his skull reminded him not to try a connection. And yet, the unfamiliar emptiness in Valor's presence was almost as unbearable. Only yards away, yet it felt like miles.

An armed guard stood right outside the window of his cell. Suddenly, Valor leapt off the roof and dived straight at the guard's head. The man gave out a shout and waved his arm uselessly as Valor pulled up with a flurry of feathers and a shrill cry. The man gripped his spear with both hands and watched the bird turn again to dive at him.

Avenging Jace's capture would only get Valor killed. But without his magic, how could he stop him?

"No! Valor!" Jace screamed and beat on the door.

The guard glanced back enough for him to see his blue eyes. In that second, Valor smashed into his helmet and almost comically knocked him over into the wall.

The man's helmet rolled away, clanking onto the stony ground. With determination he held his spear at the ready for another attack. Valor turned and dove once more. With a crash, he struck the man in the head again but not before the guard brought his spear around. With that savage strike, Valor spun and hit the ground.

"No!" Jace shouted. Not again. Please not again.

He clung to the bars, staring helplessly out at his friend. With a relieved sigh he watched the hawk hop, one wing flapping frantically. The guard laughed and stepped towards him, his spear raised.

Jace barely noticed a tiny shadow rush under his window. Something metal slid into the lock and clicked sharply. Valor hopped just out of the guard's reach down a flight of steps.

Silently the thick wooden door slipped open. Jace turned to see who it was. The small cloaked person pulled back the hood to expose a slightly familiar child's face.

"It's Evvy, silly."

He finally recognized her freckled face from the guild the last time he visited. She'd managed to lift one of his knives.

"Now hurry up and get out of there!" Little Evvy backed up, beckoning until he followed. She led him into the courtyard of the barracks.

"My friend's hurt, I've got to save him," he said. He started to go after Valor but Evvy only laughed and pulled him into the shadows.

"Don't you know your bird?"

Jace turned to see Valor now flapping both wings with ease and circling up to the rooftop. With a shrill cry of triumph he glanced over at Jace before diving off the edge. Jace smiled. He did know his bird. Their magical connection may have gone, but they had another, even more powerful, that could never be broken.

Chapter 37: The Roof

"How did you get in here?" Jace said, his voice ragged through his parched throat.

Evvy tugged at his sleeves to get him moving faster. "Picks! He saw those bad people catch you, and got us out of the caves in time, and Caspan got caught and…"

"Can you slow down a little?" Jace asked.

Quick as a bug, Evvy handed him a water flask and knelt in the shadows as he tried to quench his rabid thirst.

"He's getting too old for this, he told us. And Caspan told him where you were because he felt bad for something and Picks helped me get over NorBridge and then I saw your bird."

Jace tried to absorb all this while remaining unnoticed. He heard scuffling breaking out beyond the walls.

"How did you know he's my bird?"

Evvy shrugged. "I just knew is all."

She turned and her hood fell off. Jace caught his breath. Was that a mark, under her short brown hair? She moved out of his reach before he could look closer.

Evvy ran to an opening in the stone wall surrounding the Hall. She knelt down and backed into it. "You can maybe squeeze through here."

The Tower of Law glowed in the moon's light. "No, I have to stay. There's something I have to do."

"Picks said for me to get you out. I can help!" Evvy started to pull herself back through.

Jace knelt and took her hands. "You already have. I can take it from here, kid. Can you get to a safe place?"

"Picks told all thieves to go further up the river to the Old Guild."

Jace had a good idea where that was, though he'd only heard about it through stories. "Thanks Evvy. I'll meet you there later. I need to take care of something first."

She waved, handed him a small pack of supplies, and slid under the stone wall to safety. His stomach rumbled. He quickly ate the bread in the pack then leapt up the staircase to reach a higher vantage point. Dizziness overcame him from the motion. He needed to slow down, but not too much. If the water's image was true, Cathlyn could be here. He needed to hurry to the Library rooftop.

The Library. The last time he saw it was right before he and Straeten left to find Karanne and the others. Now, smoke filled the air, fighting broke out in the streets, and the threat of invasion loomed over the city. He had tried to warn the council. Now he had to find another way to help them. But what could he do all by himself without even a trace of magic?

And what could he do about Straeten? His best friend, now another puppet in Fay's army. Hopefully he wouldn't have to face him. First things first. He had to get to the roof.

Jace rushed through the Hall courtyard, winding his way around more skirmishes. Guards and townsfolk all senselessly fought each other. Was this what Guire and Fay's plan had been? Jace watched the sky for his friend, but couldn't see him among the low clouds and fog. Suffering ice crystals.

The Library appeared through the mist like a fortress. Several guards stood at its entrance. Instinctively he reached for his daggers only to remember all of his weapons and most of his possessions had been taken away. He needed a weapon to get past these guards.

He searched the bodies of several Beldan citizens crumpled against the tunnel wall. He found a few knives and a club. Three guards stood unwavering at the Library doors. What was he going to do? He was in no shape to take on armed soldiers.

If only he could tell Valor to help again with a distraction. Even as he told himself not to, he reached out to him with his mind. Shattering pain shot through his head and neck. He clutched at his temples and fell to a knee. The ringing in his ears lasted for nearly a minute. He staggered to his feet and leaned against the wall. Intense pain, armed soldiers and no magic? Not the best scenario.

When he was able to see clearly again, the guards at the Library doors were skirmishing with a band of younger people. While their

213

companions held off the guards' attacks with thin-bladed weapons, two others walked past the fighting through the gates.

The taller one wore a red cloak and the other wore blue robes, glowing slightly under the moonlight. A gust of wind blew off the person's hood. Long brown hair spilled out from under it.

She was here.

She raised her hand and the Library door burst apart in a clatter of splintered wood. Jace left the safety of the side tunnel to follow his friend and saw that the younger fighters still had the upper hand in the battle, pressing the guards back against the stone walls. One fighter was about to finish off a disarmed guard with a quick thrust of his rapier. Jace shouted and threw his club at him.

The youngling turned to see Jace sprinting. Jace stopped abruptly. The fighter was a young girl, a few years younger than he was.

"They don't know what they're doing!" he shouted.

The girl stared at him for a moment. The guard, his eyes shining blue, reached into his boot for a knife and stabbed her in the side. Jace yelled out again as she fell. The guard made a dash for the smashed open door. Jace picked up a chunk of wood and hurled it at his ankles.

The guard stumbled for only a second but in that time Jace leapt up and brought the hilt of a knife down upon the back of his head. He crumpled under the blow. Jace picked himself up and glanced back at the girl who had just fallen. She was so young. Why was she here? He kneeled at her side. She struggled to breathe.

"I'm sorry," he whispered and placed a piece of torn cloth on her wound. She stared at him wordlessly as he put his hands on hers to keep pressure on her side.

The other two guards quickly fell under the blades and fluid attacks of other young fighters. Jace sprinted off after Cathlyn.

"Cathlyn, stop!" he shouted out, but she was already gone from sight. He sprinted up a flight of stairs beside the main door but they led up to a short walkway and not to the roof. It had been so long since he had been up there. Nearly ten years. But he'd once known his way.

He tentatively reached for his green stone. No pain. Luckily he wasn't after its magic this time.

The memory of him racing Cathlyn filled his head, still without pain. He smiled.

His memories were his own.

He pressed further into his past. The memory guided him down a path between two tall stacks of books.

"Where are they?" a small voice called amidst his quick footfalls. His own voice from when he was much younger. His memory and the actual Library walls mixed together while he ran.

He turned a corner to see his young self talking to Cathlyn. Then Straeten crashed into him and they landed in a pile on the floor. He couldn't help but laugh. He sprinted now, more sure of his way through the twisting paths. Up a side stairway, down a long catwalk, above a room packed with manuscripts. And then the younger Cathlyn dashed straight ahead. He could almost reach her, could almost stop her from getting to the roof.

The red stone clicked as he returned it to the pouch with the others. One last winding set of stairs. He took them two, three steps at a time, until he reached a door to the wide open rooftop waiting for him.

The night sky cleared and the light of the moon shown down on the stone parapets. And on Cathlyn. Her brown hair streamed back from the gusting wind and her blue robes whipped around her. This was no memory now.

Cathlyn chanted loudly down at a vast army of Darrak, holding out her arms. Upon her right hand a familiar white artifact glinted in the moonlight. The Lock, but how could it be? Hadn't Jervis taken it? No, it was definitely here.

And Cathlyn could mean to do only one thing with it.

215

Chapter 38: The Tower

Karanne wound her way through the Hall's wide passageways and over the remains of fallen guards and townsfolk. Suffering riot. Useless deaths. At least it helped clear the way to the Tower of Law. How ironic that Dral had sent her to the one place they'd never been able to break into.

"But it wasn't about Jace before," she muttered to herself.

Her countless hours watching guards and the plans she'd memorized spun through her head. Almost there now. A part of her wished she'd let Tare come along with her. He'd be here with Turic and the others soon, but it was too late now to wait.

I'm better on my own anyway.

The sounds of battle rang through the Hall. Guards ran in and out of the barracks nursing the injured and sending reinforcements back into the streets. Who were they fighting, and who was leading them? Karanne paused to turn over the lifeless body of a young girl who lay at her feet, a rapier in her clasp.

"Shel?" she stood up quickly as if struck by a snake. "For the suffering, what's happening?" Were the children being forced to fight?

She stumbled backwards over another body. "No!" The body belonged to one of Shel's classmates, a boy named Ean. He wore the same robes and clutched the same rapier.

She closed her eyes. *I've got to focus on getting to the Tower.* With a deep breath she crept into the shadows and disappeared. She kept her eyes off the ground.

The many steps to Library entrance lay ahead, just out the door. The memory of Jace going there for his first time hit her. Her steps faltered. She'd just figured a way to get Mathes to accept him for a tour. He'd been so excited...

She slapped her face. *Focus.* No time to think about the Library now. *Just get up to the Tower.* She faded into the shadows once more as a group of guards ran towards the barracks. Dral had said Jace was up there and that was that.

With a sudden dart from her hiding spot, she left for the Tower entrance, racing between shrubs or statues to hide from watchful eyes. She kept the Fireflash at the ready, to blind any guards. It buzzed her hand as she ran past the Library.

Up the steps to the Tower she leapt, scanning as she flew. Nobody on the steps. Nobody in the entrance.

Strange. Perhaps they cleared the Tower to deal with the town's uprising. All the better for her. Maybe they left Jace unguarded upstairs.

She continued bounding upward around the massive tower. Still not a soul. Large rooms opened up to her as she passed on the stairs. Empty rooms. The echoing of her footsteps unsettled her but she pressed on, barely slowing to think.

Thief rumor held that a legal chamber lay near the top, and those tried before the Council were kept in a room nearby. But not even bribes helped confirm the layout.

She had to be nearing Jace. Just another minute of climbing. The steps led to a room with a polished wooden table and tall chairs making detainees feel smaller and less powerful. Neither a feeling Karanne cared for.

Torches crackled along the wall. She scanned the room for whoever lit them. A balcony and a barred wooden door stood to the right. Without pause she raced to the door and yanked at the handle. "Jace!" she whispered. Her voice reverberated through the room. She peered through a small opening in the door and saw someone sitting down next to a wall, his head slumped forward. "Jace!"

The person slowly stood up, only a silhouette in the dark, and walked to the door. As the light from the room shone in, Karanne noticed crystal bound the person's wrists together. "Jace? Is that you?"

The light finally revealed dark eyes peering out at her from the cell. They weren't Jace's, but she knew who they belonged to. Why was he in a cell?

"Yes, it is Dorne," a voice called out from behind her.

Karanne whipped around but didn't see anyone, only a large black bulbous mass blocking the stairway down. Something pushed into her shoulder. She spun around again, her heart pounding. Dorne was reaching through the door's window.

Had the council done this to him? Impossible. Jervis had brought him back to Fay and Guire, so why was he trapped? They probably couldn't stand the idea of sharing power.

Why wasn't Jace here? Dral. *He lied to me.* But no, there was no deception he could get past her, she knew him too well. *He* had been lied to. Her head spun.

"Jervis, let me out of here now," she warned.

"Oh, I'm not Jervis, dear."

Panic gripped Karanne's throat. She didn't recognize the voice, but she knew who it was. Guire. She settled herself with a deep breath and searched for the source of his voice. Nothing but that sickly mass. Well, that wouldn't stop her from getting to Jace.

She lit up a part of the growth with her Fireflash. To her satisfaction it popped in a splash of liquid and retreated a bit as the edges curled from the heat. Her smile faded quickly. New growths sprang from the ground like black tentacles, covering the floor and reaching towards her.

She held her hands up to cover them in flames. For every group she pushed back, two more appeared to branch off of the original mass. Sheets of them crawled up the wall to the ceiling, ever approaching. Slowly she backed away from them out onto the balcony.

Guire's laugh spilled from the room as she tried to hold off the attacks. "Just give us your necklace," his voice beckoned.

"My necklace? Why?" She reached for the white stone dangling from her neck. It felt warm to her touch.

Guire paused. Slowly his deep laugh grew from the silence. "You don't know, do you? Give it to us, and you can have your boy."

What was that in his voice? Fear? The balcony opened up to the city. The fires from below filled the sky with a soft orange glow. She peered over the edge. Dizziness swept over her. The ground was so far.

"If you push me over…"

"We can get your necklace either way," Guire responded. "Giving it to me, however, would be a lot less… messy."

She backed into the ledge while the black spell curled around the wall onto the balcony. She glanced down again for any hint of something to jump onto, and saw the top of the Library. Two people stood near the ledge overlooking the town. She squinted.

Jace?

"There is no way out." Guire stepped onto the balcony.

The necklace suddenly warmed to her touch, and then she knew. She knew why the necklace made her feel whole, knew why Guire and Fay were after it. Power welled up inside her and burned in her palm with a terrifying light.

"I always have a way out."

She raised her scorching palm. A ray of light leapt out and struck the balcony stonework with searing intensity. Veins of energy grew from where it landed and arced out seeking Guire's spell. When it reached the first vine, the bulbous growth crumpled into ashes.

Guire wavered as another of his tendrils retreated like a curling spider leg and crackled into desiccated remains. He backed away into the tower while he still had some of his magic to hide behind.

Karanne scoured away the filth with her new magic. *New magic.* The markings on her palm illuminated the darkness with strange symbols. The simple white stone pulsed with power.

Yet she knew now it was not just a simple white stone.

And she was not just a Follower.

Chapter 39: The Storm

"Cathlyn, no!" Jace shouted.

Her chanting throbbed in his ears and shook the stones beneath his feet. The white metal of the Lock wrapped itself around her wrist as she called out, slithering tighter like a constricting snake. Jace staggered out onto the roof, still reeling from the pain in his skull.

Mathes stood before him.

"What are you doing?" Jace said.

Mathes raised his sword to Jace's chest. "Stay back. She must stop this." He pushed the sword closer. Jace took a faltering step backwards.

Behind Mathes, the valley shone in the moonlight. Thousands of Darrak, the same Jace had seen in Marlec's valley, swept into the valley. But they were out of control now without Marlec to guide them, yet they still followed his call.

Jace clenched his fists. He led them here by bringing the gloves with him. How could he have been so stupid? Had he actually thought he could stop the Call himself? Why hadn't he destroyed them like Graebyrn said?

"They haven't done anything wrong yet, Cathlyn," Jace shouted. Or at least thought he shouted. His voice sounded muffled in his ears as the world around him shrunk. He could vaguely see her, a vision behind clouded glass. "You're going to kill them all!"

Cathlyn turned slightly. A wild and pained expression distorted her features. She quickly turned back to the open valley and held the Lock up higher. A sudden force gripped Jace, pulling him towards the artifact in her hands.

A ghostly image ripped from his body and appeared in front of him. He reached out for it, trying desperately to pull it back in, but his hands swept through the air. Coldness gripped his chest and his breath shortened. Did Cathlyn know what she was doing? She couldn't possibly lock the magic away without trapping everyone's souls like before. What was she thinking?

A chilling cry ran through the cold night air, a united shout from the army below. "Cathlyn?" Jace called, but this time, she did not even turn. He only barely noticed that he held his Soulkind in his hand now.

"You're too late!" Mathes shouted. He was right. It *was* too late. Jace fell to the stone roof near the ledge, his legs no longer able to support him.

"But we are not," a voice called out from behind. Bursts of fire and ice shot over Jace's head and into Cathlyn's form. Instead of hitting her, though, she simply drew the magic in like a giant vortex.

Jace spun over to see who it was this time. "Jervis?" And behind him, Fay. Through a fog, Jace saw her soul being ripped out of Lunara's body. She fell to her knees.

Mathes ducked behind a statue. Jervis rushed to Fay's side to help her up. She stared at Jace with fading blue eyes amidst the swirling storm emanating from Cathlyn. The Lock had nearly formed into the continuous loop now.

Stop her. A voice entered Jace's mind, cold and dark. Fay's voice. *You must stop her.* Fay's shadow lifted her fading hand towards him.

The ice chips on Jace's temples cracked. Relief flooded through his body followed by a surge of power. The sudden connection to all of his animal companions, his keen awareness of Fay's crumpled soul on the ground, his ability to understand the pathways of magic... it all came back to him in a flash. His ancient power was just waiting to be tapped. And yet, he also sensed it slipping out of him.

The Cathlyn he knew would never do this. Something was wrong. He reached for her with his mind like he did with Valor and Ash. Something slowed him, blocked and surrounded him with a swirl of vapor. He heard a man's voice calling to her through a cloudy haze. *Rid the world of magic.* Whose voice was it?

Jace scanned the rooftop, but only Jervis and Fay remained. They would do anything to keep their magic. Jace drew himself back towards Cathlyn's mind. Clouds and lightning prevented him from finding the source in the storm.

He had to stop her. However he could. His dark power arose like a burning brand in his head. He only needed to call it forth and everything would be over. This time, he had no choice. He summoned the flows, felt them fill him with power, but stopped short. A voice echoed in his memory.

221

Would you ever use it on me?

The burning subsided. His heart sunk. He tightened his fists and closed his eyes. He'd made a promise. There had to be some other way. There had to be.

Dimly he searched for her again amidst the whirling maelstrom, but still couldn't reach her. He slowed his own thinking and reached for his calming spell. Like a beacon lighting the night, his presence shone. The madness and confusion settled.

Calm. Quiet. Peace.

There she stood before him, as young and innocent as when he first met her.

"Cathlyn."

She turned to face him. "I don't know what to do, Jace."

"You have to let it go. You're going to kill them all, and your friends as well." She struggled to see him through the mist. He reached for her.

Slowly she raised her hands towards him. Their fingers met.

"I have to stop this magic," she said. "It's the only way to end the evil."

"There's another way."

"No. He said it's the only way."

"Who?"

Cathlyn swallowed hard and shook her head.

Jace felt around her mind, sought out the voice once again. Maybe if he saw what she saw, it would all become clear. He locked eyes with her and asked permission with his thoughts. She nodded. In a sudden sweep his mind passed behind her eyes. Her sight opened up onto the roof, staring at a statue and the man hiding behind it.

Mathes.

His twisting and manipulating, the drugs… "Don't listen to him." Jace said calmly. "Trust *me*." He pushed the distortions aside, allowed her to see behind them.

Her troubled eyes brightened, clear as the sun first rising in the day. No, she didn't want to listen to Mathes. She didn't want to end magic. That passion welled inside of her. The storm was over.

Thank the light he'd found another way.

Two bolts of ice crashed into Jace and Cathlyn, one sealing Cathlyn's hand with the Lock and the other Jace's hand with his Soulkind. Another strong gust of magic heaved him into the air and over the ledge of the Library rooftop.

But he did not fall. Cathlyn leaned over the edge, her hand outstretched. She wavered, concentration etched on her face.

"I guess I was wrong about never wanting you to pick me up," Jace said with a shaky voice. He saw the ground so far below, this time with no Soulwash to catch him.

"Jace." Cathlyn continued to struggle. A thin tear ran down her cheek.

Another blast of ice struck her in the back. Thick crystals climbed over her shoulder. Jervis and Fay walked towards her. The light of Jace's Soulkind grew distant as he, too, felt the ice creep behind his neck, over his ears, up to his temples. No!

"You fool. You could have been so much stronger if you'd used your power to *make* her stop," She turned to Jervis. "Finish them."

Jervis peered over the edge.

"I said *finish them.*"

Jervis made no move.

"For the suffering, I'll do it myself." Fay sent another blast at Cathlyn. More ice crept up her legs.

Jace dropped a foot. He tried punching his hand into the stone wall of the Library next to him. None of the ice cracked off. It began to cover his eyes.

A flash appeared at the top of the Tower of Law like a distant thunderstorm. A thin white bolt of flame shot out and arced towards him. It spun madly around the crystals covering his head.

Bits of ice sprayed everywhere. A wave of magic pulsed through his body. He was aware again of his animals. Valor circling above, Payt just outside the city, and Ash running nearby.

Fay spared a fierce glance to the tower then shifted her glare back to Jace. She raised her arms once more, Jervis cowering behind her. Again, Jace's dark magic called out. Fay was evil and needed to be stopped. Yet, his heart had already decided. The call held no sway over him now.

He had an idea.

He reached for the power of his Soulkind. He needed to pull out the memories contained in his stones, but somehow without touching them. Where was the small gemstone from Nilen's necklace? He sensed its presence and pushed towards it with his mind.

He took a deep breath. His magic flowed through him and into her stone.

"Mother?" a young voice called out from the roof.

An image of Nilen appeared in front of Fay.

It worked. He had projected the memory. Even through the ice encasing his hands he felt the glow of a new mark forming.

The soul of the ancient Master faded slightly from Lunara's body. Her mother smiled at the vision of her daughter.

Now for the next step. *Jervis*! Jace shouted into the thief's mind. *Help Cathlyn!*

Ice had nearly covered all of Cathlyn's face. Jace slipped a few feet further. Jervis glanced back at Fay who was still enthralled by the illusion.

Please.

Jervis stood and raised his hands towards Cathlyn's bonds. Flames erupted from his fingertips, weakening the ice on her body until it broke away in shards. Cathlyn dropped the Lock and grasped the roof ledge. Jace slipped jerkily, the crystal binding his hands clattering against the ledge. His pouch of stones fell off his side in horribly slow motion. Helpless, he watched them plummeting toward the ground, only to clatter among the dirt and trees below.

Cathlyn held out her hand again, her face tensing more than ever under the strain of holding him up.

Fay's peaceful expression twisted into rage. The spell was broken. A careless snap of her hand sent a blast of ice at Jervis. He crashed into the stone ledge with a sickening thud.

The valley's cool wind blew across Jace's sweating face. A call rose upon the breeze, a shrill cry calling to Jace's spirit to fly away. Valor's cry.

He laughed suddenly. It was clear to him now. His aching arms in Graebyrn's cave. The wings that enveloped him, they were feathered, not scaled Graebyrn hadn't saved him. He'd saved himself.

But not without help.

"Let me go!" he called out to Cathlyn.

"I won't!"

Don't worry about me. He pressed that thought into her mind again. Although another tear fell down her cheek, she listened. As he fell, spinning to the valley floor, he watched Cathlyn's long brown hair trail away. Wasn't that his memory of when he first fell from the roof? In a flash of light she disappeared and only Fay remained staring over the ledge.

He closed his eyes and spread his arms.

Chapter 40: Flight

The chaotic mass of Darrak writhed hundreds of feet below. Nothing but air surrounded him. Yet he wasn't falling.

He watched the distant scene through Valor's eyes then pulled back to his own vision. Nothing changed. He almost laughed at himself. Of course not. He and Valor shared the same eyes. And the same body.

He stretched his arms to catch an updraft—not his arms, Valor's wings—and yet he could control them, if only a little. The attempt slowed his forward motion and sent him spiraling downward. He strained to regain control, but Valor corrected the flight himself.

They flew toward the Tower of Law and circled the massive building. Where were his friends? He scanned the Hall, picking out faces even from this distance in the dim lights of the city, but he couldn't find any sign of them. Cathlyn had vanished. Fay could only use ice magic, but he didn't know about Jervis. Hopefully after releasing Jace, Cathlyn felt safe to escape and removed herself. But what about Straeten? And his other friends? Were they also in Beldan now? Who had caused the blast from the tower?

His mind spun with questions, skimming from one thought to another. He pitched forward into a steep dive. Valor claimed his own wings again and resumed circling.

A voice floated towards him on the wind.

Graebyrn's voice.

Valor seemed to hear it too, for he pumped his wings harder. They sped towards the cascading waters falling from the mountain behind the Hall. The cave entrance beckoned, a black eye spilling tears into the valley. They dove now, gaining vast momentum and making Jace's vision reel. At last within range of the entrance, Valor flapped rapidly and settled next to the waterfall.

Jace ripped himself out of Valor's body and slammed down beside the water in a shivering pile. He opened his clenched hand to reveal his smooth, green Soulkind inside.

"There has to be a better way of doing this," Jace said through chattering teeth. With his remaining strength he pulled himself into the cave.

A snort greeted him inside, a familiar snort. Payt's smooth tapered head breathed down on him. He reached up to scratch his chin and Payt pressed into his hand. Ash raced to his side and licked his face.

"How did you two get up here?" Jace scratched Ash's back. He peered into his eyes but already knew the answer. They came when he needed them.

He put on some clothes from his pack and peered over the edge of the waterfall at the smoldering city. The fighting appeared to have died down, but he couldn't be sure at this distance. Yet even if the internal battle had stopped, the Darrak posed an even greater threat to the people within. He had brought war to his town and now he needed to fix it.

And help Straeten.

"Fear not," a solemn voice called over the bubbling waters inside.

"Graebyrn. I'm sorry."

"You had the right intentions, young Master."

"I have to help them."

"And help them you will."

Jace nodded. With a deep sigh, he struggled to his feet. He gripped the Soulkind in his fist, feeling the metal prongs against his skin. He stood taller. Yes, they would always be there, and yet when he felt them now, they did more than remind him of his mistakes.

He had resisted the dark path.

He looked back at Ash, Valor, and Payt, all awaiting his call. And somewhere in the depths of his heart, he felt the echo of a presence he thought was gone forever. He wasn't alone nor would he ever be.

"I'm ready."

For the dangers ahead. For the challenges he would face.

And for the memory of an old friend.

The End

226

Steve Davala is a young adult fantasy novelist. He also writes science articles and blogs for a video game site. In the rest of his spare time he teaches high school chemistry and hangs out with his wife and two kids. Yes, one of them is named Jace.

Read the beginning of the Soulkind Series in **The Soulkind Awakening** and keep an eye out for the third book that will continue the story of Jace and his friends. Stay in touch with the story on Steve's web site: **www.thesoulkind.blogspot.com** or follow him on Twitter @sdavala and The Soulkind Series on Facebook.

33736526R00132

Made in the USA
San Bernardino, CA
09 May 2016